JOCK ROAD

A JOCK HARD NOVEL

USA TODAY BESTSELLING AUTHOR

SARA NEY

JOCK ROAD

Cover Design by Okay Creations

Formatting by AB Formatting & Design

FIRST FRIDAY

CHARLIE

What the actual fu…

The light behind me is so bright I squint, reaching to adjust my rear-view mirror, pink glitter nail polish catching in the light. I turn the mirror this way and that, working it so the headlights blasting my retinas are shining back at the driver, probably blinding them now, too.

Good. Serves them right.

Jerk.

I slow my car to five under the speed limit, conscious of the fact that campus security and police presence have increased since a student was assaulted by a driver of an unmarked cab first semester. More than assaulted—she ended up in the hospital.

I visibly cringe at the thought, tightening my grip on the wheel.

A car passes slowly on my left. Another pulls out in front of me, causing me to jam my foot on the brake. Ten under the speed limit, my fingers drum the steering wheel. Reach to spin the volume dial to the right, just a bit louder—this song is one of my favorites.

Upbeat.

Catchy.

Sexy.

My thoughts stray and land on a conversation I had earlier with my friend Claire about how she's breaking up with her boyfriend Donnie—Donnie the Douche, as we've started calling him behind her back, mostly because the alliteration is fun. A running back on the university's team, Donnie cannot keep his dick in his pants—or in one girl's vagina, specifically Claire's.

She used to forgive him every time and take him back. She'd forgive him for every indiscretion, probably because she's somewhat a jock chaser and Donnie was headed for the NFL—until he tore his UCL throwing a reverse pass, taking him out for the rest of the season and killing his career.

Poor Claire; she wanted to be a WAG so damn bad.

Now? No way is she willing to tolerate any of his bullshit, not with him forced to finish his business degree and take a job at his uncle's car dealership.

Football was the only thing the kid had going for him; conversations with him are mind-numbing and decreased my IQ tenfold. Just plain dumb.

I hate to call him a dumb jock, but…

Donnie is a dumb jock.

A small rock hits my windshield, knocking me out of my stupor—I realize I've been crawling along this road at barely the legal minimum and totally sober on a Friday night. I sigh when the car ahead of me stops at the light, the glare from their cell phone visible from here.

The driver is checking their damn messages.

Huffing, I glance in my mirror.

There is a truck behind me, easing up so close a body probably wouldn't fit between the two vehicles.

I inch forward a bit.

The truck inches forward.

"What the hell, dude—back off," I mutter out loud, irritated.

No—irritated is an understatement.

The annoyance grows when the car in front of me stays put, despite the fact that it's their turn to go at the four-way stop sign.

Hang a right. Hang a left. Go straight. Something!

"*Move*!" I shout, smacking the middle of my steering wheel with the palm of my hand. "Oh my god."

Lights blind me and I blink, seeing stars.

"What the hell, man!"

I hate trucks sometimes—they think they own the road. In the winter, it seems to be worse. Newsflash: just because you're heads above the rest of us peons who drive cars does not mean you *rule* the streets. It doesn't mean you get to be an asshole and blaze past everyone trying to get to their destination in one piece. Especially in the snow.

Rude.

And this jerk behind me? If he was riding my ass any closer, he'd be up my butthole.

In fact…

I bite down on my bottom lip.

It seems like…

I take my foot off the brake, moving a foot. Then another.

The truck mimics my movements.

Weird.

The car ahead of me finally lifts their foot off the brake and inches forward as the glaring set of lights flash behind me.

"Knock it off!" I loudly complain to no one.

Seriously. *Knock it off.*

But they don't. The driver of the truck flashes their lights again—this time it's their brights.

"I swear, if you do that shit one more time…" I threaten, more to myself because I'm becoming irrationally angry.

They do that shit one more time.

This is where the rubber meets the metaphorical road, and I have a choice: I can either calm down and keep going—*or* I can yank my car into park, get out, and give that reckless ass a piece of my mind.

Always a bit late to the party, my common sense rears its responsible head, and I do nothing but white-knuckle the steering wheel, my pretty pink nails filed short, the glitter in my polish once again catching a bit of light and twinkling.

I admire it despite my ire.

Get a grip, Charlie. Now is not the time. There is a psychopath riding your tail. This never ends well in the movies.

If this were a horror flick, I would put my car in park and make the fatal mistake of exiting my vehicle. I'd stalk over to the truck, probably wouldn't be able to see the driver because I bet the window tint is opaque. Then I'd get too close, the door would open, and the driver would get out with his chainsaw. Force me to retreat into a nearby alleyway or cornfield. I'd run and run and run until I'm too far from civilization or any hope of help. Then the psycho—probably in a mask—would follow me, hacking everything in his path to pieces.

Except: there is no nearby alley.

There are no cornfields.

This isn't a scary movie.

The odds of this guy having an actual working chainsaw are slim to none, but ya know what? I'm not taking any chances.

I know how the story ends, and I'd rather not end up the casualty of stupidity on the evening news.

So. I curse him out, but privately, in the safety of my car.

Oh my god, what if he follows me after I drive off? I decide if I turn left and he turns left, I'm driving to the police station. Yes, that's what I'll do—go to the cop shop.

He definitely is giving me a stalker vibe.

Flash.

Flash.

"Stop! Ugh!" I screech, scared, wishing I could see the license plate the truck is legally obligated to have affixed to its front bumper.

When it's finally my turn to go, I don't announce my direction with a signal—I just hang a left and exhale a great puff of air.

He didn't follow me.

Thank. God.

Shaking a little, I release my grip on my leather steering wheel and slump. Lean forward and adjust the dial on my radio, lowering the volume so I can hear myself think with the blood racing through my veins.

I hear it thundering in my ears.

Behind me, in the rear-view, the truck—black if my eyes don't deceive me—passes through the intersection.

Jerk.

SECOND FRIDAY

JACKSON

Goddamn I'm hungry.

Nothing new there; I could always go for food. Trouble is, I'm too far from home to dash there real quick, even with my truck on campus—fuck if I'm willing to lose my parking spot next to the athletic building over a snack—and I'm not jogging home for the frozen burrito I'm craving, even if it would burn off the calories.

Like a bear sniffing out food after a long winter, I skip the athletic dining hall—that's too far, too, because this is an emergency.

The on-campus cafeteria for regular students will have to do.

I turn my nose up at the thought, dreading the flat hamburger patties and stale lettuce I'll surely find when I get there. Chicken sounds appealing; so do a few fatty hot dogs.

I quicken my pace, not sure where this fucking joint is located; I haven't eaten there since…well, freshman year, and that one time was a mistake. The eats here are utter shit.

The perks of being a jock at a school this size are considerable. Special facilities. Massage therapist at my beck and call. Hot tubs in the training room. Free clothes through sponsorships.

I walk taller, a head above most everyone I pass. They scurry by, giving me the side-eye, some backward glances I ignore. Whispers. I don't miss the elbow jabs.

Arrogantly, I know many of them recognize me. Guys especially.

My nose leads me to the food, the room full, lines long.

Fuck.

I don't have time to stand in line—I have to be in the weight room in forty minutes, and it will take me that long to grab what I want.

I'm a big boy; this won't be a light meal. It'll be enough food to feed a family. Not having eaten since late last night, I desperately swipe a bag of potato chips on my walk to the grill. I tear it open with my teeth like a barbarian and stuff a handful in my face. Chew loudly, crumbs falling down the front of my Iowa t-shirt.

Iowa. How the fuck I ended up here is beyond me.

I was all set to attend school in my home state of Texas until, at the last minute, the scholarship money wasn't there anymore. I had a spot on the team, but not enough money to cover tuition, and my family ain't rollin' in dough.

Enter Iowa.

More money. More allowance for living expenses. More stability.

No way did I have the spare change to afford A&M on my own; I'm a great player, but not *full-ride* great.

And goddamn am I hungry.

I wad the chip bag in my fist, leaving it in my hand so I remember to pay for it. There's a line at the griddle, but I doubt anyone will object if I cut it and skip to the front.

No one complains out loud, but a few resting bitch faces judge me.

I slide in after a girl with long, blonde hair. She's bouncing on the heels of her—I glance down—brown boots. A baby blue backpack is hooked over her right shoulder. Impatient, she continues to check the watch on her wrist every few seconds, as if the action is going to speed up the process of cooking meat.

I eyeball the grill, debating about what I want. One chicken breast, lean. Two hamburger patties, fatty. Three hot dogs.

Chicken it is.

The girl checks her watch again, and I stare at the back of her head, down at the crown, into her shiny hair. It's long and a bit wavy, and I haven't touched a girl's hair in so fucking long, I'm tempted to rub a few strands between my fingers for old times' sake.

Weird, right?

She doesn't so much as cock her head to the side, so I have no idea what she looks like. I just know she has a few vulgar pins on her bag and a touchable blonde mop.

The chicken is flipped once more by the bored student running the cooktop, his sweaty and acne-covered face only accentuated by the thin black net covering his hair.

He uses the same spatula to turn the remaining meats, which I'm sure might be some health code violation—cross-contamination or some shit? Yes? No? Well, it should be—I don't want hot dog jizz on my chicken.

I groan out loud when the kid presses the spatula onto the chicken breast, squeezing out all the juice. Jesus Christ, rule number one of grilling—don't fucking dry out the meat by choking it to death.

Next, he slaps several buns onto the grill. When one is ready, he palms it, slapping the chicken into the center. Closes it, wraps it in foil. Extends his arm, holds it over the counter and into my waiting grasp.

I snatch it, immediately unwrap it, and shove the first warm bite into my mouth.

Holy shit, it's pretty damn good.

"Hey! What the hell—that was mine!"

I look down at the girl in front of me, who has spun on her heel to give me the dirtiest look anyone has ever given me. She is as mad as a hornet.

I turn to walk away. "You snooze, you lose."

"I was literally standing here waiting patiently for that thing!"

"How's that workin' for you?"

"Huh?"

"Bein' patient." I take another bite of my sandwich, moaning with pleasure because it's so delightful and just what I needed. "How's that workin' for ya? Seems to me that maybe if you were more assertive, you'd be standin' here eatin' this sammich and not me."

One more bite goes down my gullet as she stands there sputtering.

"Grab me a burger when he's done with 'em, would ya?" This sandwich isn't exactly going to fill me up, and my next meal won't come for a few hours.

"Get your own sandwich, asshole."

"Whoa, no need for name-callin', darlin'—I'm just tryin' to be polite."

"Polite? You are so rude! You stole my lunch!"

"Was it yours though?" I narrow my eyes. "You didn't pay for it."

"Neither did you—and you didn't order it, either."

Gripping the chicken and bun in my giant palm, I hold it toward her. "Want a bite? It's good."

"Oh my god, shut up." She spins on her heel, facing the kid behind the counter grilling the meat. He and I lock eyes, but he quickly averts his gaze, loading a hamburger patty onto the bun.

"You want cheese?" he asks the girl.

"No! And I don't want a burger. I wanted chicken, but you gave it to this Neanderthal!"

The kid opens his mouth; no sound comes out. Good—I don't need another opinion thrown into this conversation.

"I'll take that burger," I tell him over the girl's head.

She whips around. "That burger is for the girl behind you." She glances around me, shooting a pointed look at the mousey little co-ed standing directly behind me. "Do not let him take that hamburger."

I shoot the girl a smile. "I'm totally taking this burger."

She returns my smile with a feeble one of her own, her mouth contorting into…I'm not sure what the fuck her look is supposed to mean.

Little Miss Priss will not be deterred from her mission: keeping me from eating my damn lunch.

"Oh no you will not!"

"You're cute."

Her arms cross. "Don't you dare insult me."

Calling her cute is an insult? This is news to me. "Since when is it an insult to call someone *cute*?"

"It's an insult when the person complimenting you is an asshole."

"Darlin', you've just got your dander up. This ain't got nothin' to do with me."

Her pretty face is smug. "Ain't got nothin' to do with me? Oh my god, where were you raised?"

"Texas." Don't fucking mess with it.

She rolls her eyes.

They're bright blue.

"I've been to Texas—no one there talks like that."

I'm close to polishing off this entire chicken breast. "Talks like what?"

"Like a hick."

A hick? The fuck... "You think name-callin' is nice?"

"Name-*cawlin'*," she mocks. Now who's the asshole?

The kid behind the grill has two foil-wrapped burgers in his hand, suspended in midair—unsure of what the hell to do with them as I stand here verbally sparring with this little hellcat.

"I'll take them both," I tell him over her head.

"*I'll* take them both!" she counters, leveling me with a stare.

"You said you didn't want no burger."

"I don't have time to stand here and wait for another chicken sandwich, jerk—this is my only option."

"You're gonna eat two burgers?"

"That's none of your business."

"You can't take them both just to spite me."

"I'll do whatever I want—I'm at the front of the line." She turns her back on me, hair damn near flinging me in the face, my nose catching a whiff of shampoo. "If you give him those burgers, I will find your manager and...and..."

The bastard hands her both burgers, and I take the opportunity to shoot him a death glare, hoping he wets his pants a little.

I tail the blonde to the cash resisters, pilfering a banana, two protein bars, another bag of chips, and a rice krispy treat from a nearby snack rack as we pass it by.

"Come on, just give me one of the burgers."

"No."

"Why?"

"Some of us really do need to learn the hard way," she says to no one in particular, ignoring me completely.

"You're not going to eat both of those."

This time she does acknowledge me. "So? They're mine—I can do whatever I want with them."

"You ain't gonna waste them. You're not the type."

"Thanks for stereotyping me as not a waster."

I roll my eyes. She is as prickly as a cactus and twice as pretty as one in bloom—which is the weirdest metaphor I've ever thrown out, but there you go.

"That was a compliment."

She shoots me a look over her shoulder and keeps walking. "Are you still following me?"

"Yeah—I'm still starvin'."

The little shit rolls her eyes and throws a thumb toward the buffet. "Get in line like the rest of the general population."

"Gimme one of them burgers. Please."

She stops in her tracks at that, spinning on her heel to face me, and it's then that I get a really good, hard look at her. Wavy blonde hair framing a heart-shaped face. Blue eyes, so bright they're like a clear Texas sky on a summer day. Freckles dotted across a pert little nose and high cheekbones. Pink skin quickly dented by a small dimple appearing on her right cheek.

Well fuck me sideways and color me surprised. This little spitfire is full of gumption and prettier than a peach.

Beautiful, especially now that she's good and riled up.

"You can have the burger for ten bucks."

"Say again?" I can't have heard her right.

"I said—give me ten dollars and the sandwich is yours." It stays clutched in her grip; she makes no move to hand it over.

It's getting colder by the second, and nothing gets me grumpier than cold food.

"That's *extortion.*" I'm fucking starving and she damn well knows it!

"No," she smugly informs me. "That's supply and demand. You would know that if you attended classes."

"I attend my classes." Just like everyone else.

"Oh yeah, which ones?" The brows above her dark eyes rise. "How to be a Jock 101?"

They have a class called How to be a Jock? *Weird.* "I'm an ag major—we don't have classes like that."

"What's an egg major?"

"Ag—as in *ag*riculture."

A snicker bubbles out of her throat; she sure is a snotty little thing, something I don't appreciate.

I reach for a hamburger.

She pulls it back, out of my reach. "Ten bucks."

"Five."

"Eight."

"You haven't even paid for these yet," I remind her.

"How about you pay for all of it and let me keep these two?"

"How about I pay for all of it and you give those both to me?" I nod toward the burgers.

"I haven't eaten yet, you animal, and you've already had a chicken sandwich—*my* chicken sandwich."

Dammit, that's right—she hasn't eaten yet. I'd be a real asshole if I didn't at least buy her lunch.

"Fine. Give them here."

"Nope. Not until you've paid."

"Fine," I grind out through clenched teeth. "But I get one of those."

"A deal is a deal. I said I'd give you one and I will—after you pay for everything."

Together, we make our way to the cashier, and just like before, I skip to the front of the line.

No one objects.

Except her.

"You cannot keep doing that."

"Doing what?" I feign ignorance, head held high as I hand the cashier all my shit, including the empty wrappers, and point to the two burgers in Little Miss Priss's hands. "Those, too."

* * *

CHARLIE

This guy is the most ridiculous creature I've ever met. Stubborn. Rude. Barbaric.

Handsome—if you're into *crude* and uncultured.

And the Southern accent…it's cute—and he's *so* very good-looking. Obviously corn-fed; a down-home, bona fide country boy.

A hick?

So country I can't resist giving him shit about it, and it actually makes my stomach churn a little. I've met people from the South, but never with an accent this deep and never this pronounced.

The twang is thick, and I love it.

I hate him.

Clearly he hasn't been taught any manners, and if he has, he chooses not to use them. Or he simply doesn't care. I thought boys from the South were supposed to be all *yes ma'am* and *no ma'am* and gentlemen?

Doesn't give a fig. I chuckle to myself at my own use of the Southern metaphor.

I stand idly beside him, holding the two burgers I snatched from the griddle.

A guilty wave passes over me at my manners, which were as bad as…his. Shoot. He made me completely forget myself, and I'm ashamed I grabbed both burgers without caring who they belonged to, so hell-bent on proving a point.

Ugh.

The Neanderthal retrieves a wallet from his back pocket, pulling out cash instead of a student ID.

"Don't you have a *meal* plan?" I ask, because I'm nosy, and—I'll admit it—a bit snarky and snotty.

"No."

"Why?" It's rude of me to ask. Maybe he can't afford it. Maybe he never eats on campus. Maybe—

"I play football. We don't usually have to eat this shit, but I was desperate."

Well then. "Um…okay." I pause. "What does that even mean?"

He turns his hulking body toward me. "It means we have our own cafeteria where we get awesome food, not this slop."

I glance down at the "slop" in my hands. Two foil-wrapped burgers, no pickles, no onions, no anything. I'm a bit offended he's calling this garbage when it's the only option I have for food on campus.

"Well aren't you *special*," I goad, shooting him another eye roll, this one heavy and almost causing me to get lightheaded. Wow. Better watch that, or my eyes are going to get stuck in the back of my head. "Where is this mythical, magical place where they feed the lucky few who get to graze there?"

"Back of the stadium."

Wait—is he serious? They really have a special place where they feed the student athletes?

"For real?"

He spares me no glances as he takes the little bit of change he's offered by the cashier. The girl is gawking at him, wide-eyed and slightly spellbound.

Ugh, gross.

"Yeah, for real."

"What's up there?"

He holds a hand out for a burger now that he's paid. I slap one in his palm, secretly hoping it gets squished a little bit.

"I don't know…*stuff*. Food."

"Be specific." If he's going to throw down about this cafeteria being total crap, he better give details.

"Salad bar. Seafood. Pasta bar. Lean chicken and steak."

He tears into the silver wrapper of the burger he just grabbed from my hands, shoving one end into his mouth, biting down and chewing.

"Seafood?" What the hell! "For real?"

"Yeah."

When he says yeah, it comes out as *yee-a-ya*—three syllables—and there go those flutters in my stomach, despite him being a complete brute.

He's tall—at least six foot three—with wide shoulders, a broad back… I let my eyes wander down his torso as he gnaws on his food, down his flat stomach and thick inner thighs. He's wearing mesh athletic pants, so it's easy to make out the shape of his legs. Toned. Strong. Thick.

Did I say that already?

Crap.

His t-shirt is too tight and ill-fitting. A bit too short for how tall he is, but it doesn't look like he gives a shit about his appearance. Not one little bit.

His hair is a bit shaggy, pulled back in an elastic, strands escaping around his face. His five-o'clock shadow game is strong.

He needs a good shave.

But…

That's none of my business.

I'm not looking for a boyfriend, and if I were, it wouldn't be a guy like *this*—arrogant and offensive with no regard for anyone.

All right, that's somewhat of a lie; I would actually love a boyfriend. Like, I wouldn't be mad about it if I found one; I just haven't met anyone who felt like 'the one.' Or one who felt like Mr. Right Now—he hasn't found me, either. I'm even willing to do something casual with the right person until someone special comes sauntering my way, preferably in a clean shirt and with a shaved face.

I sniff, unwrapping my own sandwich. Wondering for a second why I'm always so picky. Why can't I just have fun and flirt with the first guy who comes along?

I've been single for two years. My boyfriend from freshman year lost interest when he joined a fraternity and found interest in the sister sorority they partied with every weekend.

Whatever. I don't need a guy like that in my life anyway. When you love someone, your eyes don't roam—that's the kind of love I'm looking for. That's the kind of love I deserve.

So, for now, I'm single.

I glance around the cafeteria at the guys scattered throughout the room, seated at tables or leaning against the walls, talking, oblivious to the looming grouch next to me.

"You're welcome," he grunts, sliding his wallet into the pocket of his mesh pants.

"Do I say thanks to the guy who stole my food?" I wonder out loud, taking a bite of my burger.

"No, you say thanks to the man who paid for it."

The may-an who paid foor it.

"Do I though?" My musing is thoughtful. "If it's by default because you stole the first round?"

"Yes."

"Hmm." I chew. "I'm conflicted about the protocol on that." Walk toward the double doors, toward the exit, leaving him to trail behind me. Push through when I reach them and walk out into the quad.

The sun hits my face and I look up, basking in it as I eat my free lunch.

"I ain't walkin' away until you use your manners and say thank you."

Thank yew.

God, it's kind of adorable.

"'Kay," I say. "Bye."

I leave him standing there staring after me and wonder if he's going to follow. Glance back over my shoulder to see him trailing along, stubborn as I am and not willing to let it go now that we've both dug our heels in.

I turn toward the English building.

"Where're your manners?"

"I ain't *got* none," I say, mimicking his accent and poor grammar. "Where are yours? You took food from me without even asking, ate it without paying, then complained about the facility where I have to eat lunch serving *slop*."

"It *is* slop."

"Well la-ti-da, you eat shrimp scampi for lunch and I have to eat hot dogs."

"Shrimp scampi has too much butter. They'd never serve that."

How did I not just roll my eyes at that comment? I miraculously restrain myself and pick up my pace, shooting a look down at my watch, searching for the time.

Shit.

Five minutes to get to class and get my ass into a seat. Bickering with this dude isn't going to get me anywhere but locked out by the professor or TA, who are both pompous windbags. They thoroughly enjoy locking tardy students out of the lecture hall.

I hike my backpack up, scarf down the remainder of my burger, and toss the wrapper in a nearby trash can. He does the same.

"I'm super glad you're so special. Enjoy the lobster for your next superior meal," I sass him.

His sneakers stop on the concrete sidewalk. Then his voice shouts toward my retreating back.

"Are you mockin' me?"

Mockin'.

"Yes!" I shout, turning to walk backward so I can laugh directly to his face, tossing my arms up for extra measure. "Yes I am mocking you!"

It takes everything I have not to throw him the middle finger.

THIRD FRIDAY

CHARLIE

I slam my car into park, impervious to the fact that I'm in the middle of a busy road in the heart of campus; that fact probably giving me the courage to shove open my driver's side door and step out into the warm air.

It's late—almost eleven o'clock—but still the perfect temperature for the tank top and jean shorts I'm sporting. Hair down and in wild waves, my sneakers hit the pavement.

Without thinking, I stalk toward the truck, arms flying into the air.

"Open your damn window, asshole!" I rage, so incensed I'm not one bit afraid of whoever is sitting behind the wheel of this honking truck. "What the hell is your problem? Are you purposely trying to blind me?"

The driver does as he's told; the window on his side starts to lower little by little, revealing the guy perched behind the wheel.

Big.

Blond.

Bulky.

Oh. My. *God*—I recognize his face immediately. It's the jocktacular asshole from the cafeteria last week! The jerk who took my chicken sandwich and then tried to take both my burgers! What the hell is he doing, driving around in the dark terrorizing people?

I walk straight up to his window so I can get in his face.

"You!" Now I'm pointing at him, forefinger aimed at the middle of his mug. "Roll down your damn window!"

He rolls it down the rest of the way. Then I hear *the laugh.*

"You don't look happy to see me again."

He's not alone, but I only spare his buddy a glance—I have my sights set on *this* one.

"Because I'm not, you…you…" Words escape me I'm so pissed. "Ugh, what the hell is your problem?" I shout into the dark, hands on my hips, indignant and outraged. I give the hood of his truck a pound with the palm of my hand for good measure, to punctuate how mad I am. "What are you doing? You're going to get someone in an accident!"

His laughing is loud, booming, and amused—three things that are pissing me off and not welcome right now. He can save his good humor for when he's not being a thoughtless imbecile.

"Well, well, well—look what the cat dragged in." His twang is lazy and drawn out and—I won't lie—really kind of cute.

Shit.

I do not have time to get mushy over that damn Southern accent. It sounds even hotter when he uses metaphors and slang that make no sense whatsoever.

Focus, Charlie.

"Your careless driving is what *dragged* me in." I use air quotes around the word, stabbing the air with my forefingers.

"There you go again, mockin' my accent." He grins, arm propped on the open window. "Not such a sweet thang, are ya?"

Damn right I'm not—especially not when it's Friday night, and I'm standing in the middle of the road yelling at the rudest guy I've ever met.

"How *dare* you tail me like that? How *dare* you! Are you trying to get me killed?"

His eyes are so blue, and with the light from passing traffic, I can see their vibrant color clearly—though they hardly need a spotlight shining on them to be beautiful.

I take another a good look at him, something I didn't do in the student union last week. Tan. Blond.

Lots of stubble. Hair still too long.

My gaze drifts to the hand that's lazily hanging half out the window; it's big and rough. He sees me looking and flexes his fingers.

Curls his lips into a knowing smile.

Cocky bastard.

When he smiles, dimples press into both cheeks like two fingers pressing into dough; a visible gap between his teeth winks at me, too.

How did I not notice that before? Oh yeah. It's because I wanted to smack him in his arrogant face.

"Babe, ya need to relax."

Babe?

I stare.

Give my head a shake to get the dust off my brain. I mean, honestly, there are cobwebs on my vagina—it makes sense that I'd be attracted to him. I simply don't know any better.

So what if he's cute? He's a danger and a menace to society.

"I need to relax? Listen to me, you *dick*, watch how you're driving. What you're doing is *dangerous.*"

"What is it I'm doing? Are your panties twisted up 'cause my truck is bigger than that piece-of-shit car you're drivin'?"

Piece of she-it yer drivin'.

My car isn't winning any beauty contests, but it's hardly a *piece of shit.*

Okay. It's a total piece of shit—but it's *mine.* I bought it myself, so Biff McBurgerThief here can shove that insult down his pie hole.

And choke on it, too.

"You need to calm down," he says again, in what he probably considers a soothing voice meant to calm me down.

I refuse.

"*You* need to take this more seriously."

Those wide shoulders shrug. "No harm, no foul."

"Are you serious? Your lights were blinding me. I could hardly see where I was going, and you were way too close to my bumper."

Still is.

"You're spittin' mad, aren't ya? Like you just chewed up nails and spit out a barbed wire fence." The brute has the nerve to laugh, as if the metal chrome of his super duty pickup truck isn't currently butted up against the tail end of my car.

The nerve.

My stance widens, fists curled at my sides, clutched into tiny fists of fury.

Ugh!

The nostrils on my nose flare. "You think you're tough shit because you're on the football team, don't you, jock strap? You think scaring defenseless girls in the middle of the night is funny? Do you?" I stab a finger in his direction, glaring.

"I don't see no defenseless girls 'round here."

Don't see no. Lord, has this guy had any formal education?

"It's me." I stab at my chest. "*I'm* the defenseless girl, you halfwit."

He is completely missing the point—hasn't picked up on my sarcasm. Either he's choosing not to, or he's dumb as a box of rocks.

I don't know for a fact that he's a complete moron, but based on stereotypes and what I'm staring at, I'm going to assume he is. Big truck. Bigger muscles. Shaggy hair. Bruised eye. Crooked smirk I want to wipe off his face.

He looks like he was raised in the backwoods and sounds like it, too.

"You hardly look defenseless." He's staring down at me from his perch in the driver's seat.

"Do you see any weapons?"

"No, but I keep hearin' one."

Huh? "What does that mean?"

"Your mouth is runnin'."

Inside the cab of the truck, his buddy laughs.

I glare at them both. "How dare you!"

"I'm not the one who slammed on her brakes and hopped out of her car in the middle of the street," he has the nerve to point out.

"Your bumper is jammed so far up my ass I can taste chrome when I swallow." Did those words just come out of my mouth? Damn, I'm kind of impressed with myself.

The kid in the passenger seat laughs, and I wish I could reach in and smack him.

"How about you be quiet?" I have to get closer to the truck to see his face, but I can make him out in the shrouded, dimly lit cab. He looks like a jockhole: big and built and strong—and smiling.

Ugh, so annoying.

"What did you expect me to do, keep driving?"

"Nope. Kind of wanted you to slam on your brakes and hop out of your car in the middle of the street."

I can't decide if he's full of crap or not. He laughs, the Adam's apple in his thick throat bobbing, tendons visible from here, even in the semi-darkness.

"Besides, if my bumper was up your ass, we'd both know it."

It doesn't sound like he's talking about car parts. It sounds like a metaphor for butt stuff, the bumper being his—

"Darlin', you look fit to be tied."

"Don't you *darlin'* me. I'm still half blind from those dumb lights, you jerk!"

He rests his forearm on the window, leaning out while talking down to me. The sleeves of his plaid shirt are rolled to the elbow. "Sorry 'bout that."

I peel my eyes off his muscles. "You're not sorry—you were doing it on purpose!"

"It worked, didn't it?" His teeth are blaring white, almost as bright as his headlights and aimed in my direction. "What's your name?"

"None of your damn business."

Wow, I sound salty.

The guy turns his body, neck craning away from me. "Tyson," he says, "listen to the mouth on *this* one." He smirks, grinning down at me, the stupid asshole. "She's spittin' fire, and I bet she's hungry for a chicken sandwich, too."

Finally, an acknowledgment that he knows who I am.

I try to get a good look at this Tyson, but it's difficult given the flickering streetlights above and the dim one in the cab of the truck.

What I do see, however, is the telltale glow from a cell phone, illuminating this mysterious passenger person's face.

"Wait a second—are you filming me?" It most definitely looks like this guy is pointing the camera of his phone in my direction.

"Yeah."

"Why?"

"Proof."

Proof? Of what! Of all the ridiculous, stupid things to say!

"Uh, excuse me, I'm the one who should be taping you—you're three times my size, and you're the one harassing me."

"No one is harassin' you, and no one made you get out of your car."

"Do I have to keep repeating that you could have gotten me in an accident with your headlights?"

He turns and says something to his friend that sounds suspiciously like, "It might be easier to forget about this one."

I strain to hear the rest, but it's difficult above the sound of cars easing their way around us on the street.

I step a bit closer, confident that although this bo-hunk is an imbecile, he's harmless—not a kidnapper, not going to sexually harass me, not going to harm me in any way.

Call it intuition.

"I'm sorry, *what* did you just say to him?"

He turns his attention back to me. "I'm not the one screamin' on the side of the road."

Huh? That makes no sense.

I might be mad, but I'm not screaming.

"That's not what you said."

McMuscles chuckles when Tyson bumps him in the universal,

bro-code kind of way. They laugh again. "Nope. It ain't."

"What did you say?" I know he was talking shit about me.

"Now why would I go and tell you that? You're already in a hair-tossin' mood—no need to ruffle them feathers more."

"What does that even *mean*?"

"It means you're pissed enough already," the other guy says from the deep recesses of the truck, translating the Southern mumbo-jumbo.

"Thanks for the translation, genius. Pretty sure I could have figured it out on my own."

Biff looks down at me, eyes shooting a cursory glance into the side mirror, finally noticing the steady line of cars gathering behind his giant vehicle.

"How 'bout you get in your car and head home—home where it's safe."

Where it's safe? "I was safe until you started riding my tail and your lights temporarily blinded me."

"Just go home." His eyes harden a bit, mouth drawing into a serious line.

"How 'bout *you* don't tell me what to do."

The nerve of this guy.

Seriously.

His giant, hulking body leans in my direction, arm still resting against the door. "Suit yourself. We'll just sit here in the middle of the road while everyone stares until you buckle your seatbelt and drive off."

Why am I still standing here arguing with this Neanderthal? Obviously he doesn't get the reason I'm pissed. It doesn't occur to him that I got out of my car because his actions were reckless.

What I should have done is call the freaking cops.

"I'll go—but not because you're telling me to."

"Good. You *should* go."

"Just so we're clear, I'm leaving so I don't keep blocking traffic, not because you're telling me to."

He winks.

"Don't wink at me."

He smiles.

My eyes narrow into suspicious slits.

"I'm watching you, bucko."

"I would love it if you were." He has the nerve to laugh again, to shoot me another cocky wink.

"Stop flirting with me." I have no interest in this guy. Not only is he a creep, he's the furthest thing from my type. I give my hair a toss over my shoulder. "Whatever. I'm leaving."

"Go." He hangs out the window a little, giving his fingers a wiggle. Revs the engine of his giant truck once when I walk in front of it, his dumb headlights a spotlight on my retreating ass.

Great. Just great.

* * *

JACKSON

The girl glares daggers at my windshield as she walks back to her car. If looks could kill, I would be a dead man.

For a split second, I have the thought that if I were interested in women and dating, she would be exactly the type of girl I'd date: a little spitfire, full of passion and sass. Any girl riled enough to climb from the safety of her car to scream at a stranger sitting in a dark truck has gumption.

"Do you know her?"

"No."

My friend and teammate Tyson pushes. "Because it definitely seemed like you know her."

I sigh, putting my car in drive. "Can't you just leave it be?"

Tyson raises his brows at me. "Goddamn I love it when y'all country boys say y'all shit like 'leave it be.'"

He totally misuses the word *y'all*, plugging it into all the wrong spots, but I don't have the time or the energy to school the idiot on its proper use. It's nothing new; Tyson loves repeating the shit I say, following me around like a puppy—or a kid chasing after his favorite player on a team.

Though we're teammates and he's a fucking fantastic football player in his own right, he has some odd hero-worship thing where I'm concerned, and I cannot shake the poor idiot.

He tags along when I'm bored and want to go driving, sitting shotgun during my cruises.

"She definitely knew you."

Yes, she definitely knows me. Not my name, or anything about me—or shit, maybe she does and just acts like she doesn't recognize me. I mean, it's not like I'm hiding who I am. I have a reputation on campus and around the country as one of the best wide receivers in the NCAA. Shit, my face is plastered on a banner hanging at the football stadium, in color and fifty feet tall.

Granted, my face is covered by the facemask of my helmet, but it's there, nonetheless.

"She's not the first girl to get out of her car because lights were shining in her eyes," Tyson says, staring out his window and tapping on the door.

No. She's not.

My truck is jacked up so high, no doubt it does blind anyone I sneak up behind. At one point, I was going to adjust the headlights and angle them downward, but the screws were rusted on too tight, and I wasn't wasting fifty bucks to have it done at a shop. Luckily, only a few brave souls have gotten out of their vehicles—dudes included—to chew my ass out, but what am I supposed to do, go spend twelve hundred dollars on a new set of smaller tires?

I don't fucking think so.

I wouldn't do it even if I could afford it. Which I can't.

"You know, we could be onto something," he says cryptically.

"Don't tell me. I don't want to know." When I put on my blinker and cut back into traffic, my passenger is already keyed up with an idea. Sits up a bit straighter in his seat, looking excited and mischievous.

"I'm just thinking out loud here, but what if…" He lets his voice trail off mysteriously. As if I'm going to be intrigued enough to ask questions.

"No."

"Let me finish."

"No."

I head toward the football house, trying to tune out the sound of Tyson's voice, wanting to end this evening. Seeing that girl—again—was enough excitement for one damn day.

We have to grab our gym bags and head to the weight room.

No rest for the weary, not with a game against Madison coming up. Besides, it's not like I have anything better to do.

No partying. No drinking. No fucking around.

Hence driving around a college town and cruising the strip—it's the only entertainment that reminds me of home. Harmless, fun, and free, if you don't count the gas my truck guzzles in the process.

"What if..." Tyson begins again, as if I didn't just shoot him down. "We make a game out of it."

"A game out of what?" My eyes haven't left the road, but my ears have perked up.

"A game out of people getting out of their cars to scream at you."

"That's a terrible idea for so many reasons. One, it's not safe. Two, I could get in fuckin' trouble."

"Why? You're not doing anything. You're just driving your own vehicle." He's turned to face me, the dumb jock actively interested in his own stupid idea. "We could come up with rules."

"That just makes it worse."

"How so?"

"Because. It just does." How does he not get it? "Besides, what kind of rules could you possibly make up for something as dumb as people getting out of their cars?"

"Dude—fun ones. Like getting one point if it's a guy who gets out, five if it's a girl."

I mean...that does sound kind of fun.

Still.

"No."

"Oh! You get ten points if the girl is a brownbagger, twenty if she's hot and you'd bang her."

"Yeah, now that just sounds like assault."

"You're not actually going to bang them—you're just earning points."

Is he in a skeevy fraternity and I don't know it? Who comes up with shit like this? Assigning a point value to a girl because she's ugly is fucking mean; I might not give two shits about dating one, but I know enough not to be a dick about what they look like.

Who the fuck am I to judge? I'm no cover model myself. I was raised on a cattle ranch in the middle of fucking nowhere, rarely had clothes that fit me properly, was always dirty, and needed braces but never got them.

"Yeah—still no."

"Why not?"

"Tyson, I ain't doin' it."

"Why?" he parrots himself. "They're getting out of their cars anyway—we should judge them for it. Five points if they scream at us, three if they just bang on the window. One point if they get out of the car but chicken out."

It sounds like he's given this some serious thought. The point values make actual sense, despite there being no way in hell I'd play a game like that.

"Think about it dude. It's such a good idea."

"Horrible, really."

He goes on, warming to the topic. "Fifteen points if the person recognizes us. Twenty if it's a girl and she starts flirting."

"Tyson. Stop."

"I'm just saying y'all could be fun."

That makes me laugh, despite myself, and I shake my head at his rambling on and on, especially his misuse of the word y'all.

"Dude. I just thought of another good one."

"Would you give it a rest?"

"I can't. Dude, I can't."

He's just called me dude four times—not a record for him, but close. Tyson is from the West Coast, California, and judging by the tan, long blond hair, and loose lingo, he spent lots of time surfing and on the water before returning to school for training camp.

His parents are boosters—wanted him to go to school locally. They wanted him under their thumb, in the family business rather than playing football.

We're opposites, he and I.

For whatever reason, the kid wouldn't leave me alone when he was recruited and has been my sidekick since. He doesn't always use the common sense God gave him, but man is he one loyal bastard. I rue the day someone tries to screw me over.

Dude has my back.

Fuck. I just said dude.

"Can you drop it for now?"

He grunts. "Fine." Pauses. "But what if I put all this down on paper, just in case?"

"Do what you want—makes no difference to me."

STILL THE THIRD FRIDAY

JACKSON

"Triple J, tell us about your angry little friend."

"My what?"

I pretend I have no idea who McMillan is talking about though I know damn well he means that chick on the side of the road, the one whose food I took last week and who I pulled up behind tonight.

Tyson must have said something—he's a little washwomen, gossiping when he has a nugget of information; the more personal the better.

Awesome.

"Your *friend.*" Why is he saying it like that? It sounds creepy.

"She's not my friend." I lift two forty-pound weights off the rack and begin doing squats. "I don't even know her name."

"Who are we talking about?" Someone else butts in from off to my right—these guys are washwomen, fueled by gossip and carb-loading the night before a game.

"No one." I grunt, bending my knees and going down as far as my legs will allow without falling. Standing. Squatting.

"Triple J has a girlfriend."

"Shut the fuck up, Tyson." I take back every nice thing I was thinking about him before—right now I need a sock to stick in his loud mouth.

"She was—what did you call it? Spitting mad at you?"

"What'd you do to her, buddy?" Another one of my teammates joins the conversation from out of nowhere, and I swear, these guys are worse than old biddies with their gossiping. Always need to be up someone's ass with their meddling.

"Nothin'." I'm trying to block them all out, but it's like we're having story time and they've all gathered 'round.

"He got all up in her grill—literally and figuratively," Tyson informs them with authority—the factotum with all the details. "We came up with a game to play while we're cruising in The Bull."

The Bull—he must be talking about my truck.

"Would you stop?" I pause. The longer I stand here blabbing nonsense, the heavier the weights in my grip become. Fuck it's heavy. Before I drop them completely, I manage to set them down and rise to my full height, the belt around my waist cinched and tightened. It supports my lower back, but it doesn't prevent the sweat from dripping down my spine, down into my ass crack.

"He means there could be a game if he'd let himself have fun for once in his boring life." Tyson cackles, garnering laughs from the rest of the lemmings.

"Tyson, give it a rest."

"I can't—it's such a good idea."

"What idea?" someone finally asks, and I sigh, unable to stop the momentum of Tyson's foolish meddling.

"Enough!" I roar. "There's no game! Me and the guys back home used to cruise the strip in town every weekend 'cause there wasn't anything else to do, and I've been doin' it here with Tyson because... You know I don't party, and there ain't anything else to do during the season. It makes me feel like I'm home."

"Cruising the strip?" A rookie wrestler by the name of Griffin Torenson scratches behind his ear and looks up at me from the bench. "What strip? We have a strip?"

"You know—Jock Row or whatever y'all call it." I pull a pair of gloves out of the pocket of my shorts and pull them on, one at a time, tightening them around the wrists. "It reminds me of home to drive it back and forth."

When I say it out loud, it sounds dumb, and my face reddens, embarrassed.

"Awww, big guy has a boner for his hometown."

Tyson slaps his hand on my shoulder as he passes by to hit the shower. "You homesick, Triple J?"

Holy shit, his tone is sincere. He's not playing around.

I shrug his hand off. "No, I'm not homesick," I scoff—even though I am, just a little. Who wouldn't be? My Aunt Beth makes the best caramel apple pie, and the family on Mama's side gets together every weekend for Sunday brunch and to watch football. I'm too fucking far away to ever visit, even a few times a semester.

So, fine. Okay. Maybe I do hanker for home more often than a twenty-one-year-old should—big fucking deal. But I can't fly, and I can't drive.

Far too expensive.

So I stay at school, even during holidays when everyone goes home.

Oh-fucking-well. You won't find me crying about it.

"It's not a crime to miss home," Griffin muses, wiping his

forehead with a white towel. "I miss my girlfriend."

"Torenson, no one gives a shit about you missing your girlfriend," a guy shouts from the machines in the middle of the weight room. "That's what your right hand is for."

"Definitely looks like his right arm is bigger than his left," another guy jokes, squirting his water bottle in Torenson's general direction but missing him by a mile.

"Gross, Rutherford—that has your backwash in it!" Griffin whines.

"At least it's not sweat from my ball sac." Rutherford laughs, grabbing a fresh towel from a nearby rack and running it over his forehead. "Enjoy a shot of moist spray from my hose."

What a fuckin' idiot.

"Asshole," Griffin grumbles, using his towel to wipe down the few drops of water that did manage to hit his chest. "You're disgusting, do you know that?"

Chuckling, I wander to the opposite side of the room to get some breathing room. These dudes are always up my butt and riding my ass. I'm almost never alone, which seems like it would be great—having people around, always keeping you company—but you know what? Occasionally I'd like privacy and some time to think without their obnoxious voices in my ear.

And I don't know why Tyson is making fun of me for cruising up and down the road on the weekends since he fucking comes along all the damn time. Idiot. He loves nothing more than riding shotgun.

We have a routine, Tyson and I—he walks his ass to the football house (where I live) Friday nights after ten. We stop along the way and grab fast food, usually several hamburgers each plus fries, onion rings, shakes—whatever sounds good at the time—I take one cheat day a week and take full advantage.

Then, we head back toward campus, going south at the end of Jock Row and slowly creeping along the road where most of the action happens. People standing around on the corners, waiting to cross the busy streets. It's almost always crowded, even during the week, usually with students walking to and from parties, downtown to the bars, or the nerdy kids heading to campus to study.

Music pumping through the speakers of my truck is a bit douchey, no doubt. I won't deny we're a bit douchey and cliché, but the weather is still freaking beautiful considering it's fall, and unless it's too cold, we put the windows down and crank the music up, which is the best way to fucking drive.

Slow, seeing who we can see, who can see us.

I'm not surprised Tyson wants to make a game of it; plenty of people get pissed off by my bright headlights, but what the hell am I supposed to do about it? I can't help it if my damn truck is higher up off the ground than your stupid car. I can't help it if the lights hit your rear-view mirror in just the perfect way. I can't take my truck back and return it, and I'm sure as shit not going to sell it for something smaller.

Back home, teenagers cruised the strip; have been for decades since carhops and Friday night lights during football season were the only forms of entertainment in our small town, population three thousand eighty-five, give or take.

That's how my mama met my daddy—though he ended up being a philandering piece of shit and the main reason I'm not in a relationship. If you can't find one person to be loyal to, don't date anyone.

I could get into more detail, but I won't. All I'll say is, I've watched my mama cry when my pops wouldn't commit, and I swear

I'll never do that to a woman unless I can give her my whole heart.

For now, football has my body and soul, and I'm gonna keep it that way.

It's the only way I'll keep my scholarship, the only way I can keep playing, and the only way I can make it in the pros.

I love football. Live for it.

It's the one and only thing that kept me going when things at home were shitty, the only time my Pops paid any attention to me, something I craved growing up. Just a bit of goddamn attention from my old man—attention I fought for. So much effort wasted on him because I didn't know any better, despite having a passion for the game.

What an ignorant kid I was.

I should have been paying more attention to my mom and how miserable she was, but I was young—what the hell did I know about love and relationships and making someone happy?

Nothing.

I wasn't a comedian, so my jokes didn't cheer her up. I wasn't sweet, or thoughtful, or studious; I knew nothing about females, and my mother never taught me. What my mother did was resent my father—then later, me, because she wanted attention from my dad and he never gave it to her.

He focused all his time on me when she wanted it—or at least *some* of it—on her.

I know *less* about women now, having steered clear of girls for the past couple of years. Shit, I haven't even had sex yet.

Yes, I've been tempted—of course I have—but it's too risky.

I'm not willing to get some rando accidentally knocked up for one orgasm—too many jersey chasers hanging around. My teammates and I never know who the fuck is honest and sincere and who's just at the house to add a notch to their athlete tally.

Anyway.

I'm single and plan to stay that way.

I don't do casual—I go all in or not at all, and right now, I don't have time for women.

I'm no Puritan; I'm not waiting for marriage to have sex, but I'm in no hurry, either. My right hand does just fine taking care of "business".

I watch the guys joke around. It's late—far later than we usually work out, but we have a game coming up against a huge rival and Coach has stepped it up to two-a-days. Practice at the ass crack of dawn then again in the afternoon.

We're also required to hit the weight room.

I won't lie—I'm fucking tired as *all* hell.

Legs weak, I sink down onto a nearby weight bench and exhale. Lower myself to my back, grip the bar that's set on the rack, the cold metal a contrast to my burning hot skin. I wish I could run it over my forehead to cool off and drench myself with water, but that will come later when I hit the shower.

I crane my neck. I can't do these without a spotter, and there is no one nearby. Too lazy to call someone over, I lie still, staring up at the ceiling and the exposed industrial HVAC vents. Wires. Fluorescent lighting tubes.

Large Iowa banners flank the perimeter, hanging down the cinder block walls. Photos of my peers—student athletes—blown up larger than life and displayed around the room. The quarterback from our football team. A few varsity women's rowers. Wrestlers. Track stars and soccer players. They're all represented, their stats and championships displayed on huge plaques near the front registration desk.

I don't get up, but I make no effort to lift.

I don't have the energy.

Then.

My thoughts stray to that girl—the one on the road who got out of her car to bitch at me. Man, she was pissed. As angry as a barn cat and ten times cuter.

That day I took her sandwich in the union, her nostrils actually flared.

Freckles.

That's what I noticed about her when she got up in my face; her adorable freckles.

Blonde hair, but don't they all? Blue eyes. Nothing special about that. Pink cheeks.

And freckles.

Right—I mentioned that already.

No doubt about it, she was cute, and kind of tall. I definitely wasn't dwarfing her by any stretch, and I'm a big dude. Most people back down when I get up in their shit, but not this girl. She was too pissed and too hungry to surrender.

And the second she climbed out of her car and came toward my truck with fire in her eyes? Shit. I don't know, my stomach did a somersault.

Really fucking inconvenient.

Whatever, I'm not interested anyway. I'm not dating, remember?

If I were, though…

But I'm not, and I best keep that in mind.

My head turns. "Bledow! Get your scrawny, good-for-nothin' ass over here," I bellow to a teammate. He's a sophomore second-stringer and is neither scrawny nor good for nothing. In fact, he's a one of the best fuckers I've ever met.

Bledow comes immediately when called.

"Spot me?"

"You got it, Triple J."

I nod, inhaling and exhaling sharp breaths, psyching myself up to lift the weight stacked on the Olympic bar, and push up.

I push everything out of my mind, focusing on the heavy, dead weight above me.

FOURTH FRIDAY

CHARLIE

This is getting ridiculous. Why do I keep seeing him, every freaking week?

Same truck.

Same spot.

Same time of night.

Same. *Guy.*

Is God punishing me? Why do I keep bumping into this idiot? Seriously. It's becoming a joke at this point, and I'm tired of it. I'm sick of seeing his stupid, smug, arrogant face.

His handsome, dumb face.

He's a cretin—one with a serious set of balls, I'll give him credit for that. One who is pulled over on the road, hogging the shoulder.

Fortunately, I'm not alone for this ride, because I'd love nothing more than to stick it to this guy; get out of the car and give him a piece of my mind. I've been daydreaming about it, as a matter of fact, since our last…encounter. Is that what I'm calling it now? An encounter?

Gosh, listen to me.

I steer my car to the side of the road, getting as close to the curb as possible so I'm pulled over on what little shoulder room there is, careful not to hop the curb. God forbid I scuff my tire—I can't afford for them to get damaged.

"What are you doing?" Savannah finally notices we're not in the turning lane—we are, in fact, pulled over. "Uh, *hellooo*."

"Give me a second here." I have to think about what I'm going to say.

"We're not stopping for a hitchhiker."

"This is a college town—there are no hitchhikers. Plus, there's Uber for that."

"Oh yeah—good point. So. What are we doing?"

I ignore her question to ask one of my own. "Roll down your window, would ya?" She has to do it for me because my car is so old, the windows are manual, not automatic.

"Why? What are you going to do?" She's so nosy.

"Can you just do it without arguing?" Ugh, when did I get so bossy? "That guy is someone I recognize and I want to, um—say hello."

Not.

My friend complies, shooting me a look as if I've lost my damn mind—and maybe I have, because I'm about to shout out the window in the middle of the road at an idiot who probably couldn't care less.

"Hey! Hey, asshole!" I'm loud, projecting as best I can so he hears me.

He straightens to stand, taking his attention away from a girl in a red compact car, turning slowly toward my idling vehicle. Crosses his arms and smiles—as if he's actually pleased to see me, pulled over and shouting at him.

"Well if it isn't Little Miss Priss."

Miss Priss? "Is that what you've been calling me?"

"Yes ma'am."

We're going to add *ma'am* to the list now?

Great.

Everyone knows it's a shortened version of the word madam, which we all know was the formal way to address a woman back when etiquette and common courtesy were common.

Yes ma'am does flow off the tongue nicely—*if* you're a Southern gentleman.

Which this guy is not.

Southern *jackass* is more accurate.

"Is this your Friday routine? Blinding unsuspecting girls and hitting on them on the side of the road?"

His laugh fills the darkness, confirming my suspicions.

"That's sick and twisted, and it could get you arrested."

Couldn't it? Surely that can't be legal. I'll have to google it later when I get home.

"Just havin' a little fun, darlin'. No harm done."

Gross. "Please stop calling me that," I shout.

"Stop calling you what?"

It sounds like '*Stop cawlin you wut?*'

Ugh. The accent is too, too much.

"What the hell is going on right now?" Savannah asks, head whipping back and forth between me and Biff McMuscles. "Charlie, do you know that guy? I think I recognize him from somewhere…"

"No, I don't know him. There was just an unfortunate incident involving chicken and a burger that I don't have time to tell you about it right now," I mutter, fixating my glare in his direction and narrowing my eyes. Lower my voice and whisper, "I wish he'd choked on it."

The big jock peels himself away from Co-Ed Barbie—whose lips I can see pursing at the interruption—to amble toward my vehicle, all toned arms and muscular legs and tight abs. I mean—allegedly.

"One of these nights, I'm going to have you arrested for harassment," I hiss to him around Savannah, whose eyes have gone wide at my tone.

I'm normally so sweet and easygoing.

Truly.

I don't know what it is about this guy that's turning me into a livid little dictator.

"For real though, how is he harassing you? You're the one shouting out the window," she mumbles. "What is happening right now? You're acting manic."

McMuscles continues walking toward my car, all cute and good-looking.

"We've got to stop meetin' like this." His deep voice is a silky Southern caress as he lumbers toward my car, large body imposing in the dim dusk of what's nearly midnight. When he reaches the passenger side door, he rests that big, monolith of a body against it and leans in, forearms propped on the metal frame.

They're tan, veins popping.

Savannah is inches away from the intrusion, reclining in my direction—as if we were in an exotic animal park or on a safari and a lion was approaching the car.

"Oh shit," she mutters. "You're…"

He winks at her, presses a forefinger to his lips so she doesn't finish her sentence—and she *sighs*.

Wait. *What?*

No.

Savannah, *no*.

Do not fall under his spell!

"At least one of you knows how to be agreeable," he drawls.

Yeah—and it isn't me.

My chin tilts up, incensed. "Can you kindly remove yourself from my car? The last thing it needs is a *dent*."

"You're feisty tonight." He laughs deep in his chest then regards Savannah. "Is she always like this?"

"Her name is Charlie."

I swat at Savannah and land a soft blow to her upper bicep, near her boob, punctuating it with a, "Shut *up*, Van." Jesus, whose side is she on? The last thing I want is him knowing my *name*.

"Charlie, eh?" Suddenly, he's keenly interested. "Like the boy's name or somethin'?" He seems to think he's amusing—I want to wipe the smirk off his face with the back of my hand. Besides, this isn't the first time someone has made a wisecrack about my male name.

I've heard it all before.

I roll my eyes at his ridiculous statement. "No. It's short for Charlotte."

"Charlotte?" His brows rise. "Charlotte." He says it twice—first as a question, then as a statement—in his Southern burr, momentarily causing my insides to twist in the most inconvenient way. He isn't just saying it. He's *saying* it, hard, like it's interesting and sexy—as if he's never heard the name before, as if he loves it and is assigning it to me.

I ignore the spark shooting to my heart, tempted to swat it away as it lingers in the air, Savannah caught in the crossfire of our barbs.

He says it again. "Charlotte."

"Yes, but no one calls me that." Not anymore. Not since I was ten, when I went through my tomboy phase and hated everything feminine, including the color pink, doing my hair, cute clothes—and my own name.

That's changed now that I'm grown, but the nickname has stuck.

"It's pretty—way prettier than Charlie. Or Chuck."

"Gee, thanks."

His smile is patronizing. "My pleasure."

Is he not picking up on my sarcasm? If he is, he's damn good at hiding it. My eyes shift around him to the platinum blonde sitting in her car, waiting for him to return. *Good.* She can have him.

"Your harem awaits. Please don't stand here in the road on my account, blocking more traffic while you try to bag another unsuspecting victim."

"Charlie!" Savannah gasps, unused to any hostility from me. "Don't be rude!"

Yeah, she's definitely siding with the devil on this one, which surprises me. Savannah is single because she's too picky; she wants a gentleman and a scholar, and those don't seem to exist anymore. This guy? He doesn't look like either, yet here she is, falling all over herself.

Drool is practically dripping from the side of her mouth.

"What!" I look to the guy for support; surely he'll back me up since we do not like each other. "A little help here—tell her we don't get along."

"I think we'd get along just fine if you minded your manners."

Oh no he did *not* just insult my manners.

"*Stealing* is minding your manners?"

His grin is wolf-like, bright white teeth vibrant in the dim light.

"Like taking candy from a baby." With that, he saunters away.

I do want to apologize for the crap that's flying out of my mouth, but not to Biff—no. I want to apologize to Savannah. I hate that she's horrified by my behavior. Her jaw couldn't have fallen any farther—she's going to have to pick it up off the floor.

Honestly—what's gotten into me? I'm not usually this big of an asshole. I guess seeing guys act like total scumbags pisses me off more than I ever thought it would. And now he's trying to schmooze me? *I don't think so, pal.*

What a dickhead.

"That was JJ Jennings."

I do not care what his name is, but Savannah wants to prattle on about it.

"He's one of the wide receivers on the football team."

Yup. Don't care.

"They call him Triple J," she drones on.

"Is now a good time to point out that his name sounds like a dude ranch in Wyoming?"

"Can you be nice for five seconds?"

"Meh—don't think so. That guy is a total ass."

"You haven't told me a damn thing, so I wouldn't know—I only know what I've heard about him."

"Which is what?"

"Let me google him, too."

"He's google-able?"

Savannah looks at me like I'm nuts. "Have you been under a rock? We go to a Big Ten school and he's on the football team—of course you can google him. He's probably going to enter the draft.

They all do if they're good enough."

"Is he?"

"Jesus, Charlie. Get with the program."

Sorry, but my eye tends to slide toward baseball players and guys who aren't as bulky and huge. Less Hulk-like and more…intellectual. Funny and cute, but smart.

JJ Jennings looks like he could bust through a wall in an action movie as a stunt double for The Rock.

"What does JJ stand for?"

Savannah's head dips as she checks her phone. "Let me check." She pauses for a brief second as her fingers fly over the screen of her cell phone. "Jackson Jennings Junior." Another pause. "Well. That's certainly a mouthful."

"That's certainly Southern."

"Bless his heart." Savannah laughs, and suddenly I find myself defending him.

"Hey, it's not his fault he's stuck with a terrible name."

"You're right, I shouldn't have said that," Savannah demurs, shooting me side-eye. "For someone who hates the guy, you sure are—"

"Don't say it."

Savannah laughs, smacking me in the arm then reaching for the radio. "I can't believe your radio has dials. This is so weird."

Yeah—my radio has actual dials and only gets a grand total of eight FM stations, and it drives my friend crazy that she can't connect her phone to my car. If I hear her bitch about it once a week, I hear it twice, but I'm the only one of us with a car, and beggars can't be choosers.

"Are you going to tell me what that was about, or are you going to pretend there's nothing going on between you and Triple J?"

"Can you not call him that? It's idiotic."

"That's his nickname. What else am I supposed to call him?"

"His name?" Jackson is a cute moniker; I could live with that, but I'd never call him Triple J if I ran into him again. "Thanks for telling him mine, you creep."

"He wanted to know."

"He didn't ask!"

"Trust me, he wanted to know."

"Whatever." My eyes are trained on the road ahead of us, and I hang a left after stopping at a stop sign, then another right, heading toward my small off-campus rental. It's the perfect distance from campus—not so close that I have to see and hear the commotion during the day when classes are in session, but close enough that I can walk and it doesn't take forever.

Plus, I'm near Jock Row. When I want to party, there's always one nearby.

"Quit stalling."

"There is nothing to tell, Savannah."

"Liar. You've met him before, and I want the details. I'd tell you, so why aren't you telling me?"

She's right—she would tell me, and in great detail.

"Fine, but just so you know, it's no big deal."

"Right. No big deal. Got it."

Her mouth is set in a straight, serious line, but it's her eyes that give her away. She's excited for more information and won't believe me when I tell her Jackson Jennings and I are never going to be a thing because Jackson Jennings and I loathe each other.

Just because he was kind of flirting with me a few minutes back doesn't mean anything; he's a jock, and jocks flirt. Like, I'm pretty sure it's in their DNA and it would go against his core nature if he didn't.

It had nothing to do with him liking me. Just so we're clear.

Great, and now I'm talking to myself.

Awesome.

"The other night when I was coming home from the library—it was Friday—"

"You were at the library on a Friday night?"

"Are you going to keep interrupting?"

"Sorry. Go." Savannah clamps her mouth shut and purses her lips tightly.

"So I'm coming back from the library. It must have been close to eleven? I'm not sure, but a truck was behind me and had its headlights right up my ass. I could hardly see—it was dangerous. Anyway. It was him, but I didn't realize it at the time."

"Mmhmm." My friend is nodding, mouth still snapped shut.

"The next week, I'm on campus grabbing a sandwich in the union—I was totally starving. I'm standing in line for food and all I want in this whole wide world is my damn chicken patty, right?" I give her a sidelong glance. "You know how I love those."

She nods enthusiastically. "You do."

"I'm about to have it in my hand and my mouth when all of a sudden, a freaking hand reaches out and takes it."

"He just took it?"

"Yes! He took my chicken sandwich and literally shoved it in his face immediately. No manners, didn't ask, just ate it like a wolf raised in the woods."

"Now you're being dramatic."

"I'm sorry, but no. He took my food and didn't even apologize."

"Okay, so then what happened?"

"Then Wyatt, the guy who works there, had two burgers ready and I took those. Because the guy with four billion Js in his name wanted to nab them, too."

"The nerve!" She's clearly outraged on my behalf—and if she's not, she's doing a great job pretending to be on my side.

"Yeah, so he wants both—*both* of them after he just scarfed down my chicken. For real, Wyatt didn't know what to do. He looked terrified, and Jackson isn't even scary. Give me a break."

"I mean, he kind of is? The guy is huge, Charlie—did you not get a good look at him? He's like six and a half feet tall."

"What. Ever. I was hardly checking him out." Not even a little—not even today when he came ambling toward me in that cutoff t-shirt and faded jeans slung low on his hips.

Brown leather flip-flops. Hair blowing in the—

Ugh, stop it, Charlie! He is not your type!

"Is that the whole story?"

"No. I told him to give me ten bucks for a burger."

"That's extortion."

I laugh. "That's what he said, and I told him it was supply and demand, but then he paid for all the food and I got a free lunch. So who was the loser in that game? Not me."

I'm on a budget; I'll take a free meal no matter what form it comes in.

"Anyway. He goes his way, I go mine, and I didn't think I'd see the asshat again, but I did the following Friday."

"I'm sensing a theme here..."

"I know, right? I need to start staying home on Fridays because I can't seem to stop running into JJ Jennings."

"So you ran into him again last weekend?"

"Yup. On the corner of University Drive and Darter. He's all up in my shit—again—but this time I'm livid. Fuming, like, I've never been so freaking mad. So I slam on my brakes and get out of my car because I have to give this butthole a piece of my mind."

"You did not get out of your car! You could have been murdered."

Solemnly, I nod. "I know. It was dumb."

"What happened?"

"I storm the truck and he rolls down his window and it's him. Ugh, that smug face." I frown, remembering how pleased he looked to see me beside his vehicle. "I don't know what the hell kind of game he and his buddy are playing, but it makes no sense. Seeing him on the side of the road like that, something has to be going on—I mean, isn't that weird? Tell me that's not weird."

"Maybe it's a coincidence?"

"Please—three Fridays, same strip of road cannot be a coincidence. They're up to something." I tap on the steering wheel, deep in thought now that the idea has taken root in my mind. "I've heard of this kind of thing, where they play for points and stuff—I wonder if it's like that."

"I think you're being paranoid. Back where I'm from, the big thing to do on the weekend was drive up and down Main Street because there is literally nothing else to do. People have been doing it since my parents were teenagers, and they're still doing it today. It's like 'see and be seen.' Triple J must be from a small town—bet you anything he is."

"I'm not going to ask him and find out. NO thanks."

"It's one way to find out what he's up to."

Why does she always make so much sense?

And why am I still thinking about Jackson Jennings?

* * *

JACKSON

"That's that same girl."

"Yup." It sure is.

"She doesn't like you."

"No shit."

Tyson gives me side-eye. "Do you like her?"

"What? No." Is he being serious? "You know I'm not datin'."

"I didn't ask if you want to date her. I asked if you like her."

"I don't know her."

He's quiet for a few seconds, thoughtful—likely putting some bullshit sentence together in his mind before saying it out loud. "Didn't look like you don't know her, and you sure do run into her a lot."

That I do.

Weird.

This is the fourth time she and I have clashed, bumped into each other randomly and gotten into a tiff.

"She's cute. I wonder if she's single," Tyson muses out loud.

I roll my eyes, not about to fall for his tactics. He's feeling me out and trying to see if I'll get jealous. Which I won't.

My shoulders rise into a shrug. "Don't care."

He replies by tapping on the window ledge and staring out at the administrative buildings on campus as we pass by them. The library.

The Registrar's Office. The alumni house.

We pass the stadium, which rises out of the ground like Goliath.

I love that fucking stadium; it's the very reason I fell in love with Iowa and the school. New, shiny, and state-of-the-art, it was like nothing I'd ever seen.

Certainly not in the small town where I grew up, though our high school stadium wasn't your typical playing field, either. No one hosts football games like Texans.

"Not even a little bit interested?" he inquires.

"Not even a little."

I can feel him staring at my profile and keep my gaze trained on the road ahead of me. I'm taking him to his place before heading home; we've had enough fun for the night and I'm beat.

That little blonde on the side of the road lost all her appeal once Charlotte and her traitorous friend pulled up. That friend of hers liked me, that I could tell—she at least knew who I was.

Charlie sure as shit didn't, and Charlie couldn't care less.

Charlotte.

The name suits her. It's feminine and beautiful and a bit old-fashioned, just like she seems to be.

FIFTH FRIDAY

JACKSON

Well, well, well, what do we have here?

Charlotte Edmonds and her crappy beige car, broken down on the side of the road, *that's* what. Not a safe place to pull over, but with a flat back tire, doesn't look like she had much choice.

How do I know her last name? Easy—I looked her up and crept on her pretty hard for someone who thinks she's a bit too salty to taste.

Charlotte Edmonds. Twenty-one. Junior. Business major who plays intramural volleyball. Kind of tall for a girl at five foot seven. Her Instagram gallery shows her doing all kinds of cutesy, adorable shit, like baking cupcakes in her tiny kitchen for the Fourth of July and volunteering at the local humane society. Spraying a hose at some little kid, wearing a bikini—that one I really could appreciate.

Boobs. Legs. Ass.

She's a trifecta of feminine perfection…

And she hates my guts.

I pull over and watch her eyeballing me, arms crossed as she leans her hip on the side of her beat-up Chevy, looking like a car model, though she would most likely disagree with that assessment.

I unfasten my seatbelt and hop out of the truck, my flip-flops hitting the ground, door slamming behind me.

"Whacha doin'?"

"My nails," she says sarcastically, rolling her eyes. "What does it *look* like I'm doing? I have a flat tire, Triple J."

She uses my nickname as if it's an insult, the little shit. As if I didn't work hard to earn it with blood, sweat, and grass stains permanently embedded in both my knees, with concussions and a few knocked-out teeth.

"Looks like you've done broke down on the side of the road. You have a flat?" I can see that she does—the ass end of her left side is slouched toward the pavement.

Her eye roll is one big *duh*. "Where is your sidekick?"

"Busy doin' somethin' else." I shrug. "Did you call someone to help you?"

"Honestly? No."

My brows shoot into my hairline. "Why not?"

"Because, Jackson, I knew you would eventually come along and rescue me. It's Friday night—isn't this your *route*?"

"You wanted me to rescue you?"

"Want? No. Need? Yes. I need help putting on my spare tire."

"So, no to the rescuin' you."

Charlotte runs out of patience. "Are you going to help me or not? I can call someone who isn't going to dick me around."

Dick me around.

Hoo-ee, the mouth on this one…

"Yeah, I'll help you. I'll show you how to change your tire, too—it's somethin' you should know how to do."

She groans. "Fine."

"Pop your trunk and let me see what you have back there."

Begrudgingly, Charlotte complies, opening the driver's side door and bending to flip the switch under her dash to release the trunk of her car.

It pops, opening a fraction, and I lift it the rest of the way up to peer inside. The spare tire is buried beneath a pile of crap: gym bag, water bottle, athletic sandals. A fuzzy purple blanket, one tennis shoe, a few paperback books.

No tools. No crowbar.

No jack.

I remove the spare with one hand, hefting it out and setting it on the ground, slamming the trunk shut.

"You're lucky it was me who came along, because you ain't got nothin' to take your tire off with. You should get a tool kit and keep it in your trunk."

"Yeah, yeah, I will," she replies in a bored, *I won't* tone. "Tool kit—gotcha."

I make short work of fishing the tools we need out of the bed of my truck then cop-a-squat next to her flat so I can wedge the jack underneath. Pump the handle until the left side of her car is suspended slightly off the ground, just enough so I can remove the tire and replace it with the smaller, temporary one.

"Come watch what I'm doin'. Pay attention."

She sighs, dragging her feet on the concrete, squatting beside me.

"First you're gonna remove all the lug nuts with this." I show her the tire iron, putting it onto one of the nuts and cranking it counterclockwise. "Sometimes they rust a little so you have to use elbow grease."

"Okay."

"Next you're gonna pull the tire off and roll it to the side." I do just that, propping it against her bumper so it doesn't roll away. "Now go ahead and pop the spare on."

"You want me to do it?" Her eyes are wide.

"Yeah. Your monkey, your circus."

"Whatever that means."

"Just put the spare on and quit rollin' your eyes. Didn't your mama ever tell you they'd get stuck back there if you did it enough?"

She laughs, arms lugging the heavy spare, struggling to fit it onto the hub. "Yes, she did—all the time."

She's watching me and not what she's doing, a small smile on her lips.

Cute.

Really fucking cute.

"Now grab the nuts and tighten them until they're snug, one at a time. Like a star, first that one, then this one," I point to each spot and the pattern I want her to follow. She hesitates. "Go on."

"What if it falls off on my way home because I did it wrong?"

"It won't fall off."

She's skeptical. "If you say so."

"I do. I've changed plenty of tires."

"*Ty-ers,*" she echoes, that smile dancing, eyes sparkling as if I've said something to amuse her.

"Stop teasin' me and keep workin'."

She grunts, her delicate hands now covered with grease and dirt, pink nail polish no doubt chipping from the contact with the metal rim. I reach in to lend a hand, forearms and biceps straining with the motion.

Charlotte's eyes stray to my muscled torso, and when I catch her gawking, she has the courtesy to blush so deep I can see it in the dim, dusky haze.

Busted.

Looks like Charlotte isn't immune to me after all. My biceps *are* pretty damn big; even dudes are impressed.

She lowers her gaze, training it on the wheel and the task at hand.

Right. Back to business.

"Next we're gonna lower the car to the ground, so grab the handle for the jack and turn it counterclockwise." I hand her the silver wrench for the jack and she gets to work lowering it. "Okay, good job," I praise. "Now finish tightening them nuts, tight as you can."

"I do that after I lower the car to the ground?"

"Yup."

"All right." Her fingers nimbly pick up the tire iron. Spin each lug nut. "Done."

"That's it."

"That's it?"

"Yup."

"I changed my own tire?"

"You did."

"I did?" She sounds excited, as if I've just surprised her with a gift or an unexpected award. "I can't freakin' believe it! I changed my own tire!"

Charlotte straightens beside me, doing a little hop beside her car—a dance, really. She squeals.

It resembles the movements my teammates might make after they've scored a touchdown and are celebrating in the end zone.

Sort of.

I stand, too, and she throws her arms around my neck—or tries to.

"Thank you so much."

Tempted to pull her in, I give her an awkward pat on the back. "Welcome."

She pulls back and looks at my face, all serious but with a megawatt grin. "No, seriously. Thank you, Jackson."

Well shit, there she goes using my real name.

No one has done that in an age, including my own parents.

"You can call me JJ."

"Meh. I don't think I will." She just has to be stubborn and difficult.

"Then I'm not callin' you Charlie."

"Fine. *Don't.*"

I cock my head to study her. "Fine, *Charlotte.*" I might be imagining it, but I think she shivers, and it isn't even cold out. "You should get home. I'll put your tire in the trunk—you need to make sure you get it to a mechanic or get a new one. You can't drive around on that donut long."

"All right." For once, she doesn't argue.

"Give me your number."

* * *

CHARLIE

"Give me your number," he says.

Ha—nice try. "Pfft. I'm not going out with you, but nice try."

"I'm not gonna ask you out. I want to make sure you make it home on this spare tire."

This spare ty-er.

Ugh, that accent. It's killing me.

"You don't trust my handiwork? You said it would be fine."

He smirks, leaning against my car and crossing those big, beefy arms across his ridiculously broad chest. Already has his phone out and fingers poised over the screen. "Just give me your dang number and quit bein' a smartass."

I guess he has a point about making sure the tire can get me home; I've never driven on a spare, let alone one I changed myself, and frankly, the idea freaks me out a bit.

It couldn't hurt to give him my number—not if he only wants to follow up and check on me. The gesture is kind, makes me feel...protected and safe, and I haven't felt that in a good, long while.

Not since I'm so far from my parents, who used to do everything for me, especially my dad.

"Maybe I could teach you to change your own oil."

Your own ole.

Jesus. I have to stop talking to this guy before he and his accent turn my girl parts to complete mush. He's an asshole with an annoyingly large truck.

"Thanks, I'm good."

"You know where to find me if you change your mind."

"On the side of the road on Friday night?"

"Ha ha. Well, you'll have my number if you ever have an emergency. Don't be afraid to use it."

Yeah, that's not going to happen, but I keep that to myself. I don't want to sound ungrateful; he just came along and helped me. I didn't have to call a tow and have a strange man pull up in the middle of the night, and I didn't have to pay out of pocket.

He hands me his phone while he sets about rearranging the contents of my trunk, making room for the flat tire, then, with one hand, slings it into the back as if it weighs nothing.

"Your number?" He nods toward his phone.

My top teeth fiddle with my bottom lip, unsure. I mean…what's the worst thing that could happen if I give him my phone number? He messages me too much and I have to block him?

Not like I haven't had to do that with people before…

"All right." My head tilts and I pop the digits into his contacts then hit save.

Have a brief panic attack.

No turning back.

Savannah will die when she hears I gave Jackson Jennings Junior my cell number, even if he isn't going to ask me out. And even if his name is ridiculous.

He has it now, and she was all gaga over him last week.

I toss him his phone and he palms it before jamming it into his back pocket. "I'll shoot ya a note in a bit to check on you."

"Thank you for stopping." I clear my throat. "I appreciate it."

"Don't worry about it." Jackson points to my driver's side door. "You should get going. I'll be in touch."

I shuffle toward my vehicle. "Thanks again."

"Yup." He watches me climb in, buckle my seatbelt. Continues watching until I glance out my window and give him a jaunty little wave.

He shoos me away before climbing into his truck, the dark tint of his windows offering no glimpse of his form. For all I know, he's sitting inside, on his phone. Or, staring at me.

I start my car, put it in drive. Turn on my left-hand turn signal and give my side mirror a glance: no oncoming traffic. I ease into the street and stop at the corner briefly before going right.

So far, so good. My wheel hasn't popped off or wobbled.

Phew.

A few more blocks.

After a couple minutes, I've made it home, safe and sound.

My entire body relaxes, sagging with relief. I don't know what I was expecting, but it sure as heck wasn't making it home safely in one piece.

I pull up to the house and slam my car into park, grab for my keys and purse. Just as I'm reaching for the door handle, my phone pings with the telltale sound of a text notification.

Unknown Number: *Did you make it?*

Ah—it's Jackson. I poke at his number and program him into my phone.

Me: Yup, just arrived safe and sound. No flying metal or screeching tires. All in one piece.

Jackson: That's good. You should be okay, just don't forget to take your tire in. You can't drive on that spare long.

Me: I'll take it home this weekend and have my dad take care of it.

Jackson: I can come grab it for you. I have a buddy at the shop in town. He's fixed my truck half a dozen times.

Me: Gosh, you don't have to do that. I can take it home.

Jackson: How far do your folks live from campus?

Folks.

Me: A few hours, no biggie.

Jackson: How many hours is a few? Two?

Me: Four? Five if I stop to go to the bathroom a few times or shop at the outlet mall.

Jackson: You can't drive four hours on a spare tire. I'll come grab it and get it patched.

Me: You don't have to do that.

Jackson: I know I don't HAVE to. I'm not letting my friend drive on a donut—it's not safe.

Friend.

Lord help me, I smile in the dark, still sitting in my car, out in the driveway. I wonder if Savannah is home and if she sees me out here grinning like an idiot at Jackson's high-handedness. Or concern. Whatever we're calling this.

Me: Oh, we're friends now, eh?

Jackson: Yup.

Me: Just like that?

Jackson: Yup.

Me: Stop doing that.

Jackson: Yup.

Jackson: Lol. FYI I'm coming to get your tire tomorrow and I'm taking it to my buddy's place. It won't be until after practice, so figure around 8:00 at night. Don't try to lift it out of the trunk on your own—I don't want you hurting yourself.

I can tell by his tone this isn't a battle I'm going to win, so I relent and acknowledge the gesture.

Me: That's…really kind of you.

Jackson: I'll remember you calling me kind next time you tell me I'm an asshole.

Me: Technically I wasn't calling YOU kind, I said taking my tire in was kind OF you…

Jackson: Same thing.

Me: Fair enough. It IS nice of you. You are being kind. I really do appreciate it since we're basically strangers.

Jackson: Strangers?? I bought you dinner—we've practically been on our first date already.

Me: OMG I knew you were going to try to ask me out! And you did not buy me dinner!

Jackson: Relax lol I'm not asking you out.

He's not? Well this is awkward. And why does it bother me that he's not asking me out?

Me: Oh, haha. Sorry.

Jackson: Unless you want me to haha.

Me: I don't. haha.

Jackson: Haha then I won't.

Me: We're going to "haha" ourselves into an idiot coma.

Jackson: I won't keep you then. You're probably sitting outside in your car on your phone when you should be inside where it's safe.

Oh lord, is he watching me?

I crane my neck to look around, to catch sight of any big, black pickup trucks lurking in the shadows.

I don't see one.

Me: Nah, I walked into the house a few minutes ago.

Lies, lies, lies.

Jackson: Good. Bet you're in one of those residential areas in a dark neighborhood that has shitty lighting no lights on the street. With mostly locals, not a lot of students?

Me: Er, yeah. I am. It's the cheapest option.

But why does he care?

Maybe he doesn't; maybe he's just being polite because he's Southern, and that's what Southern boys do. Maybe his mama raised him right.

Sheesh, listen to me.

His mama.

What am I even saying?

How did I get from cursing him out in the student union and screaming at him in the middle of the road to agreeing to allow him to help maintain my dumb car?

In any case, my parents will be relieved when they hear it's getting handled and they won't have to worry about it, my mother especially. She worries like crazy; I know she'd have a veritable fit if I drove my car home on a crappy little spare, and Dad will be glad he won't have to hoof it here to make sure everything is in working order.

I relent and play nice, thawing to Jackson Jennings and his quirky Southern-ness.

Me: I'll text you my address tomorrow.

Jackson: K, sounds like a plan. G'night little one.

Little one? What's this now?

Um…

I sit and stare at that last text from him. Little one. What? I mean, he's huge, but I'm not exactly a waif. Maybe to him I seem small?

Little one—is that weird? That must be a Southern thing, too, right? I tap open a web browser and type in *Southern slang little one* to see what will pop up. Maybe he calls all girls that when he can't remember their name?

It seems oddly specific, though, and personal.

My insides flutter.

No guy has ever said anything remotely cutesy to me like that in my entire life, let alone one I just met, or one I'm not dating—and definitely not one who is a hulking beefcake of a man-boy.

A man-boy. That sounds accurate…

A man-boy who's confusing me.

Why is he being so nice when he acted like such an asshole on the side of the road and at the union? That's not normal behavior—why is he doing it? The whole thing is total bullshit, and I'm going to pin him down and ask him about it.

* * *

Jackson: I should have that tire back to you this week, then we'll swap out the donut for the new one. It'll take ten minutes, tops.

Me: By donut, you mean the spare? Right?

Jackson: Yup, donut means spare. That's fancy auto lingo.

Me: Be quiet, it is not lol

Jackson: Okay it's not **eye roll**

Jackson: Anyway, will you be around this week if I text you and swing by? Otherwise, you can give it a go. I think you'd be fine to put it on by yourself.

Me: NO WAY AM I PUTTING THE TIRE BACK ON MYSELF. NO WAY. NUH UH. I INSIST THAT YOU HELP ME, PLEASE. I'm begging.

I'm not yelling—he's yelling.

I have no doubt I could put the new tire on myself, but do I really want to take that chance? I definitely need the help of someone more qualified than I. Plus, the last time he helped it was really nice—and not because he smelled good. Or because his muscles bulged. Or because when he got a little sweaty from heaving the heavy tire, it turned me on a tad.

A smidge, as my grandmother would say.

Jackson: Well if you insist.

Me: I do—if you can swing it.

Jackson: All right, I'll take care of you.

Jackson: I mean. Of the tire.

Jackson: I'll take care of the TIRE.

Me: Know what? I can almost hear you saying tire in your Southern accent.

Jackson: Is that a good thing or a bad thing?

Me: It's cute. I like it, I'm not making fun of you.

Jackson: Lol I didn't think you were, I just wanted to hear you say you think it's cute.

Me: You're the worst.

Jackson: Hey, so—do you ever go out on the weekends?

Me: Do you mean parties and stuff?

My heart beat skips a little. Why is he asking what I do on the weekends? Is he going to ask me out? Crap, why am I getting so excited?

Relax, Charlie. It was a basic question. It means nothing.

Jackson: Yes, parties and stuff.

Me: Yeah, sometimes, depending. Why?

Jackson: I was thinking of hitting up Jock Row for a party at the baseball house this Friday.

Me: Do you usually party on the weekends? I thought there were rules about that.

Jackson: We have a 24-hour rule. No alcohol 24 hours before a game, but we can go out and be social as long as we behave and don't break the conduct code.

Me: I see.

Me: Um. What does that have to do with me?

Jackson: Maybe you should come. If you aren't busy.

Me: Maybe I should.

Jackson: You definitely should.

Me: All right.

Jackson: Seriously?

Me: Why do you sound surprised?

Jackson: Because you hate me lol

Me: I don't hate you Jackson. I mean—you piss me off, but I'm sure you piss tons of people off.

Jackson: If you didn't hate me, you wouldn't call me Jackson.

Me: I'm NOT calling you Triple J. Or JJ, or the other nicknames they call you. That's lame.

Jackson: Junior.

Me: Huh?

Jackson: Junior. That's my other nickname. It's Jackson Jennings Junior, so sometimes they call me that. My dad does.

Me: I think I might have read that somewhere.

Jackson: Were you googling me, Miss Charlie?

I roll my eyes at him even though he can't see it. Googling him—he is so full of himself.

Me: You are so Southern sometimes…

Jackson: But were you? Googling me? You can't lie, we're best friends now.

I want to make a joke about *breast* friends but don't want to sound like a complete pervert.

Me: My friend looked you up—it wasn't me.

Jackson: And you were reading over her shoulder.

No, because I was driving and that would have been dangerous.

Me: I might have been listening when she read some shit out loud. Sue me for being curious. If I'm going to keep seeing you on the side of the road, I have to know you're not a murderer.

Jackson: Lol good.

Jackson: Hey Charlotte?

I shiver at the sight of my name.

Me: Yes?

Jackson: I'm gonna hit the hay—we have two practices tomorrow and one starts at 4:30—but I'll talk to ya soon.

Me: 4:30…in the morning?

Jackson: Yup.

Me: Dang. That's stupidly early…

Jackson: Yup, but you get used to it.

Me: I would never get used to that, solely based on principle.

Me: Anyway. See you soon.

Jackson: Later, Charlotte.

And there goes that shiver up my spine…

SIXTH FRIDAY

JACKSON

She showed up.

I mean, she *said* she was going to, but I didn't actually believe her. Not really, not even a little. I assumed she'd stand me up.

I've categorized Charlotte as one of those girls who isn't into the lifestyle I live. Surrounded by fake people. Strict routine. Strict diet (her sandwich that day did not count because I was fucking desperate). Shit tons of working out. Coaches, professors, and agents riding my ass.

It's too much for me to handle sometimes, and a girl like Charlie? No way would she deal with the bullshit that comes with being an elite college athlete.

Not that this is a date.

Just an invitation for two friends to attend the same party on a Friday night. I've never seen Charlotte out, not at a house party, not on Greek Row, not downtown at the bars. In fact, I'm beginning to wonder if she's even legal.

Granted, I don't go out that much myself, but I know I'd remember seeing her out if I did. Truthfully? I spend most of my Fridays lamely cruising up and down the street, nostalgic about home, needing something to fill my time so I don't spend it doing things I shouldn't be doing—partying, drinking, sex.

Distracting things.

Unsure about whether or not I should approach her or let her come to me, I jam my hands into the pockets of my jeans and stand rooted to the spot. I'm in the corner of the living room, near the kitchen door, with a bird's-eye view of the entire party.

Charlotte isn't alone; she's with three other girls—one from the car that I recognize and two that I don't. They're all shorter but cute. Done up like every girl in the room, they ordinarily wouldn't stand out to me.

But now I know what a smart mouth Charlie has on her, what a brat she can be. I've seen with my own two eyes how riled she gets when she's got her dander up or her panties in a twist.

The thought has my lips tipping up at the corners, and I hide the smile behind the neck of my beer bottle.

It's a nice night, not too cold, so she has foregone a jacket and stands at the door in a cute shirt tucked into dark denim. Her blonde hair is down and wavy, and tonight she's wearing more makeup than I've seen her in.

Her lips are glossy—I can see them shining from here when she cranes her neck to glance around the room and the light hits them just right.

Is she looking for someone?

I'm no fool—I know she's looking for me. I take pleasure in the fact that she hasn't spotted me yet and I can watch her for a few more undisturbed seconds before the spell is broken.

Charlie is beautiful.

So beautiful it makes me slightly uncomfortable. I might be headed to the pros and have an amazing career ahead of me, but physically, Charlie is out of my league.

I'm a brute.

Scarred.

Tall. Bulky. Bruised.

Sore.

Light on my feet for the position I play but large nonetheless.

I run a palm along my jawline. I didn't have time to shave this afternoon; my entire face is scratchy.

Fuck, my shirt is wrinkled, too, while she looks so fucking pretty. Why she agreed to meet me here is beyond me, especially after our rocky start.

It's loud in this house, packed to capacity, and takes a few minutes to weave my way through the strangers gathered for the party. Her friends have all gone their own ways and when I reach her, she's standing alone smiling, lips moving as if pleasantries are coming out of her mouth; words I can't hear because it's so damn loud in this house.

"Hey."

"Hey. Having fun?" I catch her question because I've bent myself at the waist, leaned down to listen, and tilted my head at an angle so she can talk into my ear.

"Meh."

We wouldn't be able to carry on a conversation inside if our lives depended on it, so thank God they don't.

"Want to go somewhere quiet? So we can talk?" Jesus, I'm shouting, eyes roaming the perimeter of the crowded living room. Toward the kitchen, landing on the stairs that go…well, upstairs.

Pull them away and refocus on Charlie.

She rolls a pair of eyes so blue when she catches my gaze on the stairs, I compare her irises to the ocean. Fuck. If I didn't know I was sober, I'd think I was drunk. That was a dumb notion, and she'd gag if I said it out loud.

"I'm not going upstairs with you."

"Whoa, whoa, whoa, Kemosabe. I meant outside—where it's quieter. On the porch." There's a bench swing out there big enough for two, if she can stand the thought of sitting next to me.

"Oh." She looks chagrined, shifting on her heels and readjusting the purse draped over her shoulder. "All right, we can do the porch. Let me just…" Her sentence trails off as she searches the crowd. "I don't know where my friends went. Normally they'd be hanging all over you. Haha. Let me just text them to tell them I'm going outside."

Her phone appears from the back pocket of her jeans, and she taps out a quick message. Stuffs it back inside and tilts her chin in my direction. "All set."

I hold the screen door for her after pushing through the main entrance, and we step down onto the wooden porch of the house with its wide veranda and overhang. White railings and staircase descend into a dark pit of a front yard, the streetlights lining the road doing little to illuminate the area in front of the house.

Only the flicker from two dull sconces flanking the entry provide any light.

"This isn't creepy at all," Charlie jokes sarcastically, instinctively moving to the far end, toward the swing. She rests her ass on it.

It squeaks on four rusty chains. They're thin and clinging to the ceiling by tiny, round hooks.

Shit.

Should I stand? Would that be fucking weird? Me, just staring down at her? I can see down her shirt if I stand here—what if she thinks I'm being a pervert?

Like a bull in a china shop, I sit my ass down.

The swing doesn't even swing; that's how much I'm weighing it down, and I'm afraid to give it a push with the heel of my foot. God forbid it comes crashing to the ground.

Charlie already thinks I'm a moron; that would solidify it.

"You don't look comfortable," she says after a few moments, the rusty chains yelping with every subtle movement.

I wish she'd sit still.

I give the brackets above a worried peek.

Frown.

"What?" Charlie wants to know.

"Nothin'."

"Why do you keep looking up at the ceiling? What's up there?" Now she's glancing up, only she has no idea what she's looking for. "Tell me."

"The chains don't look sturdy."

"Oh, well." Charlie goes to push us off, but I stop the swing from moving forward. "Are you scared it's going to break?"

"Yup."

"We wouldn't have far to fall." She laughs, as if me falling on my ass wouldn't be a big deal. "Why don't you relax?"

"But…" What if the swing *does* crash to the ground? I imagine the loud thud, hitting my head on the wooden planks, the rusty chains covering us with a clang.

"Jackson, re*lax*." I watch as if it's in slow motion as she reaches over and her fingers brush the denim over my knee, giving me a reassuring pat before pulling away.

My body tenses up from the contact.

That didn't help me relax.

Quite the opposite, actually.

Game face, Triple J—shake it off.

And now I'm talking about myself in the third person, using the nickname she refuses to call me because she thinks it's stupid, which she would no doubt give me major shit for.

My mind is a muddled mess; I do not want to date anyone. I do not want to have sex with her. I'm obviously attracted to her—Charlie is gorgeous—but I don't want to screw her brains out. Okay, so, I have been thinking about banging her lately, but I won't. I can think about it in passing, though…right?

Fuck.

Why did I invite her here tonight, and why am I sitting with her outside on the damn porch?

It's quiet and dim and intimate, and there's no one outside but the two of us, which is unusual. Normally, people are spilling out of the house, passing by, walking to other parties, neighboring houses—including mine—hosting their own loud, drunken keggers.

Charlie is the first to break the silence. "Do you live around here?"

I raise my arm. "I live there." Point to the white house directly across the street, its lights out because everyone I room with is inside the house behind me.

Her brows go up, surprised. "You live across the street?"

"Yeah."

"Is that the football house?"

"Yes ma'am."

"It's not as big as I thought it would be."

I chuckle, hiding my smile by turning my head. She doesn't catch it and continues prattling on.

"Bet you never get any rest."

"Yeah. It's pretty loud."

"Lots of girls, too, I bet." Charlie's sly, passive-aggressive comment isn't lost on me. She's fishing for details, wanting to know if I'm a horn dog, encouraging the groupies who hang out there, parading them in and out of my room.

"Indeed there are."

It's the truth. There *are* loads of girls hanging out at our place, almost every day of the week; some days, it feels as if they're dumped off by the truckload. Fine, not all of them are skanks—some of them are the girlfriends of my teammates. Those girls are mostly gold diggers, spreading their legs for any player with a hard-on, hoping to get pregnant, or wifed, or WAGed.

They sit around uselessly, in the living room, kitchen, and common areas, dolled up and posing. They laugh too loud, wear too much makeup and too few clothes. Fucking fake.

Desperate.

Thank God my bedroom door has a lock on the outside and a deadbolt on the inside.

I tell her so. "I have to keep my door locked. Once, I came home really late and there was a girl in my bed."

Charlie's lips tighten into a thin line, but she makes no comment about it.

I continue. "I don't think she even knew whose bed she was in. Had to get help bootin' her ass out."

Her smile is thin, the silence stretching between us. It grows incredibly awkward. Was it something I said? I'm only telling the truth, which is that girls chase after athletes all the time. Comes with the lifestyle and the territory, and not everyone is cut out for it.

Charlie isn't one of those people; I can see it written all over her face.

I'm not looking for a girlfriend, but I feel the urge to reassure Charlie I'm not the kind of dude who sleeps around, to give her the positive affirmations she obviously wants: I'm loyal. Faithful.

Pure as the driven snow.

Purer than she is, I reckon.

Her feet attempt to give the swing another shove; she's irritated. Would love nothing more than to see me flat on my ass, knocked down a peg or two. Knows I'm worried the swing is going to collapse and is punishing me for not defending my honor.

"I don't sleep around," I blurt out randomly.

She attempts a conspiratorial wink. "Sure you don't."

"You can stop stereotypin' me, thanks."

"I'm not." Her protest is feeble, to say the least.

"Bullshit you're not." I laugh at the lie.

"Fine, maybe I am, but you don't have to defend yourself to me. I'm a nobody, though I am curious why I should believe you aren't banging every girl who slips into your bedroom at night." Her blue eyes roll toward the heavens. "It's too easy."

Yeah, it would be easy, like shootin' fish in a barrel.

"So, yeah…" I draw the word out. "I'm a virgin."

I don't know what possesses me to say it, but I do, and now that it's out there, there's no taking it back. Maybe I just want her to know I'm not fucking every vagina that walks into my house.

Charlie stops trying to shove the swing into action. "Shut up."

"I'm not fuckin' around with you right now—I'm bein' serious."

"*What*?" She looks genuinely stunned.

I look down at our feet. "Forget it."

"Um, no. It's too late. I…think I heard you right? I just don't…believe you? There is no way." She's repositioned herself so she's facing me, one leg now up on the bench seat, the other dangling over the side. "Say it again."

"Nope." I cross my arms and kick my feet out, slouching with my legs spread.

"You are not a virgin."

My wide shoulders shrug. I don't care if she doesn't believe me, but I sure wish she'd lower her fuckin' voice a few decibels.

Keep tellin' yourself that, Triple J. Keep right on tellin' yourself that…

"Jackson." Here come those fingertips again, this time on my forearm. Her nails are pink, that much I can see. "Be serious."

I give her another careless shrug. "What makes you think I'm not?"

"Because, you're…" She doesn't finish her sentence. It lingers there, the spaces being filled by stereotypes and preconceived notions I can almost hear her say, even if she's not speaking them out loud:

Because you're an athlete.

Because you're popular.

Because you're a football player.

Because you live in their house.

Because you're a guy.

"So what do you usually do on Friday nights?" I ask, attempting to change the subject.

Charlie laughs. "Oh no you don't—nice try though." Her hand is still on my arm, resting like a hot iron near the crook of my elbow, branding my skin. "Jackson."

God, stop sayin' my name like that.

"Charlotte."

Her little smirk is amused—way too fucking cute and too fucking…cute. Kissable. Bratty. Sassy. She's not intimidated by me, my salty attitude, or my size.

In fact, if I didn't know any better, I'd think the little minx liked it.

"How are you a virgin?"

My thick brows go up. "Are *you*?"

Charlie removes her hand and returns it to her lap. "No."

Sex, sex, sex.

The word plays on a loop in my brain, implanted there.

"Although just barely," she adds.

Fuck, fuck, fuck.

This is not good.

"What do you mean?" I volley back.

I get an eye roll for my efforts. "Um, hello—isn't it obvious?"

"Um, no." I'm confused. What the hell is she trying to get at? How can you be barely a virgin? You are or you're not.

"I mean—look at me. Listen to me! Guys just…I think I might be too much to handle."

Too much for who? Pussies? "Please do not go down that road of self-deprecation and loathin'. I can't stomach it."

"*Loathin'*," she repeats in almost a whisper, as if the word holds some magic. Her top teeth nibble on her bottom lip. "You're right—I hate when girls do that, too. I'm not fishing for compliments, I swear. And I don't hate my body, but I like tall guys and none of them ever like me back, so I'm stuck with the short ones who can't take a joke." Her laugh sounds a bit sardonic.

Oh Charlie, if I were the dating kind…I'd date the hell out of you.

Her head is cocked and she's staring out into the dark yard.

"Why are you waiting?" Her question isn't condescending or calculated, merely quiet and curious.

"I don't…date."

A lilting little laugh fills the silence. "One has nothing to do with the other."

No, it doesn't. Still, "Sex complicates everything, and I decided a long time ago I wasn't lookin' for any. Complications, I mean."

"That sounds a tad dramatic." I don't see her eye roll, but I can hear it.

"It's the truth."

"Well it doesn't have to be complicated. It is what you make it."

"Someone always gets hurt."

"Who gets hurt? The other person? I thought guys didn't care about feelings—are you telling me you're sensitive?"

"I just know from experience—everything is one-sided and the other person loses out." My statement is vague, slightly ominous, and only makes a bit of sense.

"Are you even talking about yourself?" Charlie gives her head a shake. "I'm so confused."

That makes two of us.

I choose to be honest. "No, I guess I'm not talkin' about myself."

"Who then?"

"My parents." I let out a puff of air.

Charlie is silent a few heartbeats before leaning back against the swing's bench. "Ah, I see."

I want to ask, *What do you see?* But I'm afraid she'll actually fucking tell me what she sees when she looks at me, and the last thing I want or need is a psych eval from a pretty girl in the middle of the night on a Friday.

That's not why I brought her out onto this porch.

"Love fucks it all up."

The swing slowly sways back and forth, only its rusty chain breaking the silence. Then, "So. You're one of those, eh?"

I detect a chuckle tacked on to the end of her sentence. Charlie is amused.

"One of *what*?"

"You have to be in love to have sex with someone. You want to feel something for them. Is that it?" The way she says it oozes skepticism, as if the notion is impossible. She'd put me in a box, stuck that box on a shelf, and labeled it *Guys who fuck whomever*. Anyone with a pulse, like some of my teammates.

"No, but I'd like to have a relationship before stickin' my dick inside them. Otherwise it's just weird."

"Stickin' muh dee-uk," Charlie repeats with a laugh, full on this time, loud and boisterous and sounding fucking glorious. "You and that Southern accent of yours have a way of making everything sound so eloquent."

My lips press into a thin line. "I appreciate the sarcasm. Truly."

"Don't be a pooh. I like it," she says somewhat shyly. "The accent, I mean. I'm a bit rusty with the teasing."

I don't want to say it out loud, but most girls do love the accent. Fucking love it. Eat that shit up, in fact, driving me batshit loco with their demands: *Say something Southern, Triple J! Say y'all! Say fixin' to!*

Drives me fuckin' nutso.

Charlie here isn't immune to it, isn't the exception; she's the rule.

Same as *all* the others, really.

I have nothing more to say as she rocks the swing with the toe of her shoe, though she's the shorter one between us. I watch her leg—her calf in the tight, dark, denim skinny jeans. The toe of her leather boot pressing into the wooden floor, releasing. Pushing. Releasing. Pushing.

Controlling our movements, allowing us the chance to talk.

My eyes stray up her leg. Knee. The hand resting there.

Gold bracelets, gold ring circling. Long, delicate fingers. Nails painted a soft pink.

She taps one finger, and I blink, eyes finally reaching hers again.

Charlie is biting down on her lower lip, barely concealing her smile, head doing that little shake as if to say, *I don't even know what to do with you right now.*

"I still don't believe it."

She's back on the virgin subject again—though I don't think we ever left it.

"How did we get on this topic?" I ask, for lack of anything else to say.

"You blurted it out." Pause. "You're worse than any girl I've ever met who wanted to tell someone a secret."

"I am not."

"Yeah, 'fraid so. You just couldn't keep that information to yourself, could ya?"

"Sorry. Don't know why I fuckin' said it." Other than I'm a moron.

Charlie thinks, forehead wrinkling in concentration. "Is it hard?"

I almost choke on the beer I just took a swig of. "Excuse me?"

"Not doing it—has it been hard?"

Ummmm…yes it's been hard.

My dick. Not having a place to put it. Waiting.

Hard.

"Sure."

She waits for more but there is none. "Care to expound on that?"

"No."

With a side glance, she gets more comfortable on the swing, leaning back and letting her legs dangle. "It's not easy for girls, either." Charlie examines her fingernails. "I'm not a virgin, but sometimes wanking off with my own fingers just doesn't cut it, know what I mean?"

This time I do choke on my beer, bubbles lodging in my esophagus and causing me to cough just to clear the airway. I cover my soaking mouth with the inside of my elbow, shooting her a menacing glare.

How fucking dare she bring up masturbating?

"Care to expound on that?" I ask, once I can breathe again.

"No." I can see her cheeky grin in the dark, white teeth shining under the dim porch light. "No I do not."

"Then why did you bring it up?"

"Oh relax, it's not like I gave you any of the dirty details, like how many fingers I use—or don't use."

"*What?*"

"You should see the look on your face."

I lean back and huff out a sigh. "Whatever. I'm sure it looks like the one you gave me when I said the V word."

"Virgin. When you said you were a VIRGIN." Jesus Christ, she's practically shouting it. "There it is again." She laughs, pointing at my face until I swat her finger away with my hand, clamping my fist around her index. Place it back on her lap and cover her palm with the flat of mine.

"Could you not?"

"Pfft. It's not like anyone would believe me anyway. Jackson Jennings Junior, a *virgin*? As if." She doesn't try to move away or withdraw her hand. "Besides, no one is paying any attention—I could shout it from the rooftops and not a single person would look up."

She's got a valid point; the students around here are so fucking full of themselves, their social media feeds, and their own business that they probably wouldn't notice some girl screaming at the top of her lungs on the top deck of a house.

They'd film it on their phone, though, thinking she was going to jump.

Sick.

"Still, if you could keep your voice down, that would be great."

"You're not embarrassed, are you?"

I wasn't, no—not until I brought it up. It's the one secret I have, if you don't count how shitty my life was growing up with two parents who resented each other. A mother who resented me, a father who only cared about winning.

And the fact that I'm in Iowa and not at Clemson or Alabama or Notre Dame? He hates it, but choosing Iowa was the one thing I had control over. I felt comfortable here during the campus visits and clicked with the team members I met, and to me, that was more important than any championship.

I needed a place to feel at home, and Iowa was it.

"I'm not embarrassed to be a virgin. It's a physical act that means nothin', just like runnin' sprints or doin' a few push-ups."

Charlie's brows shoot up. "Now you're just being stubborn. If you thought sex meant nothing, you'd have done it by now."

True, I would have.

Maybe.

"Are you worried at this point you've let your virginity go so far that you'd be bad at it?"

"Please stop saying the word virgin. And no, I don't think I'd be bad at it." I snort. "Please, I fail at nothin'."

"You don't sound confident." Charlie is smirking; it's dark, but I catch it all the same as I let my hand withdraw from the top of hers. "Besides, sex isn't about failing or winning. It's about…it's…" Her voice trails off and her hands flail a little before settling back on her knees. "It's just not like trying to win or lose a game."

"How would you know? Are you a nympho?"

The look she gives me…

Shit. Why did I fuckin' ask if she was a nympho?

"I've had sex with one person exactly three times," she informs me, smoothing her palms down the front of her jeans. "It hurt the first time, was awkward the second, and unmemorable the third. I did it because I wanted to get it over with. He was a decent guy—we'd been going out about eight months, and he was…" She shrugs. "A kid. We both were." Her feet are still dangling off the swing, barely reaching the ground, making her look like a kid right now. "Anyway. I'm not a nympho." Charlie rolls her eyes. "Who even uses that word anymore?"

"You dated anyone since?"

It takes her a few moments to reply. "I've been on dates, if that's what you mean."

It's not really what I meant. I'm curious to know if she's casually banged anyone else—not that it's any of my business, but I am inquisitive. About her, her habits, hobbies…bed partners.

"You into casual sex?"

"Jackson, I literally just told you I've had sex three times, with the *same* guy, three years ago." Another eye roll goes in the books. "Thanks for being such an attentive listener."

"Right. Sorry." It's just that… "Someone who looks like you should have a boyfriend or whatever. Or at least dudes throwin' themselves at you to get your attention."

"Someone who looks like me? You're cute, but no guys throw themselves at me or try to get my attention. I could go stand inside in my underwear and still not get hit on."

Another snort leaves my nose and I swear to fucking God, if I do it one more time, I'll hate myself in the morning for acting like such a tool.

"Bull. *Shit.*"

I would notice her standing in the center of a room wearing a garbage bag. Or denim coveralls.

"It's sweet that you think so, but the truth is, I'm more the girl next door guys tell their problems to and not the girl they want to chase down to ask out."

Then those guys are fucking morons.

Except I don't have it in me to argue with her just yet—not without sounding like a dolt. Or like I care.

Which I don't. Charlie is nothing to me; nevertheless, she's slowly becoming a friend—the kind of friend I could easily do without, the complicated kind of friend who could manipulate me into doing anything she wanted me to.

I cannot afford a friend like that.

"Why are you so quiet all of a sudden?" She nudges me with her boney elbow, and I glance down at it. Then back up, into her eyes.

Shrouded but bright.

"Just tired," I lie. "It's been a long week."

That part at least is true.

"I can imagine." She looks over at me, yawns.

"Want me to walk you home?"

Charlie should say no. I'm too big, and too strong, and she barely knows me. *Say no, Charlie. Be smart and tell me no. Go inside and get your friends and walk home with them.*

"Sure."

Dammit.

"Want to go now? I just hit a wall, and bed is sounding amazing right about meow."

"Yeah...let's get you home." I stand, and the entire swing propels back from the loss of my weight—all two hundred and seventy-five pounds of me. It hits the railing behind it, Charlie swinging from the inertia.

"Oh shit!" She grunts, almost losing her balance and falling off. "Warn a girl before you go doing that."

I take a moment then to give her a once-over; eyes graze over the long legs, the dainty hands once folded over her lap are now gripping the rusty metal chains to steady herself. Long blonde hair. Sassy, upturned mouth.

I imagine the freckles scattered across her nose. The tiny indentation in her right cheek that only pops out when she's laughing.

Charlie hops up.

"You shouldn't be letting me walk you home."

They're the first words out of my mouth when she joins me on the sidewalk in front of the baseball house, instinctively facing the direction we need to walk.

"No? Why is that—are you going to assault me?" A little laugh punctuates her question.

"You think that's funny?" What is it with girls not taking this shit seriously?

"No, but I know you're not *going* to." She sounds as flippant as she looks, striding along the sidewalk by my side, not a care in the word.

"No, you don't. You're just assuming because I haven't been a prick to you tonight that it's safe to be alone with me. Didn't you take that class freshman year where they tell you all this?"

Charlie stops on the sidewalk and grabs me by the upper arm, almost pulling my body toward her, forcing me to look down into her face.

"Holy crap, Jackson—you're being serious."

"I want you to remember this next time. Do not ever walk home with some dude you don't even know. Got it?"

Her nod is slow. "Yes."

"Repeat it."

Charlie clears her throat and lowers her voice. Holds up her hand as if about to recite the pledge of allegiance. "I won't ever wawk home with some dood ay don't even know."

Great. She's being cheeky, mocking my accent. I feel my eyes narrow on her. "You little shit."

"Sorry, I'm just surprised you're so adamant about it. Do you know someone who's been, you know…"

She can't say the words to finish her sentence, but she doesn't have to.

"No. Just hear about it." It's scary as fuck and more common than even she probably knows. As an athlete, I'm privy to news and conversations other students aren't, mostly because so many things are kept under the radar, or skimmed over, or covered up—but the news always travels back to the source: the athletic department.

We're railed on relentlessly about our conduct, publicly and privately; no means no. Sometimes yes means no. Be respectful. Don't get messy, sloppy drunk. Hands to yourself.

Some guys just can't behave, and the rest of us pay the price.

"Well, no worries. I won't let anyone else walk me home in the dark." The toe of her shoe hits a small bump in the concrete sidewalk and she trips, steadying herself before saying, "It's not like I have guys beating down my door."

She could have guys beating down her door if she put more effort into it. "Why is that?"

In the dark, her shoulders move up and down in a diminutive shrug. "I don't know—you're a guy, you tell me." Her head turns and she's watching me, albeit in the dim light. Very few street lamps line the road, so I'm glad we're together and she's not walking alone.

"You look like you're in a relationship."

Even in this light, I can tell her eyes are widening. "What the heck does that mean?"

"I just mean you're the kind of girl a guy takes one look at and assumes you're already in a relationship—or fuckin' someone."

"Fucking someone—gee, thanks."

"You know what I mean."

"Okay, but what does that *mean*?"

I have to think for a second. "It means…you look…nice. You're cute and…" Shit, how do I say this without pissing her off? Not possible. I take a breath, exhale, and let her have it. "It means you don't look like you put out. Someone might have to put actual work in if they want to get in your pants, and most guys ain't lookin' to put in the effort. That's all I'm sayin'."

I don't call her the girl next door or a goody two-shoes, but I think she gets the drift. She's picking up what I'm throwing down.

Silence follows.

I expect an argument—or at least some outrage from her as she defends her look, sound, and demeanor.

"Well. I guess..." Her voice trails off. "So what you're saying is I look like I'm someone's girlfriend already?"

Yeah, that's about right. "Sure, if that's how you want to put it."

"I'm asking you. Is that what guys see when they look at me? Does that mean I don't look fun? I'm fun, goddammit! I got drunk once!"

Once.

Jesus Christ, *who is this girl?*

I choke down a laugh, covering my mouth so she doesn't get mad or offended—or smack me in the stomach to shut me up. I've never met a single person on this campus who has only been drunk once; most of them get drunk every weekend, multiple times.

There's been so much puke on the carpet and floors in our house over the past few years I've completely stopped walking through it with bare feet.

The thought of how dirty our fucking floors are makes me want to gag. It's probably worse than a hotel that rents rooms by the hour.

Anyway. Moving on.

We walk on, comforted by the sound of traffic and the wind blowing through the trees. Charlie shrinks down when a gust sweeps through the street, her shoulders slouching, arms wrapping around her middle, giving herself a hug.

I war with myself—I don't have a jacket to offer her, but I do have arms, and my body is warm. I'm a hotbox, sleeping only in a pair of boxer briefs, usually waking with my sheets wrapped around my legs.

Tempted to throw an arm around her shoulders and pull her in closer, I stuff my hands in the pockets of my jeans, shrinking down a few inches myself.

Misery loves company.

I'm not cold, but if I don't occupy my hands, they'll end up on her body to commiserate about the cold, and the last thing I want to do is send the wrong signal.

Although.

Touching a pretty girl wouldn't be the worst way to end my Friday night. She's beautiful and seems to like me, but would Charlie accept my arm around her, or would she nail me in the gut with her pointy elbow?

"You cold?" I roll my own eyes because the question is so fucking dumb; the answer obvious.

"Yeah."

"I'd offer you my jacket if I had one." Instead I'm wearing a long-sleeved cotton t-shirt with the Iowa logo on my chest. Worn with jeans, it's not dressy, but for once, what I have on coordinates somewhat. Sort of.

Not that I wanted to impress Charlie or anything.

Pfft. Whatever.

Why would I?

Suddenly I feel like a goddamn teenager. Unsure and insecure, as if she can read my mind and is going to judge me for pussing out on her.

"It's all right. We're almost to my house anyway, but thank you for saying so."

So polite. Shit, almost painfully so—she's measuring her words carefully.

"Uh. You're welcome." *For nothing.*

I can feel her sidelong glance. "Jackson, it's not a big deal. It's not your job to keep me warm."

No. Maybe not, but I want it to be.

Wow.

Holy shit—wow. No.

Just no. I did not just utter that shit to myself inside my own head.

I do not want to. I fucking don't.

Liar.

I am not having this conversation. Jesus, get out of your own head. She's just a girl—one you only just met.

Fuck that, it's been four weeks.

Wait, five? Or six Fridays—get it straight, dipshit, can't you count?

Still. You don't actually know anything about her.

Stop talking to yourself, psychopath.

"I'm sorry, did you just say, 'Stop talking to yourself, psychopath'?"

Yes. "No." I punctuate the lie with a snort then groan.

"It *definitely* sounded like you said something."

"Hmm. Nope."

Another sidelong glance, the corner of her mouth tipping up into a smirk. The brat.

"You're so full of…" She hesitates. Pauses before, "Shit. You're full of total crap, Jackson Jennings."

"I really wish you'd stop using my full name." It sounds ridiculous.

"Why? It's your name."

"Right, but…it sounds stupid when you say it like that. Can't you call me Triple J like everyone else?"

Charlie's smile widens. "Why on earth would I do that? That's not your name."

"So? Charlie isn't your name."

"It kind of is. It's not like people call me Lil C or whatever, like Tiny or something because they're pretending to be my friend."

"You're not tiny. Why would anyone call you that?"

"It was an example."

"A bad one—because you're not tiny."

"Would you stop saying that? It's insulting."

"But you're not." *Shut your mouth, Jackson. She's getting irritated.* I don't know why I'm arguing with her.

"Yes, I'm aware I'm taller than tons of other girls in the room, and no, I don't play volleyball for school, but I do intramurally, and no, I don't play basketball."

Damn shame—bet she'd look fantastic in those tight shorts they wear on the volleyball court.

"Maybe I want to be called Tiny—ever thought of that? Huh? *Huh*?"

"You want me to call you Tiny instead of Charlotte?"

"Well, no." She sounds disgruntled. "Maybe not."

I laugh, so confused. "Fine then, I won't."

"You're so annoying," she scoffs, a puff of steam from her lips fading into the night air.

"You started it."

"What are we, five?"

No, but I'm starting to feel like I am. Wanting to tug at the cute girl's braids and flirt and say all kinds of dumb shit to impress her.

We walk another hundred feet.

Charlie stops. "This is me."

This being a dinky little shit-hole, set back from the road roughly fifty feet—but aren't most college rentals shitty and in disrepair?

The place is yellow, that much I can see, with dark green shutters and a red door. It looks like something out of a children's television show, but…dilapidated?

No lights are on inside.

"Do you live alone?"

"No, I live with my friends."

"Where? It's so ti—"

"Don't you dare say tiny." Charlie laughs.

"Tiny."

She smacks me on the bicep, and I do what every hormonal guy who spends most of his time in the gym does when a female touches him:

I flex.

"You did not just flex your muscles." Her laugh is louder this time. She thinks I'm ridiculous and hilarious.

"Instinct."

"Oh. So you flex when anyone touches you?"

Translation: *So what you're saying is I'm not special?* I don't know jack shit about girls, but I know enough to read between the lines of that question.

"Surrrre." Total lie.

Lies, lies, lies.

"Right." Charlie shifts on the balls of her feet, and judging from the look on her face and the inflection of her voice, she thinks—or knows—I'm totally full of shit.

"Have I mentioned before that I'm a dumbass?" I blurt out. "Fuck. Why did I say that?" I run a hand down my face and peek at her through the spread fingers now shielding my eyes.

"Because you're a dumbass?" she answers helpfully.

"Thanks."

She shrugs. "You spent half the walk here insisting I'm not tiny enough to be called Tiny, so—that makes you a dumbass."

"Stop."

"Now, now, don't get touchy." God, the sound of that giggle makes my stomach flip. When she glances behind her, long blonde hair pulled over one shoulder, baring the porcelain skin of her neck, I let my gaze linger on her exposed collarbone. Smooth. "I should get inside."

"Okey dokey."

"You're so weird sometimes."

I am. I have no social graces, no idea how to act around a female. Fuck.

Fuck my life.

"Thanks for walking me home, Jackson."

"No problem—just make sure you're not walking home with any more strangers."

"You're not a stranger."

No. Guess I'm not.

"Besides, you didn't even try to touch me, so I know I'm safe with you." She pats me on the arm, and I fucking embarrass myself by flexing again. "Such a Southern gentleman."

Southern gentleman my ass. "Wow. You're really somethin', you realize that?"

Charlie preens. "I know."

"That wasn't a compliment."

"I know."

"You…" Charlie stares at me in the dark, eyes catching the little bit of light and shining like a thousand stars.

"Get inside," I say, throat hoarse.

She turns and begins a slow walk up her sidewalk. I wait until she turns her key in the lock, pushes through the door, and steps inside.

She turns again to face me, silhouetted by the light now shining in her house. Nothing but the outline of her body.

Tall.

Curvy.

Beautiful.

"Good night, Jackson." Her voice is a whisper in the dark.

"G'night, Charlotte."

Her irritated groan is loud enough to reach my ears, and I chuckle.

* * *

Me: Hey Charlotte?

Charlie: I feel like you're starting to abuse the privilege of having my cell phone number.

Me: Starting to? Probably.

Charlie: What's up?

Me: Nothing much. Just wondering if you were going to the next football game.

Charlie: Er. No?

Me: Ah. Gotcha **thumbs up**

Charlie: Did you…want me to?

Me: No. I mean, whatever. Do what you want, I was just asking.

Charlie: Could you not be passive-aggressive about it? If you want me to go to your game, you should come out and say it. Grow a pair of balls, Jackson.

Me: Are you always this fucking savage?

Charlie: Yes. Why, do you need me to mollycoddle you?

Me: No. I was simply asking if you were coming to a football game.

Charlie: Out of the blue, just randomly? Out of all the girls in the world you were wondering if I was coming.

Me: Don't read into it.

Charlie: I wouldn't DREAM of reading anything into it. You already told me you weren't into GIRLS.

Me: I'm into girls.

Charlie: I mean—not really.

Me: Would you knock it off?

Charlie: I cannot resist poking the bear.

Me: Forget I asked, okay? I'm bored and drunk and clearly high.

Charlie: So you weren't messaging me because you won your game today? You weren't messaging me because you think I'm cute? Damn it. I should have known **wink wink**

Me: Now you're just putting words in my mouth.

Charlie: Nope, you just said you messaged me 'cause you were bored and drunk lol

Me: Fair enough, but let's be honest—you're cuter than a button.

Me: Shit. That was such a dumb thing to say, ignore I said it.

Charlie: Too late. I'd never ignore a compliment. But let's discuss what that even means? How is a button cute?

Me: I just said it, it doesn't mean anything. Don't overthink it.

Charlie: Newsflash: I overthink EVERYTHING. In fact, my favorite saying is "I'll overthink it later." Haha

Me: I like to keep things simple.

Charlie: Most guys probably do, but sometimes if something is worth it, a little thinking on it means you care.

Me: Sounds complicated.

Charlie: Spoken like a true guy *eye roll*

SATURDAY

CHARLIE

"These seats kind of suck," Beth complains as we climb the stadium steps, one at a time, higher and higher until we're damn near touching the clouds.

Beggars can't be choosers.

"They were free, so don't complain."

"They were not free! We had to pay twelve bucks."

Fine. We had to pay—but at least it was under twenty each.

"Still, that's *practically* free compared to what those people down there had to pay. Pretty sure those seats go for well over a hundred bucks a pop." I point down—the only way to go—at the lower seats, at the alumni and network reporters televising the action.

"That's insane. Who would pay that?"

All those people? Thousands upon thousands of fans, most of them wearing some variation of our school colors—black and gold. "Football enthusiasts? Literally almost everyone?"

"Whatever." Beth shrugs. "At least it's not raining."

I get shuffled along as we take our seats, and it probably doesn't matter where we sit because so many of the seats are unoccupied this high up. Most of the fans up here have moved down to squat in far better seats, but I'm not about to get busted by the stadium police—

AKA the college student wearing a SECURITY t-shirt, holding a walkie-talkie, and glaring up at everyone walking past him.

Tim—I can read his name badge from here—wants to bust someone really bad. I can see it in his eyes. He checks the tickets of the stragglers at the end of the line, sending them back up into the nosebleeds.

He sure as hell isn't going to be busting me. Not today, Satan. Not today.

"It's not raining," Savannah complains. "But I could stand for it to be a bit warmer. And I wish I'd brought a blanket."

It's really not that cold; she's just being dramatic. The weather is gorgeous—perfect for game day, actually, although we're so high up I have no idea how we'll be expected to see any action down on the field.

"Natasha, can I borrow your *boy*noculars?"

She has a pair of black binoculars hanging around her neck on a long rope. She removes them, and they get passed down the line to me.

I give them a glance and squint over at her. "Why do you even have these?"

"My dad gave them to me so I could see if we ever came to football games or whatever and I wanted to see the field. He's still hoping I'll date one of the players—he wants a son-in-law in the NFL." My friend is picking at her pink fingernail polish then yawns into her hand.

In all my life, I've never known Natasha to give a shit about athletics, least of all football, and I've never known her to date anyone who plays. But, I'm grateful for her company, and I'm grateful for the binoculars. Holding them up to my eyes and bringing them into focus, I can clearly see the field below.

"Can someone google Jackson Jennings and tell me what number he is so I can adequately creep on him?" The words slip out before I can think twice about stopping them, and once they're out there, I'm so embarrassed a flush creeps up my neck.

"You dirty dog!" Savannah shouts. "Is that why we're here?" She is quite literally shouting, and thank God there aren't many people surrounding us. "You sneaky little hussy!"

Hussy—now there's a word I haven't been called since ever.

"Are you seeing Triple J?" Beth wants to know.

"No. I'm not seeing him—he helped fix a flat tire on my car and he has my number so he could follow up."

"And?"

"And…he texted me to see if I was coming to the game."

"And?"

"And…nothing."

"Since when do you care what a guy thinks?"

Down on the field, they're doing some kind of warm-up stretches, and I move the binoculars from player to player, trying to discern which one is Jackson but unable to figure it out. "Did you google him yet? What's his number?"

My eyes are glued to the binocs.

"Yeah, yeah, hold your horses," Natasha has her phone out, fingers tapping away. "He's a wide receiver, and his number is eighty-two."

Eighty-two, eighty-two, where are you?

Ah. There he is.

Even at this distance, Jackson is larger than life. Tight pants, wide shoulder pads, his helmet is off and he's running a gloved hand through sweat-soaked hair. It sticks up in a million directions, spiky and wild.

Black chalk or eye black or putty or *whatever the heck that gunk is* lines his upper cheekbones. Makes him look lethal and badass.

Beth is cracking open the program they handed each of us on the way in, thumbing through it, stopping toward the back. "Jackson Jennings Junior—that's a mouthful," she jokes. "Junior starter, a recruit from Texas Prep in Jasper, Texas. All-country, all-conference, all-state, all-American."

"Dang, Triple J, them's some impressive accolades," Savannah murmurs.

Beth continues. "Stats: weight, two hundred and seventy-five pounds of lean man meat. Height, six three. Wingspan…" Her voice trails off as Natasha interrupts.

"It does not say wingspan—let me see that." She tries to take the pamphlet from Beth, who laughs.

"No, it doesn't say that."

"Major, agriculture? Agriculture. Huh. Who would have thunk it."

"That sounds like tons of science."

"He's probably not that dumb, Charlie—give him some credit. He did get a full ride, and they don't give those to idiots."

Yes, they probably do. We just don't know anyone with a full ride, so none of us can accurately say.

"What else does it say?"

"That's about it. Just his hometown—where is Jasper, Texas, by the way?" Natasha inclines her head, and I know she's googling away. "It's on the border near the Louisiana state line."

Which would explain the thick accent and horrible metaphors.

"Here's more on him for anyone who cares," Natasha goes on.

"He's the only child of Jackson Jennings and Suzette Sundernan—yeesh, try saying that three times in a row."

"You can stop now." I lower the binoculars I've been holding steady against my face and hold my hand out to push down the phone Natasha is holding up. A Google search is displayed on the screen, information about Jackson pulled up. "Seriously. Stop."

"Don't be a party pooper."

"He helped me once. Stop getting your hopes up." Then he invited me to a party, then he walked me home even though I live a million miles away, then he invited me to a football game…

"And asked you to a football game."

I roll my eyes. "He won't even know I'm here. I could lie when he asks if I was here and he'd never know."

Beth tsks. "His heart will know."

Okay, drama queen. She's such a romantic.

"Guys, he doesn't like me. He likes that I give him a hard time. I bust his chops, that's all, and he likes the chase—he doesn't actually want to date me."

"How do you know?"

"He literally said the words, '*I don't date.*' That's how I know."

"He did? When?"

"Okay…maybe he didn't say those exact words, but that's what he implied, so…"

"What guys say and what they mean are two totally different things and you know it."

"No—that's girls."

"No, that's *guys.*"

Why are we arguing about this?

I sigh, leaning over and looking down the row so they can all hear me over the dull roar of the stadium noise. "Haven't you ever heard the saying, *When a guy tells you what he wants, you should listen*? They don't see things in gray like we do—they see them in black and white. I mean, not a lot of mystery there with shades in between, trust me. I read the book."

"You're turning into a giant nerd with all that reading," Natasha sasses.

I stare pointedly at her. "This from the girl who didn't even bother buying textbooks last semester."

She flips her long black hair. "I'm trying to save money."

"You are here to read books and study. That is *literally* what college is."

She points to her ears and shakes her head. "What? I can't hear you, sorry! The game is about to begin!"

The little…

As if on cue, the marching band begins playing the school fight song, and the field is cleared for the national anthem. Everyone roars, players are announced, coins are tossed, the teams take position.

It's all very loud and exciting with tons of pomp and circumstance, and I wonder why I don't come to games more often.

I raise the binoculars and locate number eighty-two. Find him on the sideline, pacing, hands on his hips. A completely different aspect of him than I'm used to seeing.

This Jackson Jennings is intense. Huge. Serious. Aggressive and ready to take the field.

I can feel his energy radiating from here, all the way up in the stands. He's like a caged tiger at the zoo desperate to be free.

Instinctively I know once Jackson takes the field, he's going to be unstoppable.

Ten minutes later, I'm proven right.

Ten minutes later, Jackson Jennings—all six foot three of his imposing height and weight—goes charging down the field, football tucked under his right armpit.

How can someone so big run so fast? It seems impossible—I don't know much about football, but aren't guys in his position usually a little smaller? Shorter? More built for speed? I would have pegged Jackson as a lineman or a tackler or something. Like I said, I know nothing about the game, the positions, or how it's played.

Not really.

Barely enough to register what's going on in front of me unless everyone around me stands, cheers, or freaks out because of what's happening down on the field.

I would make the worst girlfriend for him.

Why that thought pops into my head is beyond me, especially when I can barely tolerate the guy. Fine. *Okay.* Yes, he's had a few moments where I second-guessed my loathing for him, like when he was squatting next to me on the side of the road, helping me fix a flat tire, then bringing me a new one? Then checking up on me afterward to make sure I felt good about the work I'd done.

Really nice of him and totally unnecessary.

He could have left me there and let me call roadside assistance.

But he didn't.

He parked, got out his tools, helped.

Not to mention, when he leaned in close and got up in there…he smelled fantastic. Like cologne and shampoo and a bit dirty, like he'd showered but not that well? As if he'd rushed through it, had been so sweaty from working out he couldn't be bothered to wash it all down the drain.

Like man.

A hard-working man who cares more about getting shit done than smelling good doing it.

I recall how his shirt tightened around his pecs when he reached forward to show me how to tighten the lug nuts, how the fabric hid nothing of his tight, toned upper arms. They're ridiculously strong—not bulging, exactly, but buff. There is no other way to describe it, and for a hot minute I was tempted to curl both my hands over his biceps and cuff his muscles, just to see if my fingers could wrap all the way around.

I doubt it.

We're too far up for me to see what's going on down on the field, so my eyes stay glued to the giant screen suspended over the end zone at the far end of the stadium. The faces of young players stare down at us when one of them has the ball, their stats and information broadcasted during each short lull.

Music from the sound system and music from the band play intermittently.

It's loud—so deafeningly loud, especially when a touchdown is scored.

"How are you not banging him?" Natasha shouts across our small group of friends, and my eyes dart around to see if anyone has heard.

We're surrounded mostly by other students and families, so Jesus. Keep your damn voice down!

"You don't just *bang* a guy because you want to," I tell her with a roll of my eyes. Besides, Jackson is a virgin and isn't gonna give it up for just anyone. According to him, he isn't banging anybody and has zero plans to.

He has no time for girls, or dating—that much he has made clear.

I doubt he'd make an exception for me.

Not that I want him to.

I'm hardly on the market, and if I were… My eyes stray toward the field, searching for number eighty-two. Would it be with a guy like *that*?

* * *

Jackson: Did you show up?

Me: To what?

Jackson: Haha

Me: YES, Jackson, I showed up. I love hot dogs—how could I resist pigging out on a ballpark frank?

Jackson: You're joking, right? It's NOT called a ballpark. It's a stadium.

Me: I'm joking. Obviously I knew it wasn't a ballpark. That's where they play hockey, right?

Jackson: You're not even a little bit funny.

Me: Oh come on—I am a little bit tho. Plus I'm kind of cute, too. Amirightoramiright

Jackson: I'm ignoring you now.

Jackson: But wha'd you think? Of the game.

Me: Congrats on the win! It was fun. I haven't been to

one in a while.

Jackson: Why not?

Me: Don't know. My friends aren't really big into sports, so there's never a reason to. We haven't tailgated since our freshman year, and I'd forgotten how crazy all the alums and fans get.

Jackson: They really do, but it's not as bad here as it is at some schools.

Me: We saw more than a few black and yellow painted RVs parked in the lot with grills going. Die-hard fans, much?

Jackson: More like die-hard parents.

Me: Do your parents ever come?

Jackson: My dad, sometimes. Mom not usually unless it's a playoff game—she can't really afford it.

Me: Well...I'm glad I came today. Thanks for the invite. It was funner than I thought it would be.

Jackson: Funner? Is that a word?

Me: Don't be the grammer police.

Jackson: *grammar

Me: OMG!

Jackson: Sorry. Had to.

Jackson: Where'd you end up sitting?

Me: The cheap seats.

Jackson: Where are those?

Me: Are you being serious? You don't know where the cheap seats are?? Were you raised in a bubble?

Jackson: Dude—when do I have the chance to sit in the stands? Duh.

Me: Don't you ever go to other games? Even baseball? The cheap seats are at the 50-yard line and 50 yards up. Haha. Nosebleeds I guess you'd call them—like when you go to a concert and are up near the ceiling. Those.

Jackson: Shit, sorry. I should have left you tickets at will call.

Me: Why on earth would you do that?

Jackson: So you had better seats—so you can see? lol Those seats high up SOOK balls man.

Me: We could see just fine. My friend Natasha brought boynoculars.

Jackson: What the fuck are those?

Me: Binoculars meant specifically for staring at boys

with.

Jackson: Girls are so weird.

Me: Really, Jackson?? And you cruising the strip because you're BORED isn't?? Instead of partying or studying or staying home like a normal person, you drive up and down the street doing nothing.

Jackson: Oh, like my house is so quiet? And so conducive to studying?

Me: Have you ever heard of the library???

Jackson: First of all, stop using so many question marks.

Me: Second of all?

Jackson: Yes I've heard of the damn library. I'm there almost every Sunday night.

Me: Bull crap, you are not.

Jackson: Wanna make a bet?

Me: Yes.

Me: No.

Me: Yes. Where do you study?

Jackson: Top floor, study room on the left at the end of the second row. There's a table in it with four chairs.

That's my spot.

Me: Are you being serious?

Jackson: As a heart attack.

Me: Guess I'll just have to take your word for it.

Jackson: Or you could join me.

Me: Lol

Jackson: What's so funny?

Me: Me coming to study with you. Like it was a date.

Jackson: If I was askin' you on a date, trust me, you'd know.

Me: Well thank goodness you're not.

Jackson: But what if I was?

Me: But you're not.

Jackson: Are you always like this?

Me: Always like what?

Jackson: So argumentative.

Me: Probably. I swear to you I'm not doing it on purpose…

Jackson: Let's get serious for a second. What would it

take to get you to go out with me?

Me: I thought you didn't date.

Jackson: Pretend I'm fixin' to make a few exceptions.

Me: Starting with me?

Jackson: Yeah, starting with you.

Me: Should I feel flattered by this pretend attention?

Jackson: No, you should just say you'll let me take you out.

Me: Are we still pretending? Because it sounds like you're actually asking me out.

Jackson: For grins, let's say it's for real.

Me: All right. Where is this real pretend date taking place?

Jackson: It's a surprise.

Me: Oh brother *eye roll*

Jackson: Is that a yes?

Me: It's not a NO…

Jackson: Friday then? We have to be in early because we have a game on Saturday and it's in Ohio so I leave buttass early, but I figure if you don't have any classes in the afternoon Friday it could still work.

Me: Wow. You've actually thought this through.

Jackson: Go big or go home.

Me: Fine.

Jackson: Fine?

Me: Yeah, sure. Fine.

Jackson: Gee, try not to sound so thrilled.

Me: Do you want me to go on a date with you or not?

Jackson: Do. But could you show a little enthusiasm?

Me: All right, how's this: OMG JACKSON I WOULD LOVE TO GO OUT WITH YOU, LET'S GET MARRIED AFTERWARD AND HAVE BABIES!!

Jackson: Sarcasm, Charlotte? Really?

Me: Some sarcasm. Lil bit. But if you really want to take me out, I can't make any promises about what's gonna happen.

Jackson: What do you mean?

Me: I mean—don't go falling in love with me is all I'm saying.

Jackson: This isn't a movie. That's NOT going to

happen.

Me: That's what they say in ALL the movies…

Jackson: Guarantee that's not going to happen.

Me: Great. So Friday afternoon then?

Jackson: Yeah, Friday—if that works. 3:oo?

Me: You sure you wouldn't rather be trolling the strip in your babe-mobile?

Jackson: No. I'll be outside your house gunning the motor until you come outside.

Me: Oh god, please don't.

Jackson: Then you better not keep me waiting.

Me: SUCH a Neanderthal.

Jackson: You said it, not me. And no, Charlotte, I will not fall in love with you—as long as you promise not to fall in love with me.

Me: Don't make me laugh.

Jackson: Stranger things have happened, babe.

Me: Do me a favor and cool it with the 'babe' talk, 'kay? I just gagged in my mouth.

Jackson: Sorry, it just slipped out of my fingers. It

made me gag, too.

Me: At least we have one thing in common.

Jackson: Should I start a list and add that to it?

Me: Very cute, very cute.

Me: Hey. I'm sorry this entire time we've been talking, I totally forgot to ask how your game was.

Jackson: You were there.

Me: I know, but how do you feel?

Jackson: Feel? Uh, I have no idea how to answer that lol

Me: Are you sore?

Jackson: Ohhhh, THAT kind of feel, for a second I thought you wanted to discuss how the quarterback on the other team hurt my feelings. My one feeling.

Jackson: But yes, I'm sore as hell. It'll be fine though, it always is.

Me: Are you glad you won?

Jackson: One step closer to the championship with every win.

Me: Do professional teams only want players from championship teams?

Jackson: No, but winning games is the entire point.

Me: Ahh, I see…

Jackson: You're adorable.

Me: First I'm cute as a button, now I'm adorable. Stop, I'm blushing.

Jackson: No you're not, don't lie.

Me: Fine, I'm not. But close. I came real real close…

Jackson: I should probably say good-night before I pass out on you.

Me: Right. Well. See you Friday at 3.

Jackson: I mean—you'll probably text me before then, you won't be able to stand it.

Me: **rolling my eyes**

Jackson: Don't fight it, Edmonds.

Me: Wow. WOW.

Me: Have a good night's sleep, Jennings.

Jackson: It's a date, Little one. We have a date.

Me: Please don't remind me.

SEVENTH FRIDAY

JACKSON

What the fuck am I doing?

This is nuts—and if my pops found out I was taking a girl on a date during the football season, he'd tan my hide.

Which is why I haven't told anyone, least of all my parents.

Mama—she'd flip. Start planning the wedding and asking me all kinds of questions, but Pops?

Fuck to the no.

I have the route to Charlie's memorized since it's a straight shot from Jock Row, and I pull into her driveway a few minutes later. Seven minutes tops from door to door.

She's waiting on the porch, wearing a floral, off-the-shoulder sundress. It's pretty and dainty, her jean jacket thrown over one arm, little brown purse on the other. Wedge sandals.

A bit too summery for the season, and a bit…*chilly* for where I'm taking her, but I'm not about to send her back inside and get my ass chewed out for not telling her to dress warmer in the first place.

Jeans would have been better, but those legs…

Damn she has great calves; my eyes can't help but admire them. Tan and long and smooth. I bet she's shaved within an inch of her life.

My fingers flex over the steering wheel as I watch her before putting the in park and cutting the engine so I can walk to the porch and help her in; this is a date, after all, and even though it's maybe not going to amount to anything, I'm the Southern gentleman my mama raised me to be.

Most days.

In reality, I'm hardly—if ever—a gentleman, but occasionally I'm willing to bust out a few moves reserved for special occasions, like weddings and funerals.

When I step out of the truck, Charlie rises from the concrete stoop, a full four inches taller than normal and the perfect height. The dress is short, hitting her mid-thigh, and it's dark navy with small pink, white, and beige flowers on it. Brown belt. Brown sandals.

Yeahhh she's going to fucking kill me when she finds out where we're going. But in my defense, it *is* almost fall.

Blonde hair down, it's straight, not fussy or curled.

Fucking pretty. Too fucking pretty for me.

I feel ten feet tall and eight hundred pounds standing next to her, a giant lummox. Clumsy and aloof, I couldn't catch a ball right now if it were handed to me from one foot away.

"Hi." She shifts on her feet, which causes me to glance down at her toes.

Hot pink glitter.

Bracelets jingle on her wrists when she lifts an arm to brush back a strand of hair and tuck it behind her ear. The gold hoops in her lobes catch the light and wink.

"You look…" Nice. Gorgeous. Great. Fantastic. *Breathtaking*. "Fine."

A low laugh escapes her lips, as if she's taking pity on how pathetic I am.

"Thanks. You also look...*fine.*"

I didn't put nearly as much effort into it as she has, mostly because we're headed to a farm and I knew I'd need sturdier shoes.

I do have on clean jeans with no holes, a long-sleeved, navy polo shirt, and my usually unkempt hair is brushed and held back with a rubber band. Face is shaved. Deodorant under my pits.

So...only slightly douchey.

"Do you realize we match?" Charlie lifts the end of her skirt, letting it flow through her fingers. "We're both wearing blue."

Shit. It is indeed the same color blue.

And I'm in danger of looking like one of those pansies who gets pussy-whipped by his girlfriend and led around by his dick when he starts a new relationship.

"What were you doin' out on the porch? You're gonna catch a chill."

"The girls are home and Savannah needed the bathroom so I wanted to get out of her hair. No room."

The house is tiny.

"You're gonna need that jacket," I inform her, walking to the passenger side door and pulling it open. Giving her ass an appreciative glance when she hops up.

"I have mittens in the pockets just in case, but I figured we're going to be inside." She smiles brightly. "Right?"

Wrong.

So wrong.

My smile is weak as I shut the door on her, watching through the window as she buckles her seatbelt across a great pair of boobs.

As soon as I open my door—

"So, where *are* we going?"

"Uh…you'll see."

I can feel her checking me out in my peripheral vision, up and down, her blue eyes damn near penetrating the skin of my arms, thighs, and profile.

"Never would have pegged you for the kind of guy who likes planning surprises." The jean jacket on her lap gets spread out like a blanket, but she doesn't put it on.

Oh, you're gonna be surprised all right.

"Right."

Not interested in small talk, Charlie bites back a smile, turning her head and facing the window so I can no longer see her face. Watching as houses and campus pass us by, watching all the way until we're at the city limits and driving out of town.

Toward the country.

Finally, she turns to face me. "Are you taking me to the woods to murder me?"

I laugh. "Hardly."

"Because you could use this giant truck as the perfect way to haul my dead lifeless body to the middle of nowhere." She presses the lock and unlock button a few times, testing it against the moving vehicle.

"Lucky for you, I wouldn't want the seats in here to get stained from your blood."

Charlie gives a little *humph*. "Where the heck are we?"

"What month is it?"

"October?" She looks perturbed at my question for her question.

"What holiday is comin' up?"

"Um…Halloween?"

I laugh again. “You sure ’bout that?”

“Just tell me where we’re going!” She’s impatient now.

“See that sign right there?” We’re about to pass a giant wooden pumpkin sign that’s been pounded into the ground in the middle of a cornfield that’s already been harvested.

“Yes…” The word trails off.

“That’s where we’re goin’.”

“A pumpkin farm?”

I can’t look her in the eye, not knowing how she’s going to react. “Yup.”

“You’re taking me to a pumpkin farm.”

“Yup.”

I catch her glancing out the window again. “Huh.”

I tilt my head. “Huh—what’s that mean?”

“That’s actually really…nice. Cute.”

Cute. There’s that word we keep throwing around.

“You think?”

“Yes. I…” She casts her eyes downward at her bare legs. “I *really* wish I’d worn jeans, but this is going to be fun!”

Then Charlie does that thing girls do when they’re excited—she claps. Claps a few times and gets out her phone and snaps a photo when we pull into the farm, dust kicking up behind us as we wind down the gravel road.

“Oh my god, look at that corn maze.” She oohs. Gasps. “Oh my god, Jackson—a petting zoo!”

Shit.

Shit, shit, *shit.*

Honestly, all I planned on doing was taking the hay wagon out to the field and grabbing a pumpkin or two. Wasn’t planning on petting baby goats and feeding calves and shit.

But.

Damn she looks thrilled.

Adorable.

"Jackson! Look! We can dip our own caramel apples or stuff our own scarecrow." She looks over her shoulder at me. "Can we do that?"

Like I'm going to tell her no.

"Is that a hay wagon?" She's practically bouncing in her seat as a wagon full of families wheels by, orange pumpkins in their laps. "Are we going on that?"

"Yup."

It takes me a few more minutes to find a decent parking spot, one that's not too far away from the entrance and activities. I don't need Charlie walking a long distance and spraining her ankle on this rough road full of potholes. Not that I'd mind carrying her, but still—it would be because she'd injured herself, and not because I was trying to be romantic.

I know what a sprain feels like, and it fucking sucks.

"Maybe you should put your jacket on before we get out."

She complies, shrugging into the denim, smiling at me once she's completed the task. "All set."

Sweet and glowing, the freckles on the bridge of her nose are bright today, the tip of her pert little nose begging to be touched by the tip of my finger.

Soon, we're lined up for the wagon; I climb up behind Charlie, my hand at the small off her back in the event she topples backward. Ass parked on a hay bale, it's hard not to feel a thrill when our thighs make contact from the jostling of the wagon. Hard not to feel a stirring in my groin when Charlie's palm lands on my inner thigh to steady herself when the wagon hits a hole in the road, sending us bumping into each other.

She laughs, supporting herself by holding on to me, a bonus I hadn't accounted for when I was planning this date.

The wagon stops, the red tractor shifting into park with a jolt, its driver giving us instructions for choosing our pumpkin, where to wait once we find one, and how much it's going to be per pound.

Charlie takes a selfie, holding up two fingers and kissing the air.

Jesus.

Even that's adorable.

I meander over to where she's standing, already hovering over a medium-sized pumpkin with a ridiculously long stem.

"I found mine."

"It's been two minutes. You sure you don't wanna walk around more?"

"Nope. This here is my guy."

Her guy. Her pumpkin with the long, thick stem.

Typical female.

"You don't want one that's *bigger*?"

"Nope." She jerks her head once, nodding stubbornly. "I'm committed to *this* one. Size isn't everything, you know—he might be small, but he's mighty. Look at this stem! I can paint it or bedazzle it, or put a bow on it…" Her eyes search the ground. "You still have to pick yours out."

I do, but I'm in no rush, because who gives a fuck about a pumpkin.

Except, Charlie is eyeing me expectantly, and I'd feel like a horse's ass disappointing her since this is the reason we came.

It was my idea.

That and the fact that I wanted to impress her, and I wasn't going to do that taking her to a college bar, or to a movie, or down to the bandshell where absolutely *every*fucking*body* on campus goes on their dates.

I step three feet to my left and point to a lopsided pumpkin on the ground. "How 'bout this one?"

Charlie rolls her eyes. "Put some thought into it."

Put some thought into it? How the hell do I put thought into choosing an overgrown gourd? This was such a bad idea.

"Fine." I point again. "That one?"

My date wrinkles her nose. "Too bumpy. Plus, it's covered in dirt."

Oh my god.

"That one looks good."

Charlie examines it then shakes her head again. "Meh."

"Whose pumpkin is this? It ain't yours, so why don't you let me figure it out?"

"Because you're just pointing to random ones. Don't you want it to mean something?"

"Mean something? It's a pumpkin."

"I know, but when we get back to your place to carve them, don't you want to—"

"Whoa, whoa, whoa," I interrupt. "Back to my place to carve them? Slow your roll, Charlotte."

She tilts her head and crosses her arms. Willfully.

Shit. I know that look; I've seen it before on my mama. Charlie is about to dig her heels in for the long haul, and I doubt it's an argument I'm going to win. Not if she has her mind set on comin' back to my place, which it seems like she does.

"We can't carve these at my place," I insist, kicking at a rock with the toe of my brown leather boot.

Her arms are still tight across her chest, hair kicking up from a passing breeze. "Why not?"

"No knives."

"Oh my god, shut up." She laughs. "You do too have knives."

"Nope. No knives."

She considers me a few moments, gauging the sly grin pasted on my face, looking me over from head to toe, starting from the tips of my boots. Up the front of my jeans. The clean, navy polo I've only worn one other time and that looks brand new. Her eyes take in my broad shoulders, thick neck, and the humor playing in my eyes.

At least—I hope she interprets all that, because she's not saying anything and neither am I, and it's fucking cold and I still haven't chosen a damn pumpkin.

"Why don't you just pick one for me?" I suggest.

"Why don't we pick one out together?" she volleys back. "How about we get a cute one and carve it together."

A cute one?

Jesus.

Going back to my place and carving that little bastard sounds way too fucking domestic, and I'm not looking to be tied down.

Fun, yes.

Relationship, no.

Then what are you doing on this date, smartass?

Still…

I cave. "Fine. We'll get one."

She takes her time with the selection, dragging me around the pumpkin patch, one hay wagon having come and gone, picking people up and dropping off a few more.

Charlie has me by the elbow, using me for support; her heels or sandals or whatever get caught up so many times in divots, she's resigned to hang on to me—not that I'm complaining. Fingers pressed into the crook of my arm, her blonde hair hangs in a wave, catching light and glowing as the sun slowly begins setting in the distance.

Together, we critique different sizes and shapes of orange pumpkins, discussing various ways they could be carved.

"This might be fun with a football on it. You could put it on the steps outside with a candle inside. That would be cute."

Cute.

"It would get smashed within ten minutes."

"Ugh, you're right. I hadn't thought of that." Her eyes get wide. "Oh, Jackson! How 'bout that one?"

Fuck. I love it when she says my name.

Jackson. Not JJ, or Triple J, or Junior, like everyone else calls me, including my parents and my friends. I've always thought it was kind of impersonal in a way, though great for keeping people at arm's length.

Keeps me focused.

Keeps my eye on the prize.

Keeps my eye on the end goal: the pros.

But when Charlie says my real name, when she says Jackson—the *way* she says it? It makes my stomach curl, as if I've just done a hundred crunches and worn out my abs.

Her fingers unfurl from my arm and, on shaky legs, she makes her way to a round, smooth pumpkin, a cheery shade of orange all over with a long, coiled stem.

It's damn near perfect.

"It's almost perfect!" she exclaims, mimicking my thoughts.

I grunt. "That the one you want?"

"What do you think?"

I don't give a fuck, I want to say, but I don't, because it would hurt her feelings. She's way too jacked up about this pumpkin. "Looks good."

"So you like it?" She's hopeful.

"Sure."

"I do, too—let's get this one." We both look down at it. "Can you carry it?"

Obviously I can—I'm Goliath. Nevertheless, it makes me feel like a badass that she asked, and that she did it with a little twinkle in her blue eyes while eyeing up my biceps.

Dang, if she keeps looking at me that way—with those soft eyes and sweet smile—I'm going to forget myself and catch feelings for her, or something equally foolish.

It's bad enough that I'm about to take a goddamn pumpkin home to the house and carve it in my fucking kitchen for everyone to see.

I'm going to catch a rash of shit about it from the guys, no question.

I squat instead of bending over, scoop up the heavy vegetable, then tuck it under one arm, supporting its weight with my palm like I would a greased up baby pig, or a baby goat, or—

"The wagon's already coming back around," Charlie is saying next to me as she pulls at the collar on her denim jacket, shielding herself from the wind that's been picking up since we got here. The skirt of her dress picks up, blown up by the breeze.

Standing side by side, we wait patiently for the hay wagon to position itself. Stop.

The driver climbs off the tractor and pulls down the stoop, placing a wooden block under it like he did when we originally scrambled on, and Charlie steps one heeled foot onto it now. Then the other, until she's back up in the wagon, settling her fanny onto a hay bale. Smooths the skirt of her dress down with the palms of her hands, holding it in place when it gets kicked up by a gust of wind.

I heave myself up after her, plopping down beside her. Legs spread, I try to ignore it when she shivers.

"You cold?"

She shivers again in reply. "A little."

"Um…" I'm not good at this, but I set the pumpkin on the ground between my feet and put my arm around Charlie. Pull her in closer, tucking her under my armpit like I'd do a football—or a pumpkin. "Better?"

"Yes, thank you." She hunkers down a little more. "You're blocking the wind, which is nice."

I'm blocking the wind because I'm a fortress of strength and steel and goddamn power, and don't you forget it.

"You're like a big brick wall."

Uh.

"I prefer fortress of strength."

She laughs into the solid wall of my chest, her giggle muffled by my shirt. "Don't make me laugh."

"But I am."

Her body shakes. "Stop it, Jackson."

What the hell? "You don't think I am?"

“I mean, even if I did, I wouldn’t call you that. Who says that? Fortress of strength—that’s hilarious.”

I feel myself blush and thank God for the cold and breeze, because now that she’s teasing me, I feel like a fucking idiot for having said the words *fortress of strength* out loud to this girl.

I respond by grunting, giving her hair a nuzzle on the sly, praying she doesn’t notice.

Charlie pulls back far enough to look at my face. “Did you just sniff my hair?”

Bust my balls a little more why don’t you?

“I couldn’t breathe—you’re suffocating me.” We both roll our eyes at the lie, but when she settles back against my chest, I can actually feel her smiling against my pec.

Huh.

We get jostled and bounced around on the way back to the barn and somehow end up with straw in our hair. We also end up buying two gourds that look like mini-pumpkins and a pumpkin carving kit, stuffing a scarecrow, and noshing on caramel apples on the walk back to the truck.

I am carrying everything but Charlie’s apple.

She happily munches on it while I shove the pumpkin into the backseat of my truck, along with the scarecrow, carving kit, and gourds. I know as soon as I hit the brakes at the next light, those sonsabitches are going to fly off the seat and roll to the floor.

“We should name the scarecrow, don’t you think?” Charlie has her long legs extended, feet propped up on the dashboard with her shoes on as her teeth nibble on her apple.

“You want to name it?”

“Yeah. It needs a name.” She glances into the backseat and I steal a look at her calves.

Nice.

Smooth.

Sexy.

"It looks like a guy."

"Are you being serious?" She says it with a straight face, so I can only assume she's being serious, but it still sounds fucking ridiculous.

"Yes. I think it looks like a dude, so it needs a dude's name."

Girls are so strange. "Like what?"

"Like…Jackson Jennings the fourth."

"Ha ha, very funny."

"Randall?"

I cock my head now, getting into the game of naming our fictional new friend. "I don't mind Randall, but how about Nathan. Or Kyle?"

"Those seem too…normal. What about Biff McMuscles?" she deadpans, a glint in her eye.

"Biff McMuscles?" I give him a quick peek in my rear-view mirror. "He doesn't have muscles."

"I know, but…" Charlie ducks her head as her cheeks darken. "That's what I called you before I knew your name." Darts a glance at me. "Is that bad?"

"You called me *Biff* McMuscles?" I want to barf a little in my mouth as I say it. For real, what the fuck? "*Why*?"

I mean—Biff?

"You're all…" Her hands wave around along my torso, up and down. "Fit and buff and huge."

I force my eyes to stay planted on the road, but it's an exercise in self-control. I want to stare Charlie down so bad.

"You couldn't come up with a better nickname than that? It's terrible."

A sigh comes from the passenger side. "I know, but I didn't like you at the time so it seemed to fit."

"You didn't like me?"

"You knew that, come on." I get a patronizing pouty face as she mirrors my expression. "Why do you have that look on your face?"

"Uh, *because* I thought you liked me but you were pretending."

"Nope. I literally could not stand you. I mean—just enough to curse you out a few times. You're kind of awful."

I am?

"I've never had any complaints before."

"Who is going to complain to your *face*? No one. Yeah *right*." Charlie snorts, crossing her legs and readjusting her body. "You're Triple J, almighty wide receiver—no one is going to tell you no, let alone tell you you're being an ass or say you suck. Come on, let's get real for a second."

My mouth opens to reply but gets clamped shut again as Charlie goes on, warming to the topic of me being an ass.

"Everyone is too busy kissing your ass. When is the last time anyone told you no? Or didn't give you something you wanted? Or gave you a bad grade?" She makes an unattractive gagging sound in the back of her throat.

"Hey—I get bad grades." Why am I defending myself?

"Fine, you get bad grades." She uses air quotes around the word bad, and I get offended all over again. "When's the last time you failed a class?"

"Are you implying that I'm *given* good grades?"

Her hands go up, palms facing the ceiling in the truck. "I wouldn't know."

"See, this is where you're wrong. I study—I study my ass off. They might tailor classes for student athletes, but it's at my discretion to take them—and I don't. If I get hurt and end up on the injury list, I'm screwed. Then what? My career is shot and I'm left with nothin'—so I study and I study hard, because that's the other reason I'm here."

"Football and a degree."

"Yup."

"And that's it?"

My hands tighten over the leather steering wheel, lips drawn into an obstinate line. "*Yup.*"

"And you don't cheat?"

I turn my head to look her straight in the eyes. "No."

Her palms go up again, this time in surrender. "Okay, okay, I'm just asking, sheesh. Bring the death stare down a notch."

"Newsflash, Charlotte, you can't go around accusin' people of cheatin' based on stereotypes."

"I'm sorry."

I feel weight on my forearm, my eyes darting down to stare at the fingers resting there. The light pink manicured nails. The thin gold ring on her index finger.

It taps my muscle once, twice before pulling away and returning to its spot on her thigh, but the damage is done; I can still feel its heat on my skin long after it's gone.

"I am sorry, Jackson," she repeats, quietly this time, watching my reflection. "Hey."

I look over.

She smiles, biting down on her bottom lip. "I'm excited to carve the pumpkin with you tonight."

Fuck, the pumpkin.

My house.

The guys.

"Bet Biff McMuscles is excited, too."

I groan.

SEVENTH FRIDAY 2.0

CHARLIE

Wow. So *this* is what the football house looks like when there isn't a party going on.

We step in, Jackson closes the door behind us, and I can already hear the stirring of people inside.

Deep voices, low and hushed—according to Jackson, it's game day eve, so they're required to be home, sober, and in bed by a certain hour.

"You know we're not supposed to have guests the night before a game, Southern-fried homeboy."

"Shut up, McMillan."

The kid Jackson calls McMillan stuffs a spoonful of what looks like peanut butter into his mouth and speaks around it, following us into the kitchen. "I'm just saying."

Jackson sets the pumpkin in the center of the table, tossing down the carving kit.

"What's that?" McMillan asks, resting his hip against the counter.

"What the hell does it look like?" Jackson snips.

"A pumpkin."

Jackson goes to the cupboard and rummages around for a bowl, pulls open a drawer, and retrieves a knife and two spoons. Grabs a roll of paper towels.

Dumps it all onto the surface of the table unceremoniously.

"Can I help?" This McMillan guy loiters and now has his hands on the back of a chair, intent on pulling it out.

"No! Go do somethin' else,'" Jackson snaps. "Away from here."

"I don't have anything to do," McMillan argues, still not letting go of the chair back. He inches it out.

"Find somethin'. Get out of the kitchen."

I watch as Jackson grows increasingly frustrated, my eyes getting wide when another guy enters the room.

"What's that?" The big dude points at the center of the table, at the pumpkin.

"Oh my god," Jackson moans, but it comes out sounding like *oh my gawd*, and I smirk at his accent.

"I love carving pumpkins—is that the only one you got?"

"Yes, and you're not helpin'. You're leavin'."

"I can't leave. Coach's rules—I have to be here."

Jackson rolls his eyes, and McMillan leans over to slap the guy a high five. "Good one, Isaac."

"What are you going to carve on it?" Isaac wants to know. "Once, my sister had me carve a flying unicorn—that fucking thing took me two hours." He pauses. "Where are we putting this? The porch?"

"No, she's takin' it home." Jackson grinds the words out between clenched teeth, and it's the first time this new guy—Isaac—acknowledges I'm in the room.

He smiles at me, glancing between Jackson and myself, a slow grin taking up half his face. His teeth are white but a bit crooked, and he's missing one on the left side. Maybe he got it knocked out by an errant elbow on the playing field during practice?

"Who are you?" He's blunt, but I don't mind.

"I'm Charlie."

"That's a guy's name," he informs me rudely. Still, he's smiling, as if he knows it's going to piss Jackson off to tease me.

It does.

"It's not a guy's name, asshole. Leave her alone."

That's not what he said the first time he met me; he told me it was a guy's name, too, but far be it from me to point that out in front of his friends when he's already irritated by their presence.

"Why are you going to take the pumpkin home, Chuck? You don't think it'll look nice at this fine establishment?"

I hesitate before answering. "Jackson thinks it'll get smashed being on the porch, and I agree with him."

McMillan stands upright. "If anyone tries to smash this pumpkin after you've carved it, I'll beat their ass in."

I laugh, unable to stop myself. "Are you going to sit up watching the front steps every night?"

"No. I'll just *know*—like a fucking Jedi." He sounds pretty confident, punctuating his knowledge with a few air punches and ninja kicks.

"Wow." I don't know what else to say, but I don't have to, because a third guy walks in before I have the chance to sit down.

"Jesus H. Christ," Jackson mutters, yanking out a chair at the table and plopping down. "Charlotte, I told you this was gonna happen."

I mean, he did…but he didn't?

"Who are you?" this newcomer asks, holding a microwave bag of popcorn in one hand, a bottle of water in the other. He's bigger than the rest, not only in height, but also in size. A Mack-Truck-sized guy with a beard and belly.

"Who are *you*?" I mimic with a smile. He seems sweet, but maybe that's just because he could easily don a velvety red suit and black boots to play Santa Clause for the holidays. Jolly with a belly full of jelly.

"I'm Rodrigo."

"I'm Charlie, Jackson's friend."

Rodrigo tilts his head. "Who's Jackson?"

Everyone laughs, and McMillan claps a hand on his back. "Jackson is Southern Fried, big guy. Triple J. Otherwise known as the asshole who hogs the bathroom every morning when you're tryna take a piss."

They all laugh again, including Jackson, who seems to be staring holes into the perfectly round, perfectly shaped, perfectly colored pumpkin in the center of their kitchen table.

"What are you carving on that thing?" Rodrigo asks, fisting some popcorn and shoving it into his mouth, chasing it down with a healthy swig of water.

"We haven't decided," I let him know, joining my date at the table. Bumping his knee with mine when I scoot my chair in a bit farther. Our gazes meet, and a smile tugs at the corner of his mouth. His blue eyes sparkle, and I can see the amusement shining there.

He sounds grouchy, but he's secretly enjoying himself, this much is clear.

"One time, I carved one pumpkin for each of the Harry Potter houses even though I'm Ravenclaw," Rodrigo announces. "My two sisters are Gryffindor and my little bro is Hufflepuff, but we still carved a Slytherin."

"You're such a fucking nerd," Isaac laments, seating himself in the third chair. "I was sorted into two houses, which makes me a badass."

"I'm Hufflepuff *and* Gryffindor—you're not special. Get over yourself, Isaac."

Whoa. Where is all this coming from? And who knew jocks could be such dorks?

"What if we carve the golden snitch?" Rodrigo wonders out loud.

"Or a golden *snatch*," Isaac jokes with a laugh.

"We are not carvin' a goddamn Harry-Potter-themed pumpkin—y'all shut the fuck up about it," Jackson grumbles testily.

Y'all.

Ugh, so cute. I love it when he talks like that.

I nudge Jackson's knee under the table and shoot him a small smile. He bows his head and returns it with a tiny shake of his head as if silently apologizing for his friends' behavior.

I don't mind it; it's kind of adorable, all these big dudes standing around, arguing about what to put on an overgrown vegetable and being disappointed they can't carve one, too.

"Isaac, you should run to the grocery store and grab a few more of these. I swear they had 'em when I was there yesterday." Rodrigo squints his eyes in thought. "Big cardboard boxes full of pumpkins. Get you one."

"Yeah?" Isaac rubs his goatee in thought.

"Ah hell, I'll come with you!" Rodrigo is already out of the kitchen and in the living room, opening the front door. "Get your ass in gear, gringo. I don't want them to get too far ahead of us."

"Grab five!" McMillan calls out. "Just in case!" He seems to think about it for a few more seconds before pushing off from the counter and heading toward the door. "Wait—I'll come along, too. I don't want you buying me no stumpy gourd."

The guy—who's really just a giant kid—runs back toward the kitchen and holds his palm out to Jackson. Wiggles his meaty fingers. "Keys to your truck?"

My date grumbles but slaps them in his teammate's waiting hand, obliging—begrudgingly, but giving in just the same. "Please just get the fuck out of here."

Call me crazy, but I kind of like this grumpy, broody side of Jackson Jennings. It's ten kinds of irresistible. I'm not a fool; I know he doesn't want to be alone with me because he has romantic feelings for me. Nope. He wants to get his meddling friends out of the house.

Albeit only temporarily.

As the three leave, one more enters the room, and it's déjà vu all over again as we go through the same conversation we just had with the previous roommates: *who are you, what's that on the table, is that a pumpkin, what are you carving, why aren't there more pumpkins.*

"The guys just went to get a few more. If you want one, text McMillan," Jackson tells him as the guy takes one of the empty chairs. He stares at me, trying to place my face, and I have to admit, he looks familiar to me, too.

"You're that chick."

"You're the guy in the truck." The one who rides shotgun while Jackson drives up and down the strip. "What's your name?"

"Tyson, but everyone calls me Killer."

Is this guy for real?

"No one calls him Killer," Jackson deadpans, not looking up from his task. "Ignore him, he doesn't even live here."

"Tyson," I repeat. "I'm Charlie."

"Yeah, I know who you are." He shoots Jackson a speculative look while picking at the pumpkin topper that's been discarded on the table.

"So on these drives through campus, are you a creep much, or are you just along for the ride?"

He shrugs a set of broad shoulders. They're not as wide as my date's but fit and athletic just the same. The kind of shoulders that never miss a day in the gym. "We're not creepy—we're just bored."

How is it possible that these guys are bored? They're the people on campus most guys want to be and every girl wants to date. Or screw. They're probably surrounded by people, fanfare, coaches, and noise twenty-four hours a day. What's so boring about *that*?

"Don't they have drinking parties to cure that melancholy? Is it necessary to blind every unsuspecting female on campus with your bright lights?"

"Bright lights." He cocks his head with a smirk. "Was that an innuendo?"

I mean...it *kind* of sounds like one, but, "No, that wasn't a sexual innuendo. Jeez. I was legitimately talking about headlights."

He looks disappointed by this.

I set about ignoring him so I can peel open the cardboard packaging the pumpkin carver is sealed in, and when I free it, I hand it to Jackson. He's busy cutting the top of the pumpkin with a huge knife so we can gut it and remove the seeds.

"You need a cookie sheet." Tyson rolls his eyes, the authority on Halloween and roasting seeds, apparently. "I'll get it for you." The hulk of a man-child rises and yanks open a cabinet next to the stove, and when he does, a few pans fall out, crashing to the linoleum floor with loud clangs. "Dammit! Who put this shit away?"

As he squats to reorganize it, I chuckle at his back and the butt crack now visible over the waistband of his mesh track pants.

Not to judge, but his ass is crazy hairy; God bless the girl who gets into bed with that guy.

Why am I thinking about this? Jesus, Charlie.

Jackson catches me staring and clears this throat, tilting the pumpkin toward me so I can inspect his work. He's made clean lines—not a hack job—and removes the top so I can peer inside.

I push up the sleeves of my dress. Pick up a large spoon. "I'm ready to gut this thing." I try to sound savage but am too cheery to pull the badassery off.

The inside of the pumpkin is slimy and moist when I stick my arm in, almost up to my elbow, but I knew it would be. Years of taking the seeds out of pumpkins prepares you for the sensation, but somehow it's always still kind of gross and gag worthy.

And moist.

I root around with the utensil, slapping a spoonful of guts onto the cookie sheet Tyson has magically produced and lain on the table.

He's disappeared, blessedly leaving us alone.

"You want help?"

"No, I've got this, but thanks. You just be ready with the cookie sheet..." I glance up at him. "What else do we need to bake these? Salt? Olive oil?" I can't remember; my mom always baked the seeds.

"My mama always used some kind of spice. Let me text her."

My *mama*.

So. Southern.

"What *do* you think we should carve on this? Iowa's mascot? A witch?"

Jackson takes a few seconds to consider it. Then, "What about a sayin' or somethin'?" He pauses. "Like 'Get the fuck off my porch.' Or, I don't know. Somethin'."

A sayin' or somethin'.

I shiver at the way he says the words. Simple and basic as they are, they still flip my stomach into a dip.

"A saying is a great idea. Probably a short one since there isn't a ton of room."

"How 'bout 'Zero fucks given.'"

"That works." I laugh. "Where we putting this when it's done? Because I do not want *that* on my stoop."

"Well we can't put it on mine—it'll get smashed."

"But you have the *pumpkin patrol* to back you up."

Jackson laughs, his smile beautiful and wide, his five o'clock shadow much darker than the rest of his dark blond hair. His face is tan from practicing for hours with the sun beating down on him, and everything about him screams healthy and virile. Think mountain man meets schoolboy meets athlete.

"PP patrol." He nods.

"PP as in *pee pee*," I can't stop myself from saying. "You do like those double and triple initials."

"Ha ha, yeah—not my fault."

No, it's not—but he sure exploits them to his advantage, and who doesn't love a football player from the South with old-fashioned mannerisms and an old-school nickname?

Nobody doesn't love that.

And here I am, falling for the bastard myself.

So inconvenient. I wish he'd stop looking at me that way.

Like…a friend? Dammit. He better not be friend-zoning me.

It's really kind of annoying. Not that I want him to be all over me like a wet rag, because I'm not sure what I would do with myself then, but the least he could do is eyeball me inappropriately. Get caught staring at my boobs, try feeling me up under the table—you know, that kind of thing.

Instead, Jackson is chiseling away at the pumpkin, almost ignoring me completely, punctuating each thrust of his knife with a low grunt, as if the task of stabbing the sharp tine into the flesh is grueling. Or difficult. Or requires actual effort and muscle.

In all the years I've watched my parents—Dad usually—carving a pumpkin, it's always been a struggle sticking the knife through its thick wall and pulling it out.

Not for Jackson; he makes it look easy, probably because he's one hundred times stronger than my dad will ever be. Bigger and in shape, hundreds of hours of workouts to thank for his physique.

He chooses that moment to look up, wielding the knife in his right hand, pausing with it in the air.

"What?" He's blunt, eyes blank, unable to read my thoughts.

"Nothing." Typical response of everyone in the world who has ever been caught staring and doesn't want to admit it.

"All right." He doesn't push, returning to his task. "You sure you want this to say zero fucks given?"

"Yes?" It reminds me of a gold bracelet I have that I sometimes wear when I'm feeling sassy. It makes me feel rather empowered when I wear it, though not many people ever stop to read what it says.

"Where we puttin' this?" Jackson stands up and goes to a drawer, rummaging around and returning to the table with a black marker. "You wanna do the honors?"

"Sure." I take it from his fingers, brushing mine against his on purpose. When he repositions the pumpkin so it's in front of me, I carefully write the phrase in block letters on the slippery skin, large enough so it will be easy to carve.

Z E R O

F U X (I change the spelling so it's not as offensive.)

G I V E N

There. I sit back and study my handiwork, spinning the base so Jackson can see it, too.

"How does it look?"

"Fine."

Fy-ne. The word makes me smile. They all have today—I don't know what's gotten into me.

He smells good, too; when he stood up and sat back down, I caught a whiff of him. Masculine and clean, like a man should smell. Like a shot of testosterone. Like I suddenly want to sit in his lap and run my nose up the column of his strong, thick neck.

Our eyes meet again, and this time he doesn't ask what my problem is.

Jackson doesn't say anything—he just reaches forward and pulls the pumpkin toward him, positions it just so on the table in front of him, and takes hold of the knife.

"Here goes nothin'."

I nod dumbly, and this time, he does say something, talking toward the pumpkin as he makes the first cut.

"Sure you're all right, Charlotte? You're lookin' a little red."

He and I both know why my cheeks are flushed, but he's going to be an ass and tease me about it. A gentleman wouldn't do that; then again, no one has—or will ever—accuse Jackson Jennings Junior of being one.

"It's a little hot in here."

"Try takin' off your jacket." He grins, pulling the knife from the pumpkin's ribs with a grunt. Stabs it back in. Yanks it out.

In. Out. In. Out.

Forming the small notches comprising the words I wrote.

His concentration makes me wonder if he's got laser focus for everything he does, or if it's just football and small tasks. I have nothing to do but wonder and stare, so I do while he whittles away.

Jackson Jennings is a virgin.

The thought randomly pops into my mind on its own, with no prompting.

I look at his hands…his big, mammoth hands. Long fingers that can easily grasp an entire football. His nails are clean and blunt—he doesn't bite them. There's a smattering of light-colored hair on his knuckles that I find oddly attractive, and my mind wanders to his chest.

My eyes follow.

His polo shirt is buttoned almost to the top, and I struggle to find signs of hair lingering at the open button, doing my best to be coy about it.

Hmm.

Is he hairless or does he shave? Does he groom himself or let it grow wild?

My mind strays farther down, down to what's tucked into the fly of his jeans, not giving a crap that my thoughts are in the gutter since he's not paying me one bit of attention.

Jackson Jennings is a virgin.

How can that even be possible? What does a girl do with that information? Better question: what does a girl do with a guy who has never had sex before—especially one like *this*?

Well. I'm not likely to find out, am I? It seems like he has his shit locked down pretty tight and isn't giving it away any time soon.

If he doesn't want to see me after tonight, that's on him. I wonder if he only asked me out because he knew it would be a challenge, knowing full well guys like Jackson Jennings Junior thrive on competition. They live for the pursuit. The hunt.

But I sure hope I'm wrong and still doesn't answer the question: *What does he want from me?*

Companionship? Friendship?

It's entirely possible.

Friends with benefits would require getting handsy, since that's literally what it means. So, he can't possibly want to bang me…

…although I wouldn't mind his hands on my body.

What's it like having sex with a male virgin? Would he know where to stick it? He must watch porn—a guy his age has to get the lead out somehow, right? So he has to know which hole his dick goes into…right?

I lean back in my chair, really diving into the subject, alone in my mind.

Nature must take course, instinctively. It has to.

Even *I* knew what to do when I slept with Aaron Fletcher, my boyfriend of eight months as a senior in high school. I might never have had sex, but my body knew it was going to hurt when he pushed in for the first time and how to move my hips once it no longer did.

I smile, remembering how I did a slight crabwalk backward, scooting along the mattress when Aaron tried to jam his junk into my lady business—I have *no* pain tolerance, and it pinched. Plus, I'm a huge baby. My body rebelled, naturally.

But. I wanted to get the deed done; just shy of my eighteenth birthday, I hadn't wanted to leave for college a virgin.

How dumb I was. Sex with Aaron meant nothing, wasn't the

greatest, and made me not want to have it again since. This time, I'm in no rush.

I'm going to be crazy for my next boyfriend; he's going to give me butterflies and send my life into a tailspin. I want to be the first thing he thinks about when he wakes up and the last thing he thinks about before falling asleep—if I'm not sleeping beside him.

Jackson hacks away with the knife, seemingly lost in his own little world, tongue peeking out between his lips, not paying attention to me.

Not until a low hmm escapes from the back of my throat.

"I know you said it was *nothin'*, but I can hear you thinkin' without even lookin' up." His arm pauses, knife still, stuck inside the letter F.

Zero fux given.

"I was just wondering what we're doing."

It's too soon to have a relationship talk; I know this, but it doesn't stop me from being confused, and my mind isn't going to let this go. I have to know what Jackson wants from me or it's going to drive me insane.

"We stuffed a scarecrow, then we ate caramel apples, now we're tryin' to carve this pumpkin before them idiots get back with theirs."

Ugh, he's deliberately being obtuse. He knows damn well what I'm asking.

"No, I mean what are we *doing*." I can't make my lips say the words I'm thinking: *What do you want with me, Jackson? If you don't want to date me then we shouldn't be spending time together.*

"Hanging out."

Oh god. It's worse than I thought. Hanging out?

Hanging.

Out.

That's what guys say when they're stringing along someone they most definitely don't have any intention of dating. I've seen it a million times before; they won't use the word date, and they won't say "just fucking," so they tag the status as "hanging out" so they never have to explain the situation. Or their feelings.

I know he's not stringing me along; he's already told me he isn't going to date me.

But this is a date. He *said* it was.

I just want to know what comes next. Tomorrow. Next week.

I want to prepare myself to forget all about Jackson Jennings Junior after tonight and move on to someone who wants me to be *somethin'*—not a *nothin'*.

I won't stalk him on social media. I won't go to his football games. I won't see him if he wants to hang out again.

Because all I'll end up doing is liking him; I can already feel a crush coming on. It took root the second he took me to that farm, helped me into that hay wagon, and walked around a pumpkin field with me.

Watching him stuff Biff McMuscles, the scarecrow version, into his truck…a hulking, overgrown boy of a man…that did something to me. Something warm and melty like the caramel on my apple, sweet and salty and just the thing I didn't know I needed.

* * *

JACKSON

I know why Charlie is looking at me that way, but I'm doing my best to avoid her question by playing dumb.

This was a bad idea.

She didn't want to come out with me in the first place, but I couldn't resist the fucking challenge, and now she's sitting in my goddamn kitchen, at my goddamn table—in that dress and those shoes, with that hair and that smile.

The blush on her cheeks make the freckles across the bridge of her nose brighter.

So I say the only thing I can think of to avoid softening those blue eyes any further.

"Hanging out."

Her full lips turn down and I know I've disappointed her, but shit. Emotionally, I can't afford to actually date her—I can take her on dates, but that's it.

One date here, one date there.

When I have time, which is rare.

Girls always want more. Expect more. Demand more.

Time, energy, attention.

Everything.

I watched my mama do it to Pops for years—it was never enough attention. He was just too busy, obsessing over football from the time I could walk, and raising me to be a star athlete, like *he* was in school. When I showed promise, my daddy found his passion: getting me on track to play pro ball, something he could never do himself.

They fought. She cried. He left.

They fought. She cried. He left.

Lather. Rinse. *Repeat.*

"Hanging out," Charlie repeats. "Gotcha."

She pushes her chair back and rises from the table, taking the cookie sheet of seeds along with her, walking to the counter. Back to me, ramrod straight.

Legs, tan and smooth.

Ass, firm and round.

She's removed her jacket, pushed up her sleeves, shoulders baring, hair falling to one side of her neck, long and silky.

I clear my throat and get back to my task. "This was fun, yeah?"

"*Yup.*"

Shit. I know that particular version of yup—I've said it a dozen times myself, *in that tone.* She's pissed, but she'll deny it now that I've soured the mood with the truth.

What does she want from me?

I watch her at the counter—my counter—I feel…

Guilty as fuck.

I should never have asked her out. She's going to develop expectations, and I might not have the balls to shut her down completely when it turns out, I'm not ready.

Not really.

I have no practice dealing with women. Guys, yes. Girls? No.

I've never dated a single soul. Never taken a date to a high school dance, never made out with anyone in the back of a car. Or my truck. Or a cornfield.

I have felt tits before, but they were on a stripper, during a guys' trip to the strip club for a teammate's twenty-first, out of town and past the city limits so we wouldn't get caught—though every single person there had to have known who we were.

Man-children the size of giants don't waltz into gentlemen's clubs every day of the week.

Fake tits I paid to feel.

Not my finest moment.

"Want help with those?" I offer, desperate. The last thing I want is for her to be mad; we were having fun, and now…we're not.

"Nope. You keep doing what you're doing."

Shit.

I set the knife down, resting my hands on the table's surface, debating. Wipe my palms on the thighs of my jeans, tapping my fingers on the fabric.

Debating.

Before I can think twice, I'm standing and crossing the small space. I stand behind Charlie, my body pressed against her back, hands poised on her upper arms.

She stills.

Waits.

Hands threaded in the mush on the cookie sheet, separating pumpkin guts from seeds, an ooey, gooey mess.

"Don't be mad." Eventually my palms quit hovering and land on her shoulders.

I feel her stiffen, feel her intake of breath.

"I'm…"

She's going to deny it, but we both know it would be a lie.

I move my hands slowly, reveling in how smooth the skin on her shoulders is, so unlike mine. Watch as my calloused fingers trace along her bare flesh, over the soft curve of her neck.

"I'm just…"

Charlie's neck tilts the barest fraction to the left.

I stare at that spot—the one that no doubt smells like her. Fresh and feminine and perfect.

She's not short, and she's in heels; I'd only have to lean down slightly to place my lips in the crook of her neck. I've never done it before; I've never done lots of things guys my age have done, and for a split second I regret being so regimented.

It wasn't because I wanted to be; it was because I had to be.

Because of Pop's drive and determination.

I have drive and determination of my own, and most of it matches his, but am I my own man if everything I do is because he demanded it of me?

Because of everything he denied me?

Women make you weak, son.

Women make you lose.

I don't feel weak standing behind Charlie. I feel strong and virile and hard.

Sensitive.

I dip my head.

Rest my lips on her neck, right in the spot God intended them for.

When her arm comes up, when her goopy fingers thread through my hair, we both moan.

My hands drag down her arms and to her hips, palms grasping at her narrow waist, pulling her in against my body.

She smells so damn good, better than I was imagining but nowhere near as good as she feels. Pumpkin spice and vanilla and whatever this shampoo is that she uses—fucking fantastic. Cherries and almonds.

I can't stop my hands from exploring. They're so much bigger than she is, cover so much ground with little effort, and Charlie lets me.

Gently my fingers press into her hipbones, make a triangle like they're catching a football and go farther down to that V between her legs. Slowly up over her abs.

She's soft in all the right places.

Charlie withdraws her pumpkin-covered fingers from my hair and turns, her back pressed against the kitchen counter. Eyes widen when they rise to my hairline.

"Jackson." Just my name, but said in a way that speaks volumes: *What are you doing? Why did you kiss me? Are you going to do it again? Will I let you?*

"Charlotte." I have no idea what else to say—not when she's staring up at me with those big, bright blue eyes. They're searching mine, a bit confused and honestly, so am I.

I'm confused as fuck.

"You have pumpkin guts in your hair," she says at last, reaching up with her gunk-covered fingers to pull out a seed that's stuck in the strands.

"I don't fuckin' care." I like her touching me, dirty hands or not.

"Someone is going to notice."

"I don't fuckin' care."

"You're *so*…" Her voice trails off, catching when she finishes with the word, "Cute." She breathes it quietly, as if it's a confession and not a statement.

So. She thinks I'm cute.

Obviously, or she wouldn't be with me right now, though I'm far, far from it. I haven't been cute since…well, probably never. I was nine pounds when I was born and wearing one-year-old clothes by the time I was six months.

Not a single soul has ever called me cute before.

A big *baby*, now a big *boy*.

I'm more lummox than male model, but Charlie seems to have her rose-colored glasses on. Huge. Stubborn. Ruthless.

Handsome? Rarely.

Cute? *Never.*

"You think so?" I ask, just to be sure. Or to hear her say it again. Whichever.

She bites her lip, back still pressed against the counter, chin still tilted up in the most fetching way. "Yes."

"I think *you're* cute." God, what the hell am I doing? Listen to me—I sound ridiculous.

I don't know what's possessing me, but I want to boop her on her adorable, perky little nose; instead, I kiss it. Keep my head bent so I can kiss the small indentation in the corner of her lips.

"Jackson." She sighs as she says it.

She purses them in a slight pucker; they're so fucking soft. So, so soft—*I can't for the life of me think of a better word than soft. Stop it right now, Jackson.* And full. Pouty and pink.

They part slightly, like lips that know they're about to be kissed, and I take a few seconds to appreciate them before bringing my head all the way down.

Finally—*final*fucking*ly*—our mouths meet.

Gentle and tentative and a little unsure.

Once my tongue is in her mouth, there won't be any going back; I'll be fully committed to seeing this thing through with her.

The thought doesn't make me want to vomit or scare me shitless like it has in the past. Doesn't have me pulling back or pushing her away.

How could it when her pumpkin-gut-covered hands are sliding around my waist and lowering to my ass? How could it when her tongue tastes like sour apple and caramel? How could it when she moans my name?

Moans my name.

No one has ever done that, either, and the sound has me pulling her in tight, with no room between our bodies for negotiation.

I'll have the insides of our jack-o-lantern all over my clothes and in my hair by the time we're done kissing and I. Don't. Fucking. Care.

Since I'm out of practice, I feel myself fumbling, our lips not quite in sync.

It's distracting; I don't want Charlie to think I'm freaking terrible at it when I'm good at everything else. And I don't want her talking shit about me either. I can hear it now: *"You know Jackson Jennings? He's the worst kisser. His tongue was everywhere and he had no clue what he was doing. It was disgusting."*

I pull back and give my head a shake.

Charlie's hand goes to her mouth, fingers pressing against her lips. "What's wrong?"

"I'm so fuckin' bad at this. I'm sorry."

"Bad at what?"

"Kissin'." I hesitate, feeling like the biggest sort of asshole. "I don't… It's been a while."

Try never.

The virgin footballer who'd never been kissed—wouldn't that make a great headline in the school newspaper?

"Is this the worst kiss you've ever had?" I blurt out the question, embarrassed I even have to ask.

She laughs quietly, her hand now on the front of my shirt, pressing on my pec muscle. "No. It's not the worst kiss I've ever had. That honor goes to Benny Mayer."

"And when was this?" I sound like I'm pouting because I am.

"Eighth grade."

Great. My kisses are shit-tastic but not worse than thirteen-year-old Benny Mayer.

"When's the last time you kissed anyone?" Charlie wants to know.

"Never."

Her eyes go wide. "Never?"

My wide shoulders shrug. "Can we not talk about this? The virgin talk was hard enough."

"That's right—I'd forgotten about that."

Fuck. I just had to open my damn mouth to remind her, didn't I?

"Keep this between us, please." Suddenly, I'm agitated and paranoid about it—my private business being gossiped about by a girl I really don't know, one I'm not dating and whom I don't know if I can trust.

"I would never." Charlie brings her hand up, cups my chin, and turns my face, bringing it down so I'm looking her in the eyes. "I would never say anything to anyone about your business."

Technically it's her business too now that I've had my tongue in her mouth.

"Do you believe me?" She searches my eyes.

I don't know. I honestly don't know if I can trust her, mostly because I haven't let my thoughts go to that place. Trusting her would mean making her a part of my life.

You can only trust someone you know and have a relationship with—and I don't have that with her…yet.

"Jackson." Her shoulders fall a bit and she releases my jaw just as the front door opens. Three overgrown toddlers come bashing through, each of them carrying at least two pumpkins and a shopping bag.

I step away from Charlie and go back to the chair at the table, go back to wielding the carving knife, its tiny orange handle like a child's toy in my hand. Small and damn near impossible to grip.

"What the hell is all that shit," I complain curiously. Seriously, what the hell do they have in all those bags?

"All the shit for the Pumpkin," McMillan tells me, setting his two pumpkins on the counter then the paper bag he was holding by the handle.

"We're not having a party," I grumble.

"Calm your tits, old man—we're the party." Rodrigo is already digging through his bag, pulling out a bag of Cheetos, cheese wiz, and miniature oranges. "These are the little kind of oranges with no seeds that kids go crazy for. The theme is orange, so we got orange snacks."

Far be it from me to point out the obvious, but, "That shit is going to taste terrible together."

I get an eye roll—like I'm the moron here. "*Duh,*" Rodrigo draws out. "*That's* why we bought sherbet. It's orange *and* it's a palate cleanser."

If they say the word orange one more time, I will lose my damn mind.

"How do you know that?"

"I used to bus tables at a fancy-ass restaurant in high school for a hot minute. They served these tiny cones in between courses."

That does sound fancy as fuck.

"You're going to eat all this? Tonight?"

Rodrigo stares me down like I've done lost my mind. "It's a pumpkin party."

Jesus Christ with these guys.

At the counter, back to arranging the seeds on the cookie sheet, Charlie laughs, her back shaking with every idiotic word coming out of my friends' mouths. She moves to preheat the oven, setting it at three-fifty, then opens the cabinet next to the stove.

"Whatcha looking for?" McMillan asks.

"Salt?"

He shoots me a sly look before easing up behind her and pulling open a different door—the one directly above the stove and about six feet off the ground—high up for most people, but not for us.

Not for a household of giants.

"Here you go, darlin'." The asshole is mimicking my accent, my words, and—

Well, she's not my girlfriend, and I have no claim on her.

But you did just kiss her, I argue. *So?* I volley back at myself. *You were fucking terrible at it and she's never gonna want to see you again or put her mouth on yours, you out-of-practice, virgin piece of shit.*

I have no right to be jealous of his flirting, especially since Charlie isn't reciprocating.

"Thanks." Charlie takes the salt from my roommate, her gaze darting to me, a hesitant smile on her lips directed at McMillan, as if she knows what's going on and doesn't intend to encourage it.

She's being polite but not returning his over-the-top flirtation.

Any other girl would be playing us against each other. I'm sure of it.

But Charlie isn't any other girl.

She held out—wouldn't go out with me when I hinted at it, thinks I'm kind of an asshole.

Right?

SEVENTH FRIDAY 3.0

CHARLIE

"Thanks for tonight. I had a lot of fun." I glance at Jackson out of the corner of my eye, studying his profile in the dim cab of his truck. His strong jaw is set in a stubborn position, as if his teeth are clenched, tense. As if he no longer knows what to do with me now that we kissed in his kitchen.

That kiss.

I press two fingers to my lips, the heat from his mouth still fresh on my pout. It wasn't anything particularly sensual, just the meeting of our mouths, but the sensation lingers just the same.

My lips are soft—I exfoliated them tonight before applying gloss—so I imagine he must have liked it, green as he is.

What's it like for a guy like that to have no experience?

I could tell by the way he hesitated, nature taking over but still uneasy in his movements. Unsure.

Halting.

Refreshing.

I haven't made out with tons of people myself, but I can't imagine *never* having done it at my age. What is that like for someone in their twenties and living with a houseful of guys who screw and have casual relationships on a regular basis?

No wonder he was embarrassed and turned bright red.

Still.

I liked it, and I'm glad he doesn't have a mile-long list of conquests like most athletes; that would turn me off.

Beside me, Jackson taps on the steering wheel to the rhythm of the song softly playing on the radio—some old-school country ballad about politics, religion, and a dog named Blue—as we back out of the driveway and into the main street.

Jock Row… Jock Road. At least, that's the unofficial name for it. Stanley Drive is what it's actually called, after the alumna who donated a few million bucks to build the residences situated along the street with the sole purpose of housing athletes.

They're nice digs, way more grand than the shithole I'm shacked up in with my friends on the other side of campus. I was embarrassed the other night showing Jackson where I live knowing he's set up in the football house. The floors were disgusting, but the rest of it wasn't terrible.

At least the door wasn't falling off its hinges.

I make a mental note to send my landlord yet another message about my front door and gaze into the backseat of Jackson's truck. My date's truck.

Yup, it's official—we're on a date.

Butterflies flutter within my stomach, waking from their slumber. It's been a long time since a boy has made me nervous.

Jackson turns a corner, and the small collection of gourds in the backseat rolls from one side of the seat to the other. We didn't bring the pumpkin we carved, the guys collectively deciding they wanted to put them all out on their porch—but I have the unmarked gourds and the scarecrow, Biff, and plan on putting them on *my* porch as soon as

I get home.

Cozy my place up for the impending holiday.

"Glad you had a good time."

Good tyme.

I shiver. That accent. That voice, that tone.

Jackson taps the steering wheel again, and my eyes go to his hands.

His big, strong, masculine hands.

Before tonight, I haven't had a set of hands on my body in *God*, who knows how long.

I try not to stare at Jackson's hands or forearms, dragging my stare away and refocusing my concentration on the road ahead of us. Plucking at the hemline of my dress to distract myself, to keep my own hands busy.

"I did have a good time." I groan; we sound ridiculous. Clearing my throat, I try again. "I'm surprised you…"

I pause, self-conscious.

"Surprised I what?"

"Nothing." I zip my lip and shake my head.

His irritation is evidenced by his sigh. "I hate when people say nothin'—just tell me what you were going to say."

He's right; I hate when people do that too, and he knows damn well I had something to say. *Ugh.*

So. I do the only thing I can do: I take a breath, suck it up, and say what I was about to say. It's the only way to save face with him so he doesn't think I'm a wimp.

"I'm surprised you put the moves on me."

"I wasn't putting the moves on you."

"Oh? Then what would you call breathing all over my neck?"

Jackson laughs, gripping the wheel. "I was sweet-talkin' you because you were pissed I said we're hangin' out."

The words *I waz sweet-tawkin yew* go straight to my lady bits.

They tingle.

"You didn't have to get up and spoon me from behind. You could have just said you were sorry for being insensitive."

It's true; he could have.

But he didn't.

He put his mouth on my body—on my neck. His warm breath caressing my skin felt so, so…*oh lord, I'm going to end up touching myself tonight when I climb into bed at the memory of those lips…*

Hardly the same thing. Not even close.

Too bad I'm not desperate enough to chase after a guy who doesn't want to date me.

Have fun and hang out? Yes.

Talk and text? Yes.

Invite to parties and games? Yes.

Date? No. Have a relationship with? No. Sleep with? No.

It's just so weird to me. Here he is, this hulking hunk of a guy, outweighing me by at least one hundred and fifty pounds. Jackson Jennings is a mountain of a man with more testosterone pumping through his veins than the average college boy. It makes no sense to me that his hormones aren't raging, too, and if they are, the guy has more self-control than I can comprehend.

Most guys his age have zero self-control. None. And it shows.

"You weren't expecting me to put the moves on you. So that's what you thought I was doing, eh?"

"I mean…yeah?" Shoot, I hate when I'm wrong.

"Well." He pauses. "Maybe I was."

My head whips in his direction, eyes so wide the air from the heater in the dash is blowing them dry.

I blink.

Blink again.

"Say that again." I need clarification.

"How about we do this, Miss Know-It-All: when we turn onto the next block—onto Frat Row—if we see any people walking into a fraternity house dressed in costumes, you have to kiss me."

Whoa. Whoa, whoa, whoa, where is that coming from?

I scoff. "We kissed in the kitchen—we don't have to place bets on it."

"Nah, this is more fun. Besides, I kissed you. You barely kissed me back, and now you have to."

I turn to face him, twisting my buckled-in body like a pretzel, leaning over to get comfortable, sinking my teeth into this topic. "Okay, so let me get this straight: you're betting me when we turn onto Frat Row, there will be people wearing costumes, and if there are, I have to kiss you." I roll my eyes heavenward. "That's the dumbest thing I've ever heard."

"Why?"

I laugh. "It's just never gonna happen."

"Wanna make a bet?"

"Costumes? Jackson, it's September—no one walks around in a costume in September, let alone multiple people."

"All right, so don't take the bet."

He can't trick me into accepting a wager. "Fine. I won't."

"Okay, don't." He's laughing at me, taunting.

"I won't." Except… "I mean, what are the odds?"

"Very slim." He nods, seeming to agree with me.

Hmm. "Super slim. Vegas odds at best."

"Right. The odds are stacked against me."

"So why would you set yourself up to lose?" He reaches over and surprises me by giving my thigh a squeeze.

It takes a few seconds to recover once his hand is back on his steering wheel, my thigh branded. "Because I know I'll win."

I swear, he's driving down the road at a snail's pace on purpose, dragging out the moments we have before making a turn onto Frat Row.

"Fine. I'll take the bet! I'll take it, so would you just make the turn already so we can get this over with? The suspense is killing me."

"In a rush, are ya?"

"No." I almost roll my eyes but resist; he can scarcely see me in the dim light anyway. My sarcastic nonverbal communication is lost on him at this point; he's barely paying me any attention.

"I think you are."

"I assure you, I am not in a rush to make out with you." *Methinks thou dost protest too much…*

Jackson wrinkles his face. "No one said nothin' bout makin' out."

Ugh, I'm practically a puddle on my side of the truck; every Southern inflection out of his beautiful mouth has me melting.

I'm disgusted with myself. Well and truly disgusted.

"I meant kiss. I'm not in a rush to kiss you."

The truck makes the right turn, slowly as Jackson brakes for pedestrians and oncoming cars, the cross traffic with a blinking red light and us with a yellow. Frat Row is lit up like the Fourth of July, porch lights glowing, the entire street a welcoming beacon despite the debris on a majority of the lawns.

Red cups, wrappers, and beer cans litter the grass in front of the stately homes, dulling the luxurious properties. They're worth millions of dollars, housing the occasional douchebag who probably takes living there for granted.

People mill about in front of the Lambda house.

People dressed like a pirate, a giant panda, and a slutty nurse?

A pink bear walks out the front door and begins dry humping the leg of a guy wearing a giant sperm costume.

"Dang, do you see what I see?" Jackson has the balls to ask.

"You mean the kid lying on the ground who's dressed like a zombie? Yeah, I see it." The dude is flopping around as if seizing—and maybe he is? But probably not, since everyone is just standing around.

"Looks like some kind of costume party," he muses, going the extra mile by rubbing the stubble on his chin.

"Jackson?" When I peel my eyes off the road in front of us, it's impossible to miss the smirk on his face. "Did you set me up?"

"Me? Nooo…"

"Jackson! Oh my god, you ass! Don't lie!"

Ugh, I could kill him!

His wide shoulders shrug; he's unflappable. "I mean…I knew there was a party tonight, but it was just a lucky guess that there would be people dressed up."

"You're such a damn liar! You freaking knew we'd see costumes when we turned the corner!"

He shoots me side-eye. "Are you gonna hit me with those tiny digits of yers? 'Cause you look 'bout as mad as a wet hen."

Dammit, why is he so cute?

"Am I going to hit you? First of all, no—I don't condone violence, plus I'd probably break my hand." Jackson rolls his eyes.

"And secondly, that has got to be the weirdest metaphor I've ever heard for someone being pissed off."

"You ain't—" He stops to correct his grammar. "You haven't ever heard that before?"

"I have but still think it's weird. It makes no sense."

"Chickens hate bein' wet," he unnecessarily explains.

"The point is, you knew there would be a party."

"I'm not an idiot—of course I knew."

"That's entrapment."

His only answer is a deep laugh that reverberates through the cab of the truck, sending tingles to my nether regions in the most unladylike way.

I shift in my seat. "This was so wrong."

"Didn't no one ever tell you some athletes don't play by the rules?"

"Are you admitting you cheated, Jackson Jennings?"

"I'm admittin' I don't always play by the rules."

"So—cheating."

We both laugh, and I'm glad he's taking my teasing in stride.

"No, I don't normally cheat, never a day in my life. My daddy would have..." He pauses, shifting uncomfortably in his seat. "My parents would have killed me if I bent the rules."

He's giving me a glimpse into his personal life.

"Your parents were strict?"

"Understatement." He doesn't say any more about it, just keeps his eyes on the road and his truck from nailing any of the people now spilling into the street. As we've slowly crept along, a game of Wiffle ball has broken out in a front yard, the players racing into the road to fetch the ball, not even checking once for vehicles.

A clown leaps into the air, dodging a red minivan approaching from the opposite direction.

"Yours?"

I shrug. "Meh, not really. They never had to be—I just always did what they told me to do. Boring." I yawn for dramatic effect and pat my mouth.

"Same."

"I find that hard to believe."

He glances over. "Why?"

"Because? I don't know, you must have been popular."

"I wouldn't know if I was or not."

"How do you not know?"

Jackson lifts one of his massive shoulders. "I was usually home when everyone was out, so I don't know how popular that made me. Pops wouldn't allow it."

"Why?" I know I shouldn't pry, but…

"Wanted me to get into a good college."

I smile. "And look at you now!"

"Not *this* college." Jackson's sardonic laugh comes with a forced smile, and I'm not sure whether or not to be offended on behalf of the entire Iowa student body. But, given *his* enrollment status here, I let the comment slide.

"Where did he want you to go?"

"A bigger Big Ten school. Penn State. Notre Dame." One large hand taps the dashboard. "Anywhere but here, really.

"Ah, I see. That's why you chose Iowa." His one act of rebellion. "Do your parents come to see you play?"

"My daddy was so fuckin' pissed, he boycotted my games for the first two years." Jackson rubs his nose. "He's been to a few lately, but only b'cause…"

I wish he'd finish his sentence, so I prod him. "Because what?"

He twitches, fingers gripping the steering wheel. "Cause…" His throat clears. "This is between you and me, now, yeah?"

This is a major moment—Jackson Jennings doesn't open up to just anyone. I can see the hesitation in his eyes from my spot in the passenger seat, so him offering up information…

Huge.

I suck in a breath. Let it out. Make a tiny sign of the cross on my chest that he can't see in the near dark. *Cross my heart, hope to die, stick a needle in my eye…*

"I promise I won't say anything."

He can trust me.

"Pops is only comin' to my games because it's almost draft season and he wants me to enter, so he's bein' supportive to pressure me into it."

The draft.

Wow.

My little brain can barely comprehend what this means in the grand scheme of things. Here I am worried about my bagel supply running low and what internship I want in my hometown, and Jackson has to decide if he's entering the draft to play professional football.

My problems seem so freaking stupid. Small. Insignificant.

"Is that what you want?"

"Yes." Again, his answer is to lift one shoulder. "But…"

I wait, knowing there's more to this story. Wait while he drives, turning on my street, finding my house, and putting his truck in park.

Jackson's head hits the back of the headrest, eyes boring holes into the ceiling. "I want it on my terms, not my daddy's."

His use of the word daddy is strange to me since I call my father "Dad," but coupled with his Southern drawl, it sounds adorable rolling off his tongue.

"I want the pros for myself." His voice is low, gravelly. "Why is that so fuckin' hard for him to understand?"

I'm sorry. I'm so sorry. I wish…

I wish I could do something to cheer him up.

"Hey." I put my hand on his firm bicep, and he looks down at where my fingers rest. "Where is this kiss happening?" I swallow. "And when?"

His broad shoulders shrug. "You don't have to kiss me, Charlotte."

He sounds weary and *pathetic*, as if he's just stood in the rain, staring through a window at a room full of dry people laughing and drinking and eating, as if he will never know what it feels like to be inside. As if he *deserves* to be used by his father and doesn't know the relationship should be any other way.

"Don't have to kiss you? A deal is a deal."

"Not really."

Oh, I'm kissing you, Jackson Jennings. I'm going to kiss the Southern stuffing right out of you.

"Okay, well now you just sound pitiful. Cheer up, my gosh." I fake a bright smile, giving his muscle a flirtatious squeeze.

"Tonight then."

Yes, that's the spirit! Although a bit more enthusiasm would be preferred.

"Um, okay." I fidget, weighted down by a sudden case of nerves. I am no seductress, and even though it's just a kiss, I'm not the one who initiates them. Ever. "You can walk me to the door and, you know—I can do it there."

Jackson's laugh is loud and boisterous, truly amused. "Whatever floats your boat, darlin'."

He hasn't called me darlin' since we first met, and I'm reminded how much I hated it at first, because I didn't know him and he didn't know me and I just assumed he was a player who called women *darlin'* so he wouldn't have to remember their names.

Darlin'.

I love it.

* * *

JACKSON

"You don't have to do this," I relent, feeling like a horse's ass for making the bet in the first place. A woman should get to choose who she's intimate with, and I'm a dickhead for backing Charlie into a proverbial corner by opening my fat mouth about kissing me. "I'm not going to hold you to it."

I watch her ass as she marches up her front walkway, making a beeline for the front door.

"Nope. A bet is a bet."

"In all fairness, it wasn't so much a bet as me being a cocky asshole."

She puffs out her chest and pokes herself in the breastplate. "I'm a woman of my word."

"So what you're sayin' is, you want to kiss me."

Holy shit, she wants to kiss me.

Who am I kidding? All girls want to kiss me—this is nothing

new. I'm a fucking stud, headed for the goddamn NFL; obviously tail gets thrown in my direction from all angles on a daily basis.

But Charlie wanting to kiss me is altogether different.

Charlie is Charlie, and nothing about her is easy.

So this? This feels fucking great—fantastic, even.

Like a small victory, a euphoria I haven't felt in a lot of years, including when I'm on the playing field, running a damn football in a stadium full of screaming fans.

This…

This is better.

"I'm not saying I want to kiss you. I'm saying I'm *going* to."

Same thing, cupcake.

"And I'm saying you don't *have* to."

"Why are we arguing about this, then? Don't you want me to?" Her shoulders slump, defeated.

Shit.

"I didn't say that, either—I'm a guy, we're idiots. Why do you think I was talkin' so stupid?"

"Tawkin," she echoes, turning to face me once we reach her door. Her hands rise to brush the collar of my shirt, a smile playing at her lips. "Tawkin stoopid…"

"You makin' fun of me?" It wouldn't be the first time she mocked my accent, but this time she's doing it directly to my face, our faces and mouths and hands mere inches apart.

The heat from her body warms the skin on my neck, hands still lingering. Fingers brushing the place I painstakingly shaved not hours ago to look slightly presentable.

Earlier, when I was getting dressed, I'd been tempted to call my mama for advice—not that she'd have any. But I've never been on a date before and figured she might be able to, I don't know. Tell me what to wear. Something, I don't know. Then I thought better of it; knowing Mama would tell Pops and knowing that when he found out, he'd probably lose his shit.

Girls equals distraction.

Oddly enough, for once, I don't give a fuck what my father thinks.

I'm twenty-two years old; it's time to stop living in fear of a man who ultimately has no control over my future. I do.

Me and my agent, Brock—only we decide what I do and where I'll go when I get drafted.

And I will.

I'm predicted to go early in the second round.

Fingers crossed I go to the Cowboys, but now I'm not sure I want to be so close to home and my meddling parents. Me being a professional isn't going to chill my pops the fuck out—it's going to make him worse.

He is the male version of Kris Jenner.

I shake my head. *Stop thinking about your parents, dumbass. Charlie's hands are near your face. Focus on that.*

Focus on her.

I stand still as stone, flattening my body against the exterior side paneling of her house, letting her decide how long she's going to touch me.

I watch her eyes cast downward, sliding to my pecs. They're firm and muscular from hundreds of hours spent in the gym on the bench press. On the field running drills. On the pavement, running laps.

Charlie seems to be debating; about what, I'm not sure, but she's tentative, delicate hands now hovering over my shirt, still at the neckline.

I watch the dipped crown of her head; she might be tall, but I still tower over her, and the part in her corn silk hair has me fascinated. I want to touch it—I've never, not once, run my fingers through a girl's hair before, and I'm dying to do it right this second.

Shit.

I want her to touch me. *Just for a few minutes, Charlie.* Just for a second.

There is a light shining on her tiny porch, but it's behind her head. She's shrouded in darkness while my face is stuck in the spotlight, the glare blinding me.

I cringe, ducking my head.

"You don't like that, do ya?"

"No."

"Now you know how I feel." The little shit laughs, the palm of her hand roaming to the scruff on my face. I shaved this afternoon, but a few hours have gone by and it's grown. "I'll forgive you just this once."

Her voice is a murmur, thumbs stroking my cheekbones, almost giving me a stroke.

Shit. I'm getting a hard-on.

"Oh yeah?" I squeak out, nervously.

"Yeah. I suppose I will." Unlike mine, Charlie's palms are smooth—callous-free and roaming over the sunburn marring the flesh below my eye. "Your poor skin."

"I don't wear sunscreen," I say stupidly, wishing I'd shut my own mouth.

"I can't imagine you applying sunscreen—too big a hassle, hmm?" She hums in her throat, and I wonder when the fuck she's going to put me out of my misery and kiss me already.

Patience has never been my strongest virtue.

Charlie hums again as she studies my face with her fingers, the tips trailing from my brow bone down the bridge of my nose. The tip. The indentation above my top lip.

"You're so…" Her head gives a small shake, too bashful to finish her thought.

"So *what*?" I sound desperate for her to say what's on her mind.

Desperate for words no girl has ever said to me—and I don't even have a clue what they could be.

"Masculine."

"Is that a good thing?" Don't tell me if it's a bad thing; don't say it.

"Yes." She pauses, thumb brushing over my chin. "Yes, I like it. I like this little spot, right here."

The cleft in my chin? I've always hated it. "You do?"

"Yeah. It's…" She pauses so long I don't think she'll say it. "Sexy."

I've been called sexy before, but Charlie isn't calling me sexy—she's calling the cleft in my chin sexy, breaking me down piece by piece, identifying the parts of me that turn her on.

The meaningless nothings I've heard over the years, the same compliments and propositions from girls bestowed on my teammates…

God you're hot.

Damn you're sexy, Triple J.

I'll blow you right now in the bathroom if you'll let me…

Generic and ambivalent. I'm just a number on the back of a jersey to those women.

But I'm not just a number to Charlie.

I see it now in the way she's watching her hands move over my skin, fascinated. Like I'm good-looking when I know I'm not, not really. There are thousands of guys better looking than I am, and any of them would be happy to give Charlie what she's after—a relationship.

I don't have a clue how to be in one.

I've only touched stripper tits; what do I know about having a girlfriend?

But maybe...*just maybe*...

I'm distracted by Charlie moving closer, breasts pressed against my chest—a new sensation for me. I squirm at the tightening in the crotch of my jeans when her tits squish my pecs.

"I love this." Her palms cup my jawline.

I love this. *Love this.*

Love.

Another word I've never heard.

I lean into her warmth. She leans into me, tilting her chin up, mouth pouty.

"Do you?" I whisper.

"You know I do."

I do. I know she likes everything about me or she wouldn't be standing with me on her porch; Charlie has principles, and misleading someone isn't her style.

"What..." I clear my throat. "What else do you love?"

Her lips curl up. "Cheeseburgers."

Sassy brat.

I frown, and Charlie laughs. "Oh, don't make that face."

A *hmph* sound emerges from my throat, my hands somehow

finding their way around her midriff, spanning and clasping behind her.

She makes a happy little sound, pressing closer still. "Know what else I love?" Her palms rest on my shoulders, slowly, leisurely roaming down my biceps. "How tall you are. How strong."

I swallow the lump in my throat.

"And I love your hair."

My hair? It needs to be cut. Mustache could probably use a trim before I start to resemble my friend Sasquatch, who looks like fucking Bigfoot, hairy and unkempt. It's a damn wonder he has a girlfriend.

"I need a trim," I tell her dumbly as her fingers continue their exploration of my arms, her head giving a tiny shake.

"Mmm, no. It's perfect."

She's perfect.

I hold my breath when her hands leave my body and wind up behind my neck, fingers toying with the hair at the nape.

"At least you can see with your helmet on, hmm?"

It's the first reference to football Charlotte has ever made; not surprising since she doesn't seem to give a shit that I'm an athlete. Hasn't once pestered me about the draft, going pro, or how much I'm going to make if I get signed.

"I can see with my helmet on. It's not that long." Not yet. Sometimes I don't get it cut until Coach makes me pull it back into a bun, which makes wearing headgear a bitch. Nothing hurts worse than getting clocked on the skull when there's a fucking bun digging into your scalp.

Good times, good times.

"You know," Charlie begins. "It wasn't necessary to make a bet with me so you could kiss me."

"I'm not kissin' you."

"You know what I mean, Jackson."

Yeah, I know what she means. She would have let me kiss her if I'd have made a move on her—which I kind of did back at my house, in the kitchen, albeit passive-aggressively and by default, since my goal was to comfort her, not make out with her.

"But isn't this more fun?"

"Maybe." Her pink lips pucker. "I haven't made my move yet. I'm playing it cool."

Not cool enough. Her eyes are shining, a tell-tale sign that she's turned on, body alert. God she feels good pressed against me. We're not doing anything besides standing here, but damn if it isn't amazing.

I wait her out, letting her move at her own pace, for several reasons.

1. Because I have no idea how to make a move of my own. Mother Nature hasn't taken over yet, although she could step in any fucking day now to help me along.
2. Charlie is technically the one who should be doing all the work, since that's what the bet was about. Sort of.
3. Kind of.

I haven't felt this kind of tension since my freshman year, when the football coaching staff made cuts and, even though I had a scholarship to play, I worried my position on the team was in jeopardy.

Naïve fool.

Still am.

Still ignorant about sex and relationships, like a kid trapped in a man's body.

I might be large, but inside, I'm nothing but a virgin who has no idea what he wants or what he's doing.

Scratch that: *I know what I want*—Charlie's mouth on my lips, her body pressing against mine. And if she doesn't hurry up and kiss me, I'll lose my damn mind.

Charlotte Edmonds is everything sweet and soft and sexy, and I have my arms wrapped around her waist, the sound of her breath and the heat from her body throwing mine into turmoil.

Raging. Hormones.

Neglected libido, if you don't count my jerking off—which I don't. Masturbation doesn't count; I have heard it's a shitty substitute to actually boning someone and can't imagine it comes close. I've never sunk myself into a warm pussy, but common sense tells me there's no way my right hand feels remotely the same, even covered in lube.

"I haven't been kissed in a really long time," she finally says, eyes trained on my mouth. "Not a *real* kiss."

"Same."

"Have you ever heard that saying, 'I haven't had sex in so long I forgot how to moan—what if I fuck it up and start barking?' I feel like that's me right now, except we're not having sex. Obviously."

"I haven't heard that sayin'." A laugh escapes my throat. The quote is hilarious and embarrassingly accurate where I'm concerned. "Where's it from?"

"The internet—Instagram. I didn't make it up, but it applies to so many things." Her giggle is nervous as she fidgets, my arms still around her. Charlie has made no move to pull away—a good sign since I want her to fucking kiss me. "I like your lips."

She likes my lips. My hair. The cleft in my chin. The slope of my broad shoulders where her hands are resting, fingers fanned out, thumbs kneading the fabric of my soft t-shirt. I doubt she knows she's doing it, moving instinctually as she stands before me, stroking my upper body.

In silence, we watch each other a bit longer. It should feel weird…awkward, even, but it doesn't. No pressure. Nothing feels forced.

Charlie breaks the spell. "Technically, this isn't our first kiss."

"Technically that is true." We did kiss briefly in my kitchen before my fucking roommates barged in.

"So. No big deal." It sounds suspiciously as if she has to talk herself into not being nervous—a lot like I had to do when I was younger, psyching myself up for a football game.

"No big deal."

"I mean…this is only going to take a few seconds, right?"

Right.

"So. Yeah." She's almost sighing, fingers playing with my hair.

"Yup."

Charlie cocks her head to the side. "I'm not sure how I feel about you saying that."

"Yup?"

"Yeah. For some reason…"

"It bothers you?" Huh. An odd thing to nitpick, but, whatever. I make a mental note to use bigger words when I reply to her and not dumb ones like *yup* and *'kay*.

"Yes. I'm not sure why, though."

"Huh." Crap. That's another one.

She's stalling, and I don't blame her. I'm a ball of nerves, too. The longer we stand here, the worse it gets until I want to throw up. This is worse than the nerves I had before the College Bowl, the first big championship I'd ever played in. Fifty thousand screaming football fans do not compare to this moment.

"Charlotte." I wish my voice didn't sound so weak.

"I know, I know, I'll get there. Just give me a minute."

"Just forget it." I let my hands fall from her hips.

"No! Don't!"

"All right. Okay, sorry." I stifle a laugh as she reaches for my hands and places them back on her body. Back on her waist where it feels *right.*

They fucking belong there.

"Sorry." She smooths back a few stray hairs, gathering herself. "I didn't mean for you to stop touching me, I just… You get what I mean."

I do. She's nervous as the dickens and fidgety as a whore in church.

"All right. I'm going to kiss you now. Are you ready?"

Her pronouncement almost makes me laugh, but she's serious, and I bite down on my bottom lip to stop the noise that's creeping up my throat.

"Yu—" I pause, correcting myself. "Ready as I'll ever be."

"Okay. Here I go."

I clamp my mouth shut, trying not to press my lips together out of nerves as Charlie rises on her toes and leans forward, breasts once again pushing against my chest. It's hard to say whether or not she's wearing a padded bra, but dang—having the sensation of tits on my body is amazing.

Un*real.*

I stand ramrod straight, still as stone, trying to keep my dick from getting hard out of sheer willpower as those lips of hers hover over mine, warm breath from her nose and mouth sweeping over my skin.

She's hesitating, eyes searching my face, presumably for the perfect spot to land her kiss.

Starting in the corner of my mouth, a gentle press of her mouth hits the small indentation. Pulls away.

Hums quietly, a delicate little *hmm* before moving in a second time.

Kisses the cleft in my chin she loves so much.

It tickles and I stifle a giggle—what am I, five? Jesus, Jackson, *concentrate.*

Charlie's eyes are trained on my mouth—I can see them despite the light shining from behind her and into my eyes, blinding me. I might not be able to see anything but her silhouette, but I can still see the interest in her gaze.

The light suddenly flickers—goes out, the sound of the light bulb popping the only indication that someone didn't shut it off from inside the house.

It's dark. So dark, we stand waiting for our eyes to readjust, the only sounds our breathing and a car slowly passing by. I watch in my peripheral vision as it stops at the light, sitting far too long, its driver most likely texting.

Charlie's hands cup my jaw, reminding me how good that felt when she did it earlier, only this time, it's almost as if she's memorizing the lines in my face now that she's unable to see them.

I can finally see her better, better than I could with the porch light blinding me. The moon is full, and she's alert, interested, beautiful. Intent on her goal, almost as if I'm not standing here with her, though I'm the focus of her mission.

I suck in a breath when her lips finally hover over my mouth. Actually suck in a goddamn breath, inhaling like someone laid their freezing hands on my stomach. Or shocked me with a Taser. Or…was about to kiss me full on the mouth.

God, I'm such a damn child. My stomach positively churns from nerves—I'm in my twenties, for fuck's sake, not a freaking boy.

Charlie finally—finally—presses her mouth against mine. Firmly, our top and bottom lips meeting. Warm. Soft. Pouty. Full.

She stands there, unmoving, letting the simple kiss simmer, tattooing my mouth forever with the imprint of hers.

It burns. Singes.

Electrifies me.

Yet I don't move, instead letting my hands hover at the sides of her waist, almost touching her but not quite, too afraid to go anywhere—a deer caught in headlights.

I'm never as passive as I am right now, normally decisive and full steam ahead. A decision maker. The receiver on the team and the guy running the ball. A leader.

Not this bullshit where I'm letting some silly girl push me against the wall on her porch, calling the shots and taking control. That's usually my job.

It's refreshing.

Charlie's sweet mouth cracks open, and mine automatically does, too—just the barest of a fraction, our intentions the same: tongue.

They touch tentatively, mine hesitant, wanting and needing her to lead the way. Goddamn I wish I knew what I was doing.

Nature takes over, my tongue surprisingly meeting hers without fumbling; it's all things honey and sugar and sexy and wet. Innocent, but not quite, as Charlie opens her mouth wider so I can move my tongue deeper.

When she sucks on it, my dick stiffens in a way I haven't felt before—hard. Painful. Blood rushing from my goddamn brain to my cock. I wonder how I'll walk straight to my truck when this is over.

My hand moves up her body, gripping the back of her head at the base of her neck, pulling her closer. Her hands leave my shoulders to grip the waistband of my jeans, fingers hooking through the belt loops and tugging.

Our pelvises don't line up—I'm too tall for that—but they're close enough to alleviate this throbbing between my legs as our lips and tongues clash.

A bump on the wall digs into my ass, but I couldn't care less. All I care about is Charlie kissing me. The little moans coming from her throat. The fact that we're alone, the only two people who matter right now.

What team? What coaches? What career?

Nothing matters.

There is no one but Charlie Edmonds.

A WEDNESDAY

JACKSON

I couldn't sleep for shit last night.

I can't eat at breakfast.

I can't do anything but let my mind drift.

It's the first time I've been this distracted in my entire life, at least that I can recall.

My ass has been lodged on the same weight bench for the past ten minutes, except I haven't lifted a single barbell or weight.

One name plays itself on a loop in my mind: *Charlie, Charlie, Charlie.*

Shit, what happens if I sleep with her? What will that do to my football career? I have no fucking idea, and I'm not sure I'm brave enough to find out. My entire life I've been told by Pops and my coaches that girls are nothing but a distraction—career killers.

The wrong girl can make or break you, the way my pops blames Mama for him not playing college ball, although I can't imagine getting some girl knocked up doing that much damage. You do what you have to fucking do and hustle harder.

That's the difference between my father and me—he obviously never had the drive, instead blaming his shortcomings on the person closest to him: my mother. She didn't get herself pregnant, but he blamed her my whole life.

Which is why he pushes me so hard not to screw myself by screwing women.

That's not what this is, though. Charlie isn't…

Our relationship isn't the same.

She wants what's best for me, and if I told her tomorrow that I wanted space, she'd back off and give it to me.

Charlie would disappear.

The thought makes me fucking sick to my stomach, along with the thought of being alone for the rest of my life.

Sure, when I make a pro football team, I'll have more money than I've ever seen—more than I'll know what to do with, more than my family has ever seen. I know my parents expect me to support them after I'm drafted; that's the motivation behind my father's big push.

Then what? I pay off their house, buy a swank pad of my own—and sit in it alone? I immediately envision a backyard with a pool, grill, and lots of space. Inviting friends over and watching them with their children and families while I'm off to the side watching.

Jealous.

Cleaning up the mess, alone. Going to bed, alone. Waking up in the morning, alone. Heading to practice and coming home to an empty house.

Sounds fucking awful.

All because I've been told and taught a relationship will squash my goals.

What's the worst thing that could happen if I stick my dick inside Charlie? We give each other a few orgasms and go on our merry way.

Easy.

It's not like I'll get attached to her. Boom, one and done.

Okay, maybe twice.

Liar.

You're a fucking liar, Jackson. You're already attached or you wouldn't be thinking about sleeping with her at all. You'd be doing what you're supposed to be doing—these squats.

I'm staring off into the distance, at a banner hanging from the far wall, down the cinderblock confines of the giant workout facility. It's a blown-up photo of one of the rowers on the women's crew, her expression one of elation as the team crosses the finish line first at a meet.

I pan to another banner: baseball. A grunting pitcher on the mound, face pinched, one eye shut as he takes aim before releasing the hard ball.

Wrestling. Dark and broody Zeke Daniels, an alumna. Kind of a bastard, if my memory serves me correctly; I've only met the guy a few times, but he wasn't pleasant. I believe he's engaged to be married.

Which means he had a girlfriend when he was winning championships. Their other team captain did too.

Legs spread, a white towel in my hand, I wipe the sweat from my brow, mind ticking through a mental roster of my teammates—which of them have serious girlfriends?

Devin Sanchez, linebacker. Peter Van Waldendorf, quarterback. Stuart White, linebacker. Kevin O'Toole, tight-end.

Tick. Tick. Tick.

Fuck, fuck, fuck. What have I been doing the past three years? No personal life, just football. No going out, just football. No drinking, no sex, no nothing.

Just football.

I lean forward, burying my face in my hands, drying my sweaty forehead on the towel. Close my eyes and breathe.

This isn't my fault.

I did what I thought I had to do.

But for what?

For your career, idiot, I argue.

But why? You're twenty-two, not fifty.

Because that's the only thing I've been taught.

There—I just saved myself hundreds of dollars on a shrink and therapy, because Lord knows I probably need one after the head case my father has turned me into.

Damn him.

Fucking Pops.

He's at home sitting in his recliner, armchair quarterback for the past two decades, calling shots on my life from Texas while I bust my ass in Iowa. *Me.* Injuries, arguments, grunt work—for him. Sweat, plenty of tears, and sometimes blood.

Speaking of tears…

The white terrycloth towel absorbs the salt dripping from my tear ducts, and I squeeze my eyes harder, willing the little bastards to stop.

Shit.

"Hey man, you all right?"

When I lift my head, Rodrigo is standing there, head cocked, dark skin bright red from overexertion, muscles bulging.

"I'm fine."

"You don't look fine."

It's on the tip of my tongue to tell him to piss off, but he actually looks concerned, and if I'm being honest, I haven't let myself become friends with these guys. Always keeping a safe distance for whatever reason—who the fuck knows.

"I don't know what I'm doing anymore."

"Do any of us?"

Yes, actually. I think Rodrigo plays ball because he's talented, but he loves it, too. It's in the way he runs on the field, how he digs his heels into the turf before dashing during sprints, the look on his face when someone scores.

Do I love this as much as he does, or am I so programmed I sleepwalk through it? A member of the Jackson Jennings Senior cult—the one and only acolyte.

Rodrigo—first name, Carlos—stands hovering above me, and if I don't say something soon, he's going to put his hand on my shoulder to console me, I just fucking know it. Dude is sensitive, having been raised with three meddling sisters and a mama who occasionally brings enchiladas to the house on game day. Stocks the fridge with water bottles and snacks, hands down discipline better than any coach in the locker room.

Typical mother.

Actually, that's not true; my mama hasn't come to visit once, not even to move me in freshman year. Pops told her to stay home, but she could have insisted. Looking back at all the mothers on move-in day, mine was noticeably absent and has been every year since.

I'm not bitter about it.

"Yeah, Carlos, I do think most of you know what you're fucking doing here."

He doesn't know what to say, so he continues lingering near me like an unwanted fly; the truth is, I don't mind it.

"Dude, were you crying?"

My shoulders shrug. "I don't know."

"So that's a yes."

I shrug again.

"Hey, I cried last weekend when my parents and sister left."

Twist the knife in my back, why don't you? "Oh."

"Seriously, man—what's wrong? You look sick."

I am sick—sick of the bullshit around me and needing a change.

A weak smile crosses my lips. "I've just been overthinking everything, that's all."

Rodrigo doesn't believe me, and he does what I didn't want him to do: touches me. Places a mammoth paw on the ball of my shoulder and gives it a squeeze. "Get it out, man."

"Are you tryin' to therapy me, man?"

"Probably." He shifts on his heels. "This is why it sucks having three sisters—turns you into a pansy ass." Pauses. "I was the same way when I had a girlfriend. Fucking sap."

I lift my chin. "Girlfriend? When was this?"

"Last year. She dumped me for someone else. Holy fuck, I was in bad shape for a while after that."

"I don't remember that."

"That's because I didn't say anything to anyone. I went home when it happened and mi madre baked for me all weekend, fed me, and listened to me lloriquear como un bebé."

"Huh?"

"I whined like a baby." He laughs.

"But you didn't play ball like shit." Our coaches always warn us about the pitfalls of a relationship, one of them being a breakup. Falling off the wagon as a player and having a shitty season because you lose focus. No one wants to be the dickhead crying in the corner because his girlfriend dumped him or he's hung up on some girl who strings him along. No one wants to be the guy who gets mixed up with a gold-digging user.

Rodrigo looks nonplussed. "No. I was too pissed off about it. I channeled it into positive energy, bro."

"How?"

"I don't know—meditation?"

Meditation? Huh, who knew. "I didn't realize you had a girlfriend. Sorry I wasn't there for you, man." What a shitty friend.

"Yeah, her name was Sunny. We met at a party."

"Was she a jock chaser?"

"No. The guy she broke up with me for is in the drama department. She was..." He trails off. Swallows. I feel shitty that we're talking about someone he obviously hasn't thought of in quite some time; it's clear in the quiet way he's measuring every sentence. Sunny was special.

And she didn't fuck up his game.

How is that possible? Isn't that what girlfriends do? Fuck your shit up?

Superstitions among athletes run deep, and a girlfriend can jinx the locker room, jinx the playing field, and jinx the house football players live in—especially during a losing streak. One loss in a season can be blamed on someone's new girlfriend, old girlfriend, side piece, or fiancée.

"Did you ever feel pressure when you were with her?"

Carlos looks confused. "What do you mean by pressure?"

"Pressure, you know—to break up with her."

He scrunches up his face. "Why would I have broken up with her? I *loved* her."

Now I feel like an idiot for asking, but I go on to explain, "Because bein' in a relationship can fuck up your game on the field."

My teammate watches me, staring down before taking a seat on the weight bench across from me. Rests his elbows on his knees. Clasps his hands and leans forward. "Triple J. *Dude*—life isn't all about the game. Other shit is important, too, like family and friends."

"Right." It's the only thing I can think of to say.

"Jackson, mi hermano, listen to me." He leans closer still, and I'm shocked to hear my name on his lips—I honestly wasn't sure anyone knew my real name. Other than Charlie, who has no problem overusing it. "At the end of the day, the field isn't the one who is there for you. It's this." He points a finger at me, then at himself, running it back and forth between our two bodies. "Family. La *familia.*"

Brother, listen to me...

He reclines back on the bench and scrutinizes me. "Your parents really fucked you up, didn't they?" His voice is almost a damn whisper, and it makes me twitchy, because yeah—they really did a number on me. "No offense."

"None taken."

"So were you? Crying?"

"Yes." A laugh escapes my throat, thank God, breaking the somber mood. I already look like a pussy; I don't need him feeling sorry for me.

"Why?"

My gaze darts around the workout room, judging the distance between us and the nearest athlete. A few girls—volleyball or basketball players judging solely by their height—are loitering by the fridge with the waters, and a few beefy dudes are at the free weights, all of them grunting out reps.

The sounds of metal barbells clinking, air conditioning units pumping out cold air, and trainers giving directions drown out any conversation I'm having with Rodrigo.

So I tell him.

"I feel like I've wasted too much fuckin' time on this sport and not enough time on myself." Does it sound like I'm whining? Hope not.

"What do you mean?"

"I have no life, dude."

My teammate nods and stays silent.

"It's like I woke up this mornin' and realized…I'm sleepwalkin' through my own damn life."

"Sure." He measures his next words. "I think a lot of guys feel like that at one point or another."

"Do *you*?"

He looks embarrassed. "Well, no, but that's because I'm Mexican. Dude, when I have a birthday party, eight hundred people show up. When I take a dump, mi madre is there to wipe my ass. I grew up in a tiny house with no privacy and we traveled in packs.

"So…I didn't have the chance to sink too much time into playing ball, because family always came first." He smiles at a memory. "Once, I skipped the grand march for my little sister's homecoming dance, and I caught *hell* for it. She cried, mi padre cursed. You would have thought I got a girl *embarazada*." Pregnant—even I know what that word is in Spanish. "Or committed a felony."

"Yeah, I don't know what that's like." I don't recall having a birthday party, let alone attending a homecoming dance…or a dance, period, even though I was nominated a few times for the court.

Whatever, the past is in the past.

Is it, though?

"I'm sorry, man. You can borrow mi familia if you want—they're enough to make a man loco." Rodrigo reaches out and gives my knee a tap with the tips of his fingers. "Cheer up, brother. You have all the family you need right here, you know. Do you forget that?"

He's talking about the football team, coaching staff, and the community as a whole. It's been ingrained in us from the beginning that we are one—no man left behind, team spirit, we can't win alone, yada yada and all that inspirational bullshit—only I never cared to foster any of the friendships at my disposal.

"Jennings, we're your family when you're not home."

Jesus Christ with this guy—what's he trying to do, make me start crying again? I can live without the waterworks in public.

I wipe my eye.

Shit.

"Look at you. Should we change your name to Sally?"

"Shut up, Rodrigo."

"Aww, aren't you cute when you're sappy." He's giving me shit and it feels great. "Seriously, man—we're brothers. We play together, work together, and bleed on that field together. Remember that when you're feeling lost and alone."

Damn, the kid could write speeches.

"What are you, a lit major?"

"Nah, international studies." Rodrigo stands, stretching to the full six foot four his bio boasts in the football program. "I wanna be a translator for the government."

"Shit, Carlos. What the fuck? How did I not know this?"

"You do now, and that's all that matters, eh, amigo?" His open palm gives me a smack on the cheek then pats it twice. "You have nothing to cry about. Count your blessings, asshole."

He's right; it's time to count my fucking blessings.

* * *

Me: Hey, what are you up to?

Charlie: Not much. You?

Me: Lots of thinking and now I can't concentrate. You want to come over?

Charlie: Um, to your place?

Me: Lol yes. To my place.

Charlie: Are your roommates home?

Me: It's Wednesday, so yeah. Is that a big deal?

Charlie: No! No. I just wanted to know what I'm walking into.

Me: Everyone is either eating or studying. It's quiet, safe to come over. Hint hint.

Charlie: Well since you put it that way…

Me: I have something I want to talk about.

Charlie: Oh crap. You want to TALK??? What guy ever wants to talk? Answer: none of them. Are you sick? Do I need to take your temperature?

Me: Lol no I'm not sick. But you could come take my temperature.

Charlie: Are you sure? It's a rectal thermometer.

Me: A WHAT?

Charlie: Rectal. You know, you insert it up your **wiggles eyebrows**

Me: Don't ever say the word rectal and wiggle your eyebrows in the same sentence ever again.

Charlie: You're a virgin—how do you know you wouldn't like a rectal?

Me: How dare you rub my virginity in my face.

Charlie: I'm not rubbing it in your face! I'm just asking how you know you wouldn't like it.

Me: Um, I don't think you can just bring up butt stuff randomly—this escalated so quickly.

Charlie: Oh? How so?!

Me: Uh, I asked you to come over and talk, and now you're discussing rectals…

Charlie: Oh. Shit. That's right, you did ask me to come over…sorry. Sometimes I get off track.

Me: Lol I don't even know what just happened there. Weirdo.

Charlie: I've been called worse things than weirdo.

Me: Seriously?

Charlie: Well. No…

Me: Lol

Me: You coming over or not?

Charlie: When?

Me: Now?

Me: You don't have to if you don't want to. It feels like you're stalling.

Charlie: I'm not.

Charlie: It's not like this is a date and I have anything to be nervous about **nervous, crazy laugh**

Me: Guess that depends.

Charlie: Oh shit.

Me: Just get your cute little ass over here.

Charlie: Whoa. WHOA. I cannot believe you said that.

Me: Neither can I.

...STILL WEDNESDAY

CHARLIE

Okay. This feels strange.

I raise my hand to knock on Jackson's door—nay, the door of the football house—and pause halfway up, clenched hand poised just beneath the rusty, brass doorknocker.

Do it, a little voice whispers. *Stop being a chicken.*

Knock.

Low, masculine baritones are the only sounds I can hear. They're not raucous or wild or loud, so I know nothing crazy is going on inside. I mean, Jackson already said the only thing happening is studying, but I don't think I actually believed him.

They're football players, for heaven's sake; why would they be sitting quietly around their house on a Wednesday night?

You're being ridiculous, Charlie. Knock on the damn door.

I pull at the hem of my shirt so it's down over the waistband of my jeans. Then fuss with my hair for a few seconds, smoothing down the strands though I can't see what they even look like. I've gone from my place to my car, then from my car to this porch—there's no way it could have gotten mussed.

Still.

I'm nervous.

More nervous than I was for the biology midterm I had to take and pass so I could begin my application to enter the nursing program. (Totally aced it, by the way.)

Knocking on the front door of the football house is weird. The last time I was here, I entered with Jackson, which made me feel protected.

I feel like a sitting duck here on the porch by myself.

Ugh, why did I wear these stupid shoes? Heels.

Well, fine, they're wedges—high or tall or however you want to describe them, and I wore them because Jackson is crazy tall and…dammit, I'll probably wind up taking them off as soon as I step into the foyer. Shouldn't have bothered.

So why did I?

Because you want him to think you're pretty.

This isn't a date, and we're not buddies—I don't think? Fine, we're friends…I'm just not sure what kind. Being here is an odd place to be. I have no idea what to expect when I get inside. Who's going to be sitting around, what they're going to say, how I'm supposed to be behave…

…like a normal person?

Wow. Calm yourself, Charlie. Get into the house and overthink it later.

I text him to let him know I'm standing outside.

Me: I'm here

Jackson: K

Ugh. I hate when people use the letter K as a reply. It's enough to send me over the damn edge, but I get it; what kind of reply was he supposed to give me?

He needs to come get me like, right now, because I am about to start actually talking to myself out loud.

The door swings open, but it's not Jackson standing there; it's the outline of the Hispanic guy I remember from the pumpkin-carving party.

"Hey Charlotte, what's up?" He pulls the door open wider so I can step through, and I'm shocked—shocked and in awe that he remembers my name.

They must have dozens of girls here on a weekly basis.

"Triple J is upstairs, probably wanking it to cheap porn." The guy smiles—for the life of me I can't remember his name and I feel horrible about it—not flinching at what's obviously a lie.

Jackson wouldn't be jerking off knowing I was downstairs, would he?

Nah.

"Right." I laugh, feet on the small patch of hardwood floor closest to the door, looking around to see who has their shoes on and off. A large dude is sprawled out on the couch, yellow headphones around his neck, glasses on his nose, laptop glowing, fingers typing faster than mine do.

Another guy is in the kitchen nearby…washing dishes?

A sight I wouldn't have expected to see, but there you go—football players do chores. Who would have thunk?

"You want to go upstairs? His lady dungeon is the second room on the left."

When he says lady dungeon, I laugh again, his speech laced with a sexy Spanish inflection.

Muy caliente.

Stop it, Charlie. Focus.

Up the stairs and to the left.

"Thanks, I'll just…" I point to the staircase, and the big guy closes the door behind me.

"You kids behave yourselves. Don't do anything we wouldn't do."

"And wrap it up!" the guy in the kitchen shouts. "No pumping and dumping. Keep that shit on lockdown."

Jeez. With friends like these, who needs enemies? If Jackson were down here, he'd be positively red, I'm certain of it.

I climb the staircase slowly, hand gliding along the shiny wooden railing, counting them out.

One…four, five.

Nine…twelve.

When I'm at the top I go the only way I can go: left. Pass one room then stop at the closed door, wondering why Jackson hasn't come crashing through it yet, knowing he needed to come get me from the front porch.

For the second time tonight, I raise my arm to knock.

And just as my hand hits the solid wood door, it goes flying open, Jackson Jennings filling the entire space. Broad. Huge.

"Hi," I say dumbly. "Your friend let me in."

"Sorry, as soon as I sent that last text my mom called."

Oh?

"She never calls, so…"

He stuffs his hands into the pockets of his track pants and steps aside. "You comfortable chillin' in my room? Or we could go downstairs?"

"Yeah, this is fine. I doubt you're going to put the moves on me, haha." Jackson is barely a womanizer; there's no doubt I'm safe going into his... "Your roommate called this your lady dungeon."

"My what?"

"Lady dungeon?" I laugh; it sounds so stupid leaving my mouth.

"Jesus Christ, what does that even mean?"

"No clue. It sounds more like he's referring to my lady business." I point to my private parts as a joke then catch the look on Jackson's face. His brows have shot up into his hairline, eyes wide, mouth gaping. "Oh relax, I'm kidding. But it does."

He stares at me for a few awkward seconds. "Er...'kay. Well, come on into my dungeon."

I cross the threshold of his bedroom, busying myself by setting my purse on the desk against the far wall. Slowly, I let myself look around, taking in my surroundings.

"This looks more like a lair than a dungeon, if I'm being honest."

"No it doesn't." His deep laugh echoes in the space that's way too small for a guy his size. He dwarfs the room, larger than life.

It's painted deep forest green, the trim a golden brown. It's a dark man cave with a studious, library vibe. Two bookshelves flank the desk where I set my things, both of them filled edge to edge.

"You moved all these here from Texas?" I finger the spines of the books sitting on the third shelf down, the majority of them paperbacks.

"Some. The rest I've read over the past few years. I've lived in this room since I was a freshman."

"You've read all these?"

"Most, yeah."

"Huh. Another layer to your onion." I smile, toying with a tiny action figure. "Who is this?"

I glance at him over my shoulder; Jackson still has his hands jammed in his pockets.

"Um...He-Man."

Hmm, never heard of him. "And this?" The next figurine looks like a wolverine.

"That's Wolverine."

"Oh."

The entire collection is organized neatly in a straight line, lined up one by one toward the front of the shelf. Tiny toy soldiers. A piece from a Monopoly board game—the dog, to be exact.

"What's the significance of this?"

"Stole it."

"Why?"

Jackson shrugs. "I don't know. Dumb, right?"

Yeah, kind of, but who am I to judge? I once stole the head from a Pez dispenser and had it on my desk for the longest time. Some things have no logic behind them.

More trinkets. Tons of football memorabilia: awards, medals, articles. I pick up a newspaper clipping about Jackson and a teammate named Adam who passed away from an aneurism. It's dated two years ago.

"Did your mom frame this?"

"No. I did."

I glance at him again then back at the myriad of articles; not all of them are about him. "Did you frame all of these?"

"Yu—" He stops himself. "Yes."

Interesting.

Jackson is sentimental.

And sweet.

He looks…*lost*, standing there watching me, unsure what to do with himself as I invade his space. Insecure, as I felt on his porch, uncertain whether to knock or turn tail and run.

I set down a newspaper article about some bowl championship and give him my full attention. Take the few paces to the bed and plop myself down on the mattress. Lean back on my elbows and stare up at him.

His eyes scan my body, starting at my denim-covered knees and working their way up my torso. Over my abs and stomach. Stalling on my breasts.

They're full—mostly because I'm not the thinnest girl around and always seem to carry around a few unwanted pounds, but sometimes, it's nice having a decent pair of boobs. Times like this, when an attractive boy is paying them attention, staring at them as if they're the most fascinating things he's ever seen.

And he hasn't even seen them naked.

My chest heaves, adrenaline coursing through my veins from a sudden rush of blood through my quickly beating heart—how easily Jackson is able to make it palpitate. I wish I could calm it, pressing my right hand to the left side of my chest, taking a few steadying breaths as he continues watching me.

Studying me sitting on his bed, I must look like a foreign object to him, out of place. Blonde and light in contrast to this dark bedroom filled with memorabilia and guy stuff.

Green walls. Dark wooden trim and shelves. Headboard. Deep, navy blue bedspread with plaid pillowcases. It's lodge-y and homey and I bet super toasty in the winter.

Jackson's blue eyes get darker the longer they stay fastened on me, his bottom teeth pulling at his top lip. He wants to say something but, for whatever reason, can't.

Or won't.

Or doesn't know how to.

"Maybe this was a bad idea."

I watch him from my spot on his bed. "What's a bad idea?"

"You bein' here."

"You said you wanted to talk—did you change your mind?" I sit up, straightening, then scoot back so I'm in the center of the mattress, crisscross my legs.

Jackson looks miserable.

"What's wrong?" I cock my head to the side. "Come sit down—you look like you're going to throw up."

He does totally look like he's going to toss his cookies all over the hardwood floor, the poor thing; probably hasn't talked about his feelings much like he was intending to tonight.

I assume that's why he wanted me to come over.

I might never know since he's stalling so badly.

Jackson's gaze burns a hole into the quilt where my hand is patting it down, inviting him to take a seat next to me. On the bed.

Hesitantly, he shuffles his feet across the floor. Uncrosses his arms and lowers himself to the mattress. It dips from his weight.

I'm graced with a view of his broad back. It's wide and strong, the cords from each muscle visible beneath his soft, threadbare t-shirt, which I'm tempted to touch, to slide my fingers across to see his reaction.

I bet he'd jump clear across the room. The little devil inside me laughs. *Maybe you should touch him, just to see…*

When he clasps his hands in his lap, the cotton stretches with movements, which I follow intently.

That back is a pure power, and I marvel at it while he has his eyes focused on the door.

The closed door.

Jackson clears his throat and shifts his rear.

Turns, back to the headboard, pulling his heavy legs onto the mattress, letting his head fall to the wall behind him. Heaves a sigh.

I wait, not wanting to steamroll over him. Wanting him to talk and say what he wants to say, because clearly, there is something weighing on his chest.

His strong. Masculine. Chest.

I peel my eyes away from his pecs, and he catches me.

"Jackson, anything you tell me, I promise not to repeat." It's something I feel I have to say, to let him know he can trust me with whatever information he wants to share.

He shakes his head. "It's nothin' like that."

"What is it then?" He has a lot on his mind, that much is clear, especially if he asked me to come over. So unlike him. I know he's never had a relationship, keeps primarily to himself, lives and breathes football.

He is never going to live and breathe for a girl.

"So, I've been thinkin'," he begins, voice husky, hands still clasped in his lap. He studies his fingers, head bowed, unable to make eye contact. "Um. About us."

Us?

What's this now?

I sit up straighter, at full attention. He wants to talk about us? What us? What does this mean?

My imagination and mind go into overdrive before he's gotten any further words out of his gorgeous mouth. Surely he wouldn't have called me over to tell me our friendship wasn't working out, right?

Not his style; he'd ghost me instead.

"Us," I deadpan coolly. Nonchalant. *Casual.*

Fake as fuck, because my heart has spun into a tailspin, deceiving me.

Jackson has no idea how to proceed, that much is obvious. His face is pink as a newborn baby's bottom that's just been scrubbed in the tub, and he hasn't raised his gaze to look at me, eyes fastened to the bookshelves in front of us.

"I was thinkin' that maybe..." His voice hitches, caught. "That...we...um..."

Oh my god, he's so cute I can't even handle it right now.

Big and taking up half the bed, I can't wrap my brain around him being nervous. This boy who is going to play professional football, who's a head taller than half the people I know. Twice as wide. Stronger and larger than life.

Because of me.

I, Charlotte Edmonds, make him nervous.

Jackson says, "Um," one more time before tilting his head back and staring up at the ceiling for help.

"Do you not want to hang out anymore?" I ask innocently, knowing full well the answer is going to be *no* but providing him a springboard for the words he wants to say. A prompt, if you will...

"No." His head shakes back and forth. "I mean, yes. That's not it."

"Okay." I'm biting back a smile because I really suck at maintaining a poker face. Honestly, though—he's *adorable.* I could smush his face right now, he's so clueless and naïve.

So mystified.

Jackson finally glances over at me, quickly skimming my body with his blue eyes. His perusal sends an involuntary electric shiver down my spine. Tingles between my closed legs momentarily distract me, and I offer him a weak smile when he makes it to my face.

"You're..." He swallows. "So. Pretty."

Now I'm swallowing; his nerves are contagious. "We've kissed twice before—it wouldn't kill you to do it a third time, would it?"

"I..."

I let my back hit the headboard so we're matched, sitting on the bed beside one another, both facing the opposite wall. Jackson's hands unclasp, then spread. Palms get set on his knees, until he lets his left hand drop to the bed. Flat on the mattress, it rests next to mine, our fingers mere centimeters away from touching.

I look down.

Jackson looks down.

I watch as his long, strong pinky finger moves toward mine, slowly but surely creeping those few millimeters to close the gap. Suck in a breath when he strokes my pinky with his. Moves his entire palm over my skin; it's warm and calloused. Huge.

Engulfs my hand entirely, dwarfing it like a tide sweeping in, onto the beach and swallowing the shore whole. I'm enthralled by the sight of our hands together on his dark blue bedding. Mine pale and light, his tan and weathered. Bruised and battered.

Abused.

It's rough, but still it sends nerves bouncing around my body when it caresses the skin of my knuckles, the tips of his fingers lightly brushing back and forth. Curious.

"Your hand is so soft."

It is.

"I, um, use a lot of lotion." Was that a stupid thing to say?

We sit like this a little too long, neither of us really knowing what to do or say, how to make the next move. And since Jackson still hasn't said whatever it is he invited me over for…I let him. Let him stroke my hand.

"You haven't dated anyone in three years?" His question is random and out of the blue. Unexpected.

"Yeah, it's been three years."

"Why?"

I shrug. "No reason. I guess I just haven't felt…" My shoulders rise and fall again. "I haven't met anyone I clicked with."

"Do you click with me?"

"Are you asking because you think we have a connection? Or because you genuinely don't know if we have chemistry?"

"I want to hear your answer first." So annoying, but I get it; he's insecure and wants reassurance. Isn't about to open himself up until he knows how I feel.

Fine with me.

"I think we click. I hope we do? Maybe I'm wrong, but…" I shift on the bed but don't move my hand. "I think we get along."

Get along? Ugh, I want to face-palm myself.

"I don't mean get along—I meant we're attracted to each other. I think we're…that. I think we have a connection? Don't we?" *My god, why are you still talking? Shut up, Charlie.* "I'll stop talking." I sneak a peek at him. "What do you think?"

"I agree."

"Is that why you wanted to talk?"

Jackson nods. "I've been thinkin' 'bout a bunch of stuff, mainly 'bout how I've been wastin' time—not wastin' time, that's not the right word." He pauses, searching. "My focus has always been on football, but I think I might be ready for it to…not be only on football. Do you know what I'm tryin' to say, Charlotte?"

Yes, but I want to hear you say it. "Not really? Could you be more clear?"

Jackson's face turns as red as a beet. "I'm sayin'… Shit, I'm sayin' I want to spend time with you. In a romantic capacity."

Romantic capacity? Welp, that's the most unromantic way to put it, but beggars can't be choosers, and the poor boy looks as if he's going to shit himself.

Plus, he's from the South, and don't they say flowery shit like that? No offense.

"We already have a head start since we've already been on our first date." I bite my lower lip, remembering how fun that date was. The pumpkins and the boys who live in this house crashing the entire thing. Giant children, the entire lot of them. If I dated Jackson, I'd be spending more time with the football team.

"I'll probably fuck most of this up. I won't have any idea what I'm doing."

"Who does?"

"Plenty of people."

"Jackson, all you have to do is be sweet and, uh…kiss me when you want to." I straighten my spine against the headboard, knowing—expecting—him to take the hint. Expecting him to seize the moment and plant one on me.

"Whenever I want to, eh?"

"Eh."

"I can do that?"

"Yes."

"Huh." We watch each other until the energy inside the room crackles. Until he moves his hand from my palm to my thigh, sliding it up my jeans, causing my breath to hitch—it's so unexpected.

Our shoulders bump when he tries to lean in and kiss me, and we're in such an awkward position—side by side—making it difficult. His shoulders are way too wide. Even when he tries twisting his torso to reposition himself, it's just as uncomfortable. And impossible.

Maybe not for someone with experience, but it is for us, because Jackson has none.

All this is so new to him; I don't want him to get discouraged and stop because we're plopped on the bed like morons.

So.

I do the only thing a girl can do in this situation: shift out of the spot I'm in, get on my knees, and crawl over to him. Straddle his legs so we're face t0 face, my ass resting on his thighs.

"Hi."

"*Hi.*" His voice is gruff, and his hands? He's not quite sure what to do with them. Nature takes over a few seconds later, though, and those big paws get planted on my hips. Gripping them gently, holding me steady.

"Is this okay?" I ask. "I feel like I'm manhandling you."

"If I'd known you were this bossy…"

"You would have what?"

"Invited you over weeks ago."

"You didn't know me weeks ago."

"But I know you now."

Jackson is still, eyes fastened on my mouth. His chest heaves up and down, a physical sign his heart is racing—like mine is.

"You know…" I lean in close—so close. My loose hair hangs

around my face, brushing his chest as I whisper, "At some point, you're going to have to be the one to kiss me. I'm not going to make the first move all the time."

He gives a definitive jerk of the head. "Deal."

Then.

I kiss him.

Cup his beautiful face in my delicate hands and kiss him square on the mouth. My palms slide over his skin, relishing how warm it is. His ruddy cheeks, burned from the sun. Freckles on the bridge of a nose that looks like it's been broken in a few places and probably has.

I kiss the freckles. I kiss the sunburn.

The corner of his bushy eyebrow, first one, then the other. They're dirty blond, like he is, and unkempt—like he is. Jackson needs a haircut, and I weave my fingers through the longish locks, pulling them back as if I'm going to tie them with an elastic band.

I have one on my wrist, but I don't use it, instead letting his silky strands slip through. Again. And again.

My body dips so my lips can kiss the column of his neck, just below his ears, and Jackson groans when they make contact. Mouth brushing along the sensitive skin just below the lobe. Give it a teasing nip and suck.

"Do you like that?" I whisper.

His reply is a jerky nod.

I can feel him getting hard, the valley between my thighs settled straight on his dick; he's wearing thin athletic pants that do nothing to conceal the erection, and I wish I'd worn yoga pants and not denim.

So I could feel every inch of it.

Our mouths connect again, this time because Jackson can't wait to taste me. Bless his hands, they begin to wander, straying up my ribcage, thumbs spanning, flirting with the sides of my breasts.

His movements are a little rigid and jerky, as if he's not quite sure what he's allowed to do, as if waiting for me to yell at him.

"Is this okay?"

"Yes." Higher, as a matter of fact, and to the left.

Touch my boobs, touch my boobs, touch my boobs…

He doesn't.

His mouth is perfection, tastes delicious, if that's considered a thing—like minty toothpaste, saliva, and need. If Jackson has never kissed anyone before, I never would have guessed it. Either that or we were meant to be together.

I want his lips everywhere.

Patience, Charlie…

Little by little, my hips rotate. Little by little, I watch Jackson's expression go from one of wonder to one of…bliss. And agony.

His eyes close when I line us up and grind gently, my head tipping back as I mimic riding him on top. Even though we're both wearing bottoms, I can still feel the head of his dick creeping up inside me. It's deliciously old school and I feel like I'm in high school again, making out with my boyfriend in his parents' basement, listening for the sound of them coming along to bust us.

But no one does.

It's just me and Jackson and a locked door in a college rental. No one is going to bust us; there are no parents here.

His friends didn't bat an eye when I walked through the living room, and if they thought it was strange Triple J was finally having a girl up to his room, no one said a word.

Maybe they'll give him shit for it later; maybe they won't.

I grind.

I grind and bite my lower lip, closing my eyes for a second—crack them open again to watch Jackson close his. His head is against the headboard, mouth falling open, heavy brows bent in concentration. Or pain.

"Am I hurting you?"

He jerks his head. "No."

"Good." Because it feels good—and would feel even better if his pants were off.

He gives my hips a tap when I speed up my rhythm, a warning tap. "Be careful, Charlotte. I don't w-wanna…don't wanna…"

Come in your shorts?

I don't want him too, either, but I love watching his expressions. They're my new favorite thing in the world, passing across his face in flashes. Shock, surprise, euphoria.

I lean down and suck on his neck, careful not to leave a mark. Kiss his throat, right on top of his Adam's apple. He's shaved and smells incredible. Clean. Masculine and sexy.

I kiss his exposed collarbone along the scooped neck of his t-shirt, sniffing there, too.

Yum.

Nuzzle between his pecs as I make the slow, languid crawl down his body.

"W-What are you doin'?" He's raised his head, eyes blazing and unfocused as he looks down at me.

Giving you a blow job—what do you think I'm doin'? I want to ask but bite my tongue.

I press a finger to my lips. "Shhh."

"Oh god." His head slams against the headboard again, and I note him white-knuckling his navy coverlet.

It's been an age since I've had a dick inside my mouth, and I wonder if I'll remember how to suck one. I let my fingers find the waistband of his pants and tug.

Jackson lifts his hips, jerking them when I pull at the fabric. Ass scooting down a bit farther, settling in. He unclenches his fingers, lifts his arms, and clasps his hands behind his head.

I can't tell if he's even breathing, he's holding so still. Watching me with baited breath.

I want to tell him to breathe; I also want to laugh, he looks so damn serious.

He's concentrating harder than I am, his forehead scrunched, brows knitted so furiously he's likely to combust.

He's never had a blow job...

This thought gives me a renewed sense of confidence—no matter how bad I screw it up, there's no way I'll suck at it.

Pun intended.

Jackson has nothing to compare it to. I'm his first: first kiss, first blowie, first...

My pussy tingles at the thought of having sex with him, making my mouth positively water when I hook my fingers in his boxers and work them down his hips. Hold a breath of my own when the fabric of his drawers catches on the tip of his dick, snagging but freeing itself when I give another gentle tug.

I've never been one of those girls who was a huge fan of dicks—I think I'd gag if a guy sent me an unsolicited picture of his—but Jackson's penis? It's...

Perfect.

He gasps when I cup my hand and run it over him, down toward the base and up again. Slowly. Slowly. Up and down, again and again.

"*Fuck*, Charlotte. F-Fuck, fuck…"

His words are music to my ears. They're a tribute to how good I'm making him feel—and I haven't even done anything yet.

I stare at his junk for a few moments, studying it. I can see that it's throbbing, involuntarily twitching the longer I look. I'm close, my hot breathing warming the tip. My tongue darts out so I can lick it. Flick it.

I watch his eyes flutter closed, his biceps flexing. Nostrils flaring.

Thighs clenching, too.

His whole body is tense, trying to gain some semblance of control, and I love it. I want him to lose it. I want him to…

I want to make him feel like he's never felt before.

No amount of jerking off and masturbating is going to feel like my mouth on his cock, and we both know it.

I free his business up a bit more by yanking his pants and underwear down so they're around his thick thighs, noting that everything about Jackson is big. Thick. Hot.

So beautiful and well put together, he's a work of art that's gone unappreciated for twenty-two years—and I plan to make up for lost time if he'll let me.

I lower my head and…suck. He damn near jerks his ass off the mattress.

"Holy fuck!

I suck a bit harder, as best I can given the size of his dick.

"Charlotte, *stop*."

I raise my head. "You want me to *stop*?"

"No! Yes. No, oh my god, don't stop."

"Okay." I laugh.

I get back to it, deciding to enjoy myself (let's face it, who actually enjoys having a cock jammed down their throat?), deriving all my own pleasure from the pleasure I'm giving Jackson. Hearing his moans and sighs and grunts and cursing.

It sounds like he's being tortured.

Just as I begin to wonder how long he's going to last with my mouth wrapped around him, his hands come down from behind his head and hit the mattress, grabbing fistfuls of comforter.

I'm not timing this, but it can't have been more than five minutes.

"Shit, oh shit…" He's mumbling, moaning. "Christ…oh god…"

Wow. I knew this would be easy, but I didn't think it would be *this* easy. I've heard horror stories from my friends about guys taking half an hour to come from a blow job, which would be my worst nightmare.

I'd probably get lockjaw! God, wouldn't that be a freaking train wreck.

"Charlotte…Ch-Charlotte," Jackson mutters above me, lifting one arm, tapping me on the shoulder. "I'm…I'm gonna…"

He taps again, warning me.

But I don't plan on spitting once he goes. He gets the full treatment, swallowing and all.

I'm no spitter—that would make me a quitter.

The poor boy deserves to come inside my mouth. His dick has been neglected for so, so long.

"Charlotte." He sounds desperate in his attempts to get me to lift my head, to spare me from his sperm. Honestly, if it hits the back of my throat, who even cares? I won't taste it.

I can't explain this to him, though—by doing so, I'd have to lift my head and talk, and we can't have that now can we?

Giving my head a shake, I let him know we're finishing this together.

Jackson moans again—this time so loud, my cheeks flush with embarrassment, knowing someone in the house had to have heard. Moans again, head thrashing against the headboard.

Knuckles white. Rising from the bed, fingers flexing. Hitting the mattress. Hips shaking.

It's intoxicating, this level of control and making him feel this way. I'm the one giving him an orgasm—*me.*

He chose me to be his first.

Jackson comes as I suck, taking him as deep as I can without choking, waiting until he's done trembling.

Pull back and glance up at his face; it's flushed, hotter than mine. Eyes closed, his chest moves up and down, breathing labored like he's just run the fifty-yard dash.

"Are you all right?" is the first thing I ask when his body stops convulsing.

It's adorable.

He nods. Sort of?

"You sure?"

"Come here." He spreads his arms wide, and I scramble to my knees. "Here." Jackson pats his thighs.

I climb back on top, facing him, and he wraps those strong arms around my middle, pulling me close. Hugging me tight. Kissing the top of my head.

I lean back a bit so I can see his face, two sets of shining, glassy eyes. Jackson inches forward, kissing my mouth.

Opening mine, he deepens the kiss. Tongue.

Oddly, it's romantic; this post-blow-job make-out session makes me feel close to him. The fact that he didn't push me away or want to clean off, didn't act disgusted because I had cum in my mouth? It's nice.

I weave my hands around the back of his neck, fingers raking through his hair. Tilting my head, letting him hold me as I sit on his naked lap, his dick flaccid and squished beneath my ass.

Ah, modern romance…

* * *

JACKSON

Hours after Charlie blows my cock, we're flat on our backs staring at the ceiling. It's late as fuck and I have to be up at the ass crack of dawn for practice, but I didn't have the heart to send her home.

I like having her next to me, her warm body pressed into the side of mine.

It's always been something I thought would annoy me—just assumed it would. Not the case, though.

We're both still awake, the mood calm. My nerves are shot, body sated from a mouth-induced orgasm.

There were actual, important *things* I wanted to discuss with her before she got down on her hands and knees and sucked my dick. Things I wanted to discuss about our relationship.

I owe it to myself to get the words out.

I have to stop being a pussy.

"What are you thinkin' 'bout?" I find myself saying, and then I groan, because it's such a dumb fucking thing to ask. So cliché. I don't know a whole hell of a lot, but I do know it's the one thing you're not supposed to ask someone. *What are you thinking about right now?* The trap question so many of my friends have fallen into that's started so many fucking fights with their girlfriends.

And here I am asking it.

"I'm thinking about...hmm." She shifts beside me, rolling to her side so she can face me head on, tucks her arm beneath her head to prop herself up.

Her face is beautiful as she regards me; like a fucking angel, pink cheeks surrounded by a halo of blonde hair. I catch some between my thumb and forefinger and rub the silky strands together.

"I'm thinking about how I like being here with you, and it's nice just lying here, not talking."

Yeah—it is. Usually I lie here alone, staring up at the ceiling. Night after night, by myself.

"And I'm wondering if you meant what you said about spending time with me in the romantic capacity." She giggles.

"Yeah, I meant it." I release the hold I have on her hair and stroke her smooth cheek. "Why you laughin'?"

"Romantic capacity—it sounds so official."

"I s'pose."

"Don't get all salty—I'm just teasing. It's cute." Her index finger extends, and I watch it boop the middle of my nose. "*You're* cute."

"Just cute?" Jesus, listen to me, fishing for compliments. Who am I?

"No—you're sexy. I like the noises you make."

"What noises?"

She giggles again. "Your sex noises."

We didn't have sex, so I'm not sure what she...Oh. *Ohhh*. The sounds I made when she was blowing me! Ah. I see. I try not to blush but fail. I can actually feel the heat rising to my face.

"Oh yeah?"

"Mm hmm," Charlotte hums, that index finger trailing down my breastplate, between my pecs. I flex without meaning to, dammit. "I love your body. I know you probably hear that all the time, but I do. You're *so* strong."

Oh fuck.

My dick twitches.

"Is that the part you like? That I'm strong?"

Her hands caress my muscles, and I want to purr like a goddamn kitten.

"I feel so…safe lying here with you."

Well. Shit.

Not what I was expecting her to say—not when I'm six foot three of solid meat that can cut through a defensive line and press four hundred pounds of weight.

I make her feel safe.

Cool.

"My size doesn't intimidate you?"

"No. No, sir. I like it too much to be intimidated by it." Her finger traces down my sternum.

"Huh." Imagine that. I've been accused of using my size to intimidate people, and the psychologist at my high school once told me I had to knock that shit off. I've been huge since I was young—hit six feet by the time I was eleven, so…I've been taking advantage of it ever since. No shame.

Charlie yawns, patting her mouth with her perfect, petite hand.

"Tired?" We've barely talked.

"Getting there."

"Do you want to spend the night?" It's a big move for me,

inviting her to sleep over.

Charlie cocks a brow. "Are we actually going to sleep?"

"Yes? I'm fuckin' tired—what else would we be doing?"

Charlie's laugh tears through the silence. "Wow, I have my work cut out for me here. I'm no nymphomaniac, but use your imagination for once, would you? What else would we be doing in a bed besides sleeping, Jackson? Think about it, you goof."

Shit. I'm an idiot.

"Do you really just want to sleep? Because if you do, I'll have to try hard to keep my hands from wandering south of the border." She gives her brows a creepy wiggle.

"Yeah, we should probably sleep." The last thing I want is for her to think I'm taking advantage, or that I asked her to spend the night so I could bang her. Even though she knows I've never screwed anyone, I'm not trying to make her think tonight's going to be the night.

Although…

My mind can't help but go to that place. That naked, sweaty, orgasmy place.

But. I don't have condoms.

The guys do—the communal bathroom has a whole drawer full of them.

But I wouldn't even know how to put one on.

Shut up, loser. How hard could it fucking be? Get a grip.

My dick twitches when Charlie runs the tip of her finger around and around my areola; it's firm beneath my t-shirt.

"I don't have pajamas." No, she doesn't, and I don't have any for her. My t-shirts would be ginormous on her.

"You can borrow something if you want." How the hell did we

go from me wanting to talk to her blowing me to me inviting her to spend the night? Jesus, I work fast.

The whole thing escalated quickly.

But I'm ready for it.

I think.

"You really want me to spend the night? Seriously?"

"Yeah—I think I really do." And I realize I mean it. I've never slept next to anyone, just Pops those times we shared a hotel room for an out-of-town football game growing up when I played for an elite traveling team.

He'd get a double, and we'd share a bed. Or, I'd sleep on the floor next to it. *Builds character being humbled*, he'd say. *You'll appreciate it someday, and besides, I'm payin' for the goddamn room. Someday you'll repay the favor.*

What will it be like sharing a bed with a girl? Will I roll over in the middle of the night and crush her? Will I snore and wake her up? Shit—will *she* snore and wake me up? Kick me all night, tossing and turning?

I size her up. "How do you sleep?"

She considers the question. "On my back? I think I sleep like I'm in a coma—at least, my blankets are usually in the same spot when I wake up every morning. I can usually just flip the covers back into place without remaking the entire bed, so…yeah."

"All right."

"Why? What are you like when you sleep?"

"Honestly, I have no idea."

"Guess there's only one way to find out." Charlie rests her hand on my shoulder. "Are we sure we're not rushing this?"

No. We're definitely rushing it.

It's too soon.

I'm not ready for it.

But I'm going to fucking suck it up; I've known her for weeks already, and chickening out is the coward's way. If I was one of my friends, I would have fucked Charlie by now, not invited her to spend the night. Anyone else would have let her suck him off, fucked her, and kicked her out.

I'm doing this entirely the wrong way and don't freaking care.

If my father found out, he'd tan my hide…

Your father isn't here.

No one is.

Just you and Charlotte.

And ten other dudes, but who's counting?

"The bathroom isn't private, but I don't think anyone will bother you if you want to go use it real quick. Most of the guys are still studyin'." Enough chicks come through here that you learn to ignore them—although, if someone has to take a piss, they're going to tell Charlie to get the fuck out of the bathroom.

It's ours, not for the use of random women, and that's how we treat it. Like a private sanctuary for taking shits and showering, not as a glam room for hook-ups.

"So it's okay if I go freshen up or whatever?"

"Yeah." I shift on the bed, sit up. "Why don't I come with you and stand outside the door, just in case. I don't need you gettin' hassled."

Charlie smiles at me like I've been sent from heaven. She's sweet—goddamn angelic. Her rosy cheeks and that little dent in her cheek flirting with the insides of my stomach.

"Thank you." When she scoots off the bed, she pecks me on the lips before hopping onto the floor and sliding her shoes back on. Makes for the door, glancing over her shoulder to see if I'm following.

I rise. Push down my semi-wood with a shrug; not much I can do about it. Lead her to the bathroom and give the door a tap before pushing it wide open. It's empty, and clean—the cleaning people were here this morning, scrubbing the kitchen, floors, and shared bathrooms.

Breathing a sigh of relief that the place isn't disgusting (usually there are pubes all over the toilet seat), my hand rests on the brass doorknob, poised to pull it closed behind me so Charlie can do her thing alone.

"Let me know if ya need anything, 'kay?"

"Mmkay." She beams up at me, pushing a strand of silky blonde hair behind her ear. "Do you have a toothbrush I can borrow?"

"Sure—I mean, no. You can use mine if you don't think it's gross.

"It's gross, but I'd rather not have bad breath. Haha." She pulls the cutest sour expression, followed by a long pause. I strain to hear her muttering. "In any case, my mouth was on your dick—does it matter if I have my mouth on your toothbrush?"

Wow.

Wow, wow, *wow*.

"Uh…good point? My toothbrush is…" I lean into the bathroom, reaching for the closest drawer. Yank it open. "Here." Hand her the blue toothbrush, along with the toothpaste. "All my shit is in here and on the top shelf in the closet behind the door, like towels and stuff."

"I love how you say stuff. It's so cute."

I laugh—she's so weird. "How do I say it?"

"I don't know, like, *stuuf*. I can't describe it. All I can say is that it's adorable."

Oh. Well in that case. "Stuff."

Charlie shifts on the balls of her feet. "Give me five minutes."

"Duh! Sorry." I back out of the room, pulling the door along with me. "Knock if you need me."

I hear her laugh through the door as I lean against it, back pressed against the wood. I cross my arms and ankles, standing vigil like a guard. The water runs. The toothbrush gets tapped on the sink.

I try not to hear her pee, but it's impossible—the walls are thin, and the hall is quiet, so I'm relieved she doesn't take a dump. I'd never be able to look her in the eye otherwise.

The toilet flushes.

While Charlie is washing her hands, a door at the end of the corridor opens and out walks Carlos. We regard each other, and both his black eyebrows shoot to his hairline.

"What the fuck are you doing?" He doesn't mince words.

"Waitin'."

"For what? Since when do we wait for someone to finish taking a dump to use the bathroom?"

A laugh escapes my throat. "I have a guest."

I didn't think it was possible, but his brows shoot higher. "A guest? Is it Charlie? The cutie who was here carving pumpkins?"

Another laugh. "Yes."

"Is it okay if I giver her a nickname, like George? Frank?"

"*No.*"

"Right." Now he's standing next to me. "What's she doing in there, shaving her pussy bald?"

"No, she's brushin' her teeth."

"She brought her own toothbrush?!"

"No. She's usin' mine."

"That's asquerosa. *Disgusting.*"

"Tell me how you really feel."

"You know, I can hear you," Charlie calls through the door with a laugh—thank God.

"Sorry," Rodrigo calls back, but he shakes his head at me. "Not sorry. It's disgusting, sorry bro."

"I can still hear you." At least Charlie is giggling as she turns the sink back on. "I'm ignoring you now—you can keep talking about me!"

"I like her," my friend says.

"Same." He continues standing next to me, watching the wall—as if Charlie is going to materialize so he can entertain her with his wit and charm and good looks. "You can go now," I tell him.

"Don't really have anywhere to be."

"Then why'd you come out of your room?"

"'Cause I was bored, *amigo.*"

"Please go away."

"Why? I like Charlie. I wanna hang out with you guys."

I stare at him, hard. Is he fucking serious? "Carlos, I'm not… You know how I am. This is a big deal." I can't be more eloquent than that, can't speak any more plainly. If he doesn't walk away before Charlie comes out of the bathroom, I swear I'll have a stroke.

"I'm just giving you a rash of shit, buddy. Calm down—your face is so fucking red."

I can feel the heat covering my entire body, not just my face, blood pressure surely shot up past what's considered healthy. Simply because I have a girl in my house and she's about to spend the night.

"Maybe this was a mistake."

Carlos puts a lip to his finger, hissing, "Shh, she'll hear you!" He steps in closer and puts his paws on my shoulders, squeezing his palms into my muscles—hard. "Listen to me: relax. Take a deep breath. You earned this, mi hermano. *Relax.*"

Relax. I can do that.

"She likes you. You." Now his palms give me a resounding smack in a show of solidarity. "You got this."

I got this. "Right."

"Have your balls shrunk? Why you being such a pussy?"

"Fuck off!"

My roommate laughs. "That's the fighting spirit. Put on your big-boy pants and bone her tonight. Take one for the team—no one else is getting laid."

"*Eww*! You did not just use the words 'bone her'!" Charlie cackles through the bathroom door beyond my back.

"Goddammit, Rodrigo! Get the fuck out of here."

"I'm going, I'm going." His laughter fades as he makes his way down the hall, retreats down the stairs to the lower level.

On cue, the bathroom door behind me comes flying open, and I spin. She's wearing the same clothes she had on before, but her hair looks combed, face scrubbed a shiny pink.

My overnight guest is grinning from ear to ear, clearly amused by my teammate's antics. "I can't say I'm not sorry I had to hear that. Bone her? Really?" Charlie breezes past me, brushing my shoulder and glancing at me over hers. "I'll wait in here while you, you know—get your own business handled."

She winks before disappearing into my bedroom. My door clicks shut.

I stare a bit too long from my spot in the hall, finally walking into the bathroom and going through my own routine. Take a piss. Brush my teeth. Wash my balls with a towel. Pull open the second drawer down and gaze into it.

Gold wrappers. Black wrappers. Blue, red, glow-in-the-dark.

Should I grab a condom, just in case?

I reach down, fingers closing around a gold one. Release it, letting it fall back into the drawer. Stand and stare down a little longer.

As I bite my lip, the penis inside my pants throbs. Still, I give the drawer a nudge with my knee until it closes.

Charlie doesn't want to have sex with me tonight—assuming she does makes me the biggest kind of douchebag. We've only been on one date; what's the rule about sleeping with someone?

Three dates? Five?

Six months?

Fuck, I don't know, and I don't want to find out the hard way that she has no interest in…boning me, despite the fact that she just sucked on my cock.

Said cock thickens.

Shit.

I glance down at it. Is this normal behavior for a dick?

"She just sucked you off, asshole. *Calm down.*"

Great. Now I'm talking to my penis—definitely not normal behavior.

I splash some cold water on my face and dry it off; that's not part of my nightly routine, but I'm stalling, afraid to go back in my bedroom, heart rate still accelerated.

I take my pulse, counting the seconds and beats.

"You're gonna live. Relax, amigo," I say to my reflection. Run a hand over my scruff. "Damn, you couldn't have shaved before she came over?" Too late now. If I get out the razor and cream, she'll wonder what the fuck is taking so long.

Inhale. Exhale.

In and out. Out and in.

"What are you waiting for, you pussy?" Damn. If I acted like this before a game, I'd be kicked off the team so fucking fast my head would spin.

I screw around for another couple of minutes before heading to my bedroom. Give a few raps on the door with my knuckles before slowly turning the handle and pushing it open.

Charlie has all the lights off except one, the small lamp on my bedside table, its dim glow casting a light no brighter than a single candle would.

She's in bed.

Not wearing one of my shirts.

Her shoulders and arms are bare, comforter pulled up to her chin. I can make out a pair of white bra straps; they're lacy and stark against her pale skin. Blonde hair falls over one shoulder.

I gulp.

Step all the way inside and shut the door behind me, sliding the deadbolt to the left. "Um, I'm not lockin' you in or nothin'—I'm lockin' everyone else out." I feel the need to explain. "Is that okay?"

"Yeah, I don't want anyone walking in while we're trying to, you know—sleep."

Is she being sarcastic? I can't tell.

I walk the few paces to my dresser, pull it open—though, do I really need a shirt? Shouldn't I just go to bed without one tonight? The tit-baby in me is tempted to text Rodrigo and ask, but he'd just give me shit for it.

I reach for the hem of my shirt and pull it up my torso. Fold it into a neat square. Set it on my dresser.

Now the pants. On or off?

I'm wearing boxers under my mesh athletic pants, but are those enough? It's underwear—is that weird?

My stomach forms a knot, a pool of indecision, uncertainty, self-consciousness and regret that has me wanting to vomit all over my bedroom floor.

If I don't get my head out of my ass and in the game, I'm going to be filming the sequel to *The 40-Year-Old Virgin.*

My fingers hook the inside of my pants and push.

I inhale when they catch the tip of my dick, the same way my breath hitched when Charlie pushed them down earlier.

Anticipation makes my heart thrum and my dick stiffen.

My pants also get folded into a neat square and set atop my shirt. Then socks.

I leave the stack and turn, glancing around the room like a tiger backed into a corner and looking for an escape route. I school my features; the last thing she needs to see is me panicking.

I know I have a great body; it's part of my job as an athlete to be in peak physical condition. It's my mental sanity that could use some work right now.

Charlie sweetly smiles.

"Good choice on the bottoms. I wouldn't want to wear pants to bed, either." She grins as I shuffle to the side of the bed closest to the door, pull back the comforter, and slide in.

I shoot her a stiff smile, nausea bubbling up in my throat.

"Are you okay, Jackson? You look a little…" Her head tilts as she studies me, sitting up to get a better look at my face. "Sick."

She's definitely only wearing a lacy bra.

"I'm fine."

I can't tell her I've never been this nervous—she'll think I'm a sissy, not the strong guy she's attracted to.

"Hmm. I don't think you are, but I'm not going to pry." She plops back down, head hitting the pillow, hair fanning out against the navy pillowcase. She looks like a fucking angel.

Beautiful. Serene.

Pure.

"I can leave if you want me to." Her voice is soft and sincere.

"I don't want you to." My voice catches, but I manage to say the words. If she touches me right now, I'll probably fall off the fucking bed and embarrass myself more than I already have this evening.

My back flattens and I relax. Sort of.

For her part, Charlie is silent, rolling to her side and looking over at me as I try to get comfortable. She tucks a hand under her chin—the same way she did earlier when we were just talking—and studies me some more.

Smiles.

Then, "What's it like being out on that field with so many people watching?"

"It's…" I don't know how to describe it to her.

It's not like this is the first time someone has asked, but it's the first time I try to dig deep for an actual answer. Usually I go with a generic reply—indescribable, nuts, loud—but because Charlie is genuinely curious, I put actual thought into my answer.

"It is nerve-rackin', but also one of the best adrenaline rushes you can have. The pressure of havin' every eye on you durin' an entire game is somethin' you can't…you just can't duplicate it. If you make a mistake, everyone knows it was you and they boo you, but if you make an excitin' play, everyone cheers. For you. So, it can be a kind of horrifyin' experience? Or it can be one of the greatest feelins ever." I lower my voice as I think out loud. "Hearin' the crowd all cheer at once brings chills all over your body."

Charlie lets my last line linger, giving it a little time before saying, "Wow. I can't even imagine what that would feel like."

It's something not many people will ever experience. I'm one of the lucky few who gets to know what it's like—the minority of people who get to play in a damn stadium. Surreal.

Never gets old. You never get over it, and I hope I never do.

Charlie's blue eyes are bright and full of wonder as she regards me across the mattress. "Has there ever been a time you haven't wanted to walk out there?"

I try not to stare at her cleavage, but it's almost impossible; she has a great rack—full and pushed up to her throat because of the way she's lying on her side. "Uh." I yank my eyes off her boobs. "No. But there have been a few times I've been sick and probably should have stayed in bed."

"What happened then? What do you do when you're sick?"

"Nothin'. You play through it." That's what you do when it's your job and you have scholarships and agents and people depending on you to perform.

That's just what you do. You walk out onto the field whether you want to or not. Whether you're sick as a dog or not.

You just do it.

Suck it up, JJ, Pops would shout from the sidelines. *If you're going to puke, do it in the end zone.* I was never allowed to be home sick in bed.

"I don't think I could do it. I'm too big of a wimp. Like, I get my period and the cramps alone turn me into the biggest baby. No way could I walk out onto a field if I didn't feel good."

"You would. Trust me—you would."

"Mmm, I'm not so sure. You're built of sterner stuff than I am."

"Maybe," I agree, knowing she's right. I might have been raised—trained—to play, but I also believe people are born with the qualities that make them stick with it. People are born fighters, winners, follow-throughers.

You can't teach it or learn it; you have it or you don't.

"How many cold baths do you take in a week?" she asks.

Cold bath? "Um, none?"

"You know, that pool thing filled with ice?"

Oh, she means the ice bath. "A few times a week, dependin'. It helps recovery after a game or hard workout, for inflammation and shit."

"Is it actually filled with ice?"

"No. I mean, some of them are, but ours are more state-of-the-art. It's a fancy tub with really fucking cold water. Then you get out and get into the hot tub, then back into the ice bath." It's a form of torture.

"That sounds awful."

It really is. "Anything else you want to know?"

"Are you sorry you chose Iowa? Will it hurt your chances once you graduate?"

Maybe. But I doubt it. "Not accordin' to my agent. I'm at the top of my game."

"*Top of your game*—what does that mean?"

"It means..." How do I say this without sounding like an

arrogant prick? "It means I'm one of the best players in my position."

"At Iowa?"

"No. In the country."

Charlie's eyes get wide. "*Really*?"

Seriously. How does she not know this—hasn't she googled me yet? "Yes, really. Do you not follow along? Are you not my biggest fan?"

She laughs, and her boobs seem to get even bigger. "I don't follow along, sorry. The game you invited me to was the only one I've been to in forever."

"It's America's pastime—how do you not have a team?"

"America's pastime is baseball."

Is she for real? "No, it's football."

"Hmm." She purses her lips. "Agree to disagree."

"Do you even watch baseball?"

I can see her blushing from here. "No."

Her disgruntled reply makes me laugh, and without thinking, I reach for her, extending my arm and resting my large palm on her bare shoulder.

We both freeze.

It's my knee-jerk reaction to apologize, but Charlie isn't giving me a look of disgust. Nope. She's biting her lip and smiling, white teeth illuminating her face.

God she's so pretty.

Palm splayed, my fingers fan out. Stroke her soft skin, thumb moving over her clavicle. I knew girls were softer and more delicate, but I've never actually touched one like this.

Charlie's face changes the longer my hand stays on her body; I watch it go from surprised to fascinated to…turned on? Her pupils are dilating and her chest is starting to heave, which is weird. Is that right? My hand on her shoulder is actually getting her aroused?

Shit. This is too easy. Maybe I don't have to have much experience—maybe it has to do with the person you're with.

Maybe if you're really into someone, you don't have to be smooth or suave—maybe just being myself is enough.

I test the theory.

Move my hand south.

Charlie's nostrils flare as her eyelids droop.

Huh.

"Tired?" I move my hand back up to her shoulder. Let it trail down her upper arm.

"Um…not really."

Man her skin feels amazing. Mine is sunburned and chafed and rough in comparison. I could touch her all night, and I'm confident now that she'd let me.

She continues watching me, still rolled to her side. Boobs still deliciously squished together and on display, her stark white bra a lacy little number that leaves little to my imagination—I can see her dark nipples through the fabric. Try not to notice them pucker when I let the pads of my fingertips linger on her bicep.

We lie like this for who knows how long, my hand resting in the same spot, fingers exploring but not to their full potential. I don't have the balls to put my hands anywhere else; what if she slugs me? What if she likes it and I don't know how to handle it?

What if, what if, what if.

Fuck!

"Jackson. Stop overthinking everything." She's whispering, and it's sexy as fuck despite the words being cajoling. "You're not going to screw it up."

How does she know what's on my mind? Is it that obvious?

"You're so cute," she adds.

"I'm *cute*?" No I'm not. Puppies are cute. Kittens are cute. Babies are cute. I'm *Goliath*. A huge bastard who fights battles on the grass—a guy who happens to have raw talent and not much else going for him.

"Say, 'Thank you, Charlie.'"

I roll my eyes.

"Say, 'I'm cute.'"

I shake my head. "Nope."

Charlie narrows her beautiful blue eyes. "Say it and I'll move closer to you."

That has my attention. "How close we talkin'?"

She wiggles her eyebrows, lending a smarmy air to her comment. "*Real* close."

"I'm cute." I punctuate the sentence with another eye roll, but a smile has bloomed on my mouth. The little shit could probably get me to do anything, include eating a pile of shit.

"You are cute," she agrees, inching forward. "Real, real cute." Charlie has to push back the covers so she can get her body closer—so she doesn't get wrapped in them—and when she does, I get a full body shot. An up-close-and-personal introduction to her tits. Stomach. Hips. Skimpy underwear.

Oh my fucking god.

My dick? He's noticed, too, and he fucking loves it.

Charlie scoots across the mattress, across my navy sheets. Sliding inch by inch with her beautiful, perfect body that's not perfect at all, until her tits are against my chest. The only parts of us that are joined.

Our faces are inches apart.

"So *now* what are you going to do?" She's challenging me.

When my palm finally finds her hip beneath the covers, Charlie moans deep in her throat—as if her body's been waiting for it to happen and sighs, too. Moans again when my palm glides down to her ass cheek and slowly caresses her there. Pulls her in closer so our pelvises meet, my cock wanting to burrow in the space between her thighs.

"You feel so good," she whispers, leaning in to kiss my mouth, bringing an arm up and running her fingers through my hair. Nails gently scraping my scalp.

She's adorable and fucking sexy and I love when she teases me.

"I like you so much, Jackson." Her fingers graze my cheek. "You don't even realize…" By the look on her face, I'd say she means every word. The hand cupping my face is as tender as the soft set of her eyes.

We lean in at the same time, mouths connecting. Lips pressed together, they open simultaneously. Tongues unhurriedly dragging and languid, like a drug. Intoxicating and delicious, like toothpaste and arousal.

I remember her mouth on my dick, which is already stiff, and the thought makes the blood pumping through my body completely harden it.

Charlie's soft groan spurs me on, and my hand roams from her hip to her ribcage. Up and over, my thumb catches a glorious amount of side boob, and her tongue goes deeper into my mouth. It's wet and hot. Wanton.

I hesitate briefly; I've never felt a girl up, and I've certainly never removed anyone's bra.

Sliding my hand over her breast, cupping it in my palm, I swear to fucking God, my balls tighten painfully. And when Charlie disconnects from my kiss to tip her head back, I seize the opportunity to latch onto her throat. Kiss the column of her neck, inhaling her perfume and lingering on her pulse point.

Kiss my way down. Collarbone. Valley between her breasts.

Hook the strap of her bra with my thumb and drag it down her shoulder.

Charlie's breast is hot. Everything I pictured the times I pictured her naked. Round, with dark, rosy nipples. Pert and puckered, it wants my mouth on it.

I inch down on the mattress, pulling the lacy material aside.

Know I'm making all the right moves because Charlie inhales a breath and jams her fingers into my hair as my lips latch onto her nipple. Lick it and blow, watching the skin tighten with fascination. Run my thumb over the hardened nub, around and around, before flattening my tongue and dragging it over the perky tip.

Another inhaled breath. A sigh. My name.

"Oh *Jackson.*"

Oh Jackson—goddamn right, that's my name.

Charlie rolls so she's flat on her back, arching her spine, giving me full access to her flesh, fingers still buried in my hair. Twirling the longer strands around the index, languishing under my touch.

I explore, raising my head and letting my hand drift. Trailing it down her bare torso, palm gliding toward her panties. They match her bra—white lace, a bit see-through. I glimpse the dark hair between her legs.

Slowly hitch the waistband and raise it to peek at what lies underneath.

Charlie grips the bedspread, breath catching with every

movement I make inside her drawers.

She has hair down there.

It's dim inside the bedroom, but I can still see it. Neatly trimmed but still—hair.

"Is that okay?" she timidly asks.

"It's not my body," I gruffly reply, not caring that she isn't bare.

"I know, but still. Does it bother y-you?"

"Why would it bother me?"

I catch her shrug. "You know—if you put your mouth down there?"

Oh, I'm definitely putting my mouth down there…

She pushes the point. "If you want me to shave it, I will."

"Darlin', I don't think I mind a little grass on the playin' field."

She giggles, a nervous laugh made prominent by the mood.

"And I don't need ya to shave it." I slide my palm over the soft patch of fuzz between her legs. "It's sexy."

It's the first pussy I've had my hand on, and I'm insatiably curious, index finger running up and down the hot, slick slit heating up her thighs. My thumb begins a steady rotation at that spot right at the top—exactly the same spot I see actors in porn rub. My hands are so huge, that thumb covers a lot of ground, digging a bit deeper as it parts her the smallest bit.

The friction has Charlie moaning.

Her thighs squirm.

Spreading her legs, I wedge myself between her thighs, elbows nudging her wider. Resting on my arms, I take two thumbs and gently spread her pussy. Stare, fascinated, at the parts of Charlie that make her a woman: clit, vulva. The spot above her asshole that I'm tempted to touch.

Using my right thumb, I run it over her labia.

"Jesus, Jackson, would you stop staring at it!"

"I can't help it—I've never seen one up close."

She throws an arm over her eyes and groans miserably. "It's so embarrassing."

"Why? Your clit is fuckin' sexy."

"Oh my god, shut up. Clits are not sexy."

"Fuckin' yes they are."

If I looked up, I know I'd catch her rolling those pretty blue eyes. "You're only saying that because you've never had sex with one," she grumbles.

"Why do you have to rub it in?"

"Because, if you don't stop staring at it, I'm going to make you rub one *out* instead."

Rub one out. *Jerk off.* Masturbate.

My girl is clever.

Say your prayers, Charlie Edmonds. I might be a virgin, but I'm about to make up for lost time, starting with worshiping at the altar of your delicious pussy.

"You better give your heart to Jesus, 'cause your ass is about to be mine."

She raises her head and looks down at me. "Huh?"

I lower my mouth and make contact, flattening my tongue and dragging it straight down the center. Give my head a shake, like I've seen them do in pornos. I dig in deeper. *Everything I learned I learned from porn…*

"Oh. My. God."

Just like everything I do, I put every last bit of effort into going down on Charlie, relying on her sounds for feedback, knowing I'm doing a damn good job when she loudly gasps and pulls at my shoulders.

Spreads her legs wider, bending at the knees.

I grab an ankle and prop it on my shoulder.

"Oh J-Jesus."

That's right, darlin'. Pray to Jesus.

Charlie's hips rise off the mattress and I seize the opportunity, sliding my hands under her ass. Bury my face and go to town. My mission: make her moan and beg for it.

It doesn't even take two minutes; the sounds coming from Charlie's throat—from her mouth—are loud, almost tortured. I shush her, not wanting to lift my head and ruin the moment, but fuck, she's noisy.

I don't have time to worry about it or be embarrassed, because when I start sucking on her clit, Charlie makes the tell-tale sound of a girl who's about to orgasm. Thrashes her head on the pillow and grasps for my head, giving my hair a tug. Pushes at me, trying to inch away.

I know better—I've seen the movie.

I know how this ends, have envisioned it so many times in my mind the past few weeks since I met her—how'd she'd look when I made her come. Yeah, I've thought about it. I'm a virgin, not dead below the waist.

"Jackson, oh my god Jackson."

My tongue swirls. Dips. Licks.

"Oh shit." She groans, guttural—a sound I wouldn't imagine a girl making. "Fuck."

I love the dirty talk—it's erotic and unexpected. I've never heard Charlie talk dirty, and the fact that she's doing it during sex—or, oral—is hot as hell.

It has me hard as a fucking rock, grinding my dick against the mattress at the same time I'm eating her out. Dry humping the bedding like a teenage horn dog, about to come myself and inevitably squirt jizz on my own damn comforter.

Fuck.

There's no stopping the train once it's in motion, and we both moan—me into her pussy, Charlie into the dim bedroom. Me, grinding my hips.

I might be inexperienced, but I know she's about to come by the swivel of her pelvis on the bed—she's damn near grinding her crotch into my face, fucking it. First, little pulses. Then, louder moaning. Then, she's shoving at my shoulders, pushing me away but not really wanting me to pull away; she simply doesn't know what to fucking do with herself as her body begins shaking with shocks of pleasure.

Now I can feel it on my tongue, the jolts. Her body humming. Convulsing, for lack of a better term.

I can feel the whole thing happening on the surface of my tongue. My lips. I grin into her pussy, knowing I'm going to smell like sex for days—the smell from her imprinted on my skin. Under my nose. My fingers.

Mmm.

I like the idea that I'm going to smell her after tonight, when I'm sitting in class or pulling on my helmet on the football field.

Charlotte Edmonds' cum.

Fucking. Delicious.

Who knew?

I could get used to this, dining on her pussy. The insatiable part of me that has to do better and be better fuels me on; I want to be the best fucking oral she's ever had, or will have.

Remember this moment—it might never happen again…

I shrug off the thought. Nope. It won't be the last time, Jackson—you're hooked on her and you damn well know it. Stop denying it.

She says my name over and over like a mantra, a psalm spoken to God, repeated and memorized; words to live by.

"*Jackson*, oh *Jackson*…yes…God *Jackson*, oh Jesus…"

It's a rush.

The best rush.

Nothing will ever replace the sound of it, not the noise in the stadium during a game or fans shouting my name in unison when I make a play. Not the sound of the press calling to me for an interview. Not students saying my name as I walk past them on campus, heading to class. Not the little kids who want my autograph if they see me at the grocery store.

This.

This beats all of it.

My name. Her lips.

WEDNESDAY 3.0

CHARLIE

So tired…

I crack an eyelid, blinking against the pitch-black bedroom, hearing only the sound of our breathing and the fan gently whirring above us.

I can't see anything, not even the ceiling.

We've been lying here for hours—after Jackson went down on me, he rolled off the bed and went to the bathroom to get ready for bed. Brushed his teeth, washed up, came back, and climbed across the mattress. Awkward, he wasn't quite sure what to do with me afterward. Reached for me then pulled back, unsure.

I made it easy on him. Wanting to cuddle, I rolled into his giant, warm body and little-spooned him—little-spooned the shit out of him, actually, until he relaxed and his arms went around me. One hand resting on my hip, the other under his head, he rested his chin on the crook of my shoulder and inhaled my shampoo, smelling me.

Mmm.

This beats all of it.

The mediocre dates that fizzled, resulting in and meaning nothing. The sex I had with my ex-boyfriend.

I must have rolled away from him in my sleep, and the space

between us is cold, so I scoot back, inching toward him in the dark. Press my back against him where it belongs, my ass firmly planted against his front—his resting dick no longer at full mast and stiffly begging for attention.

I cuddle deeper, loving the warmth from his big body. He's kicking off heat like an inferno—*a hotbox*, my mother would call him. His gentle snore reminds me of a slumbering bear.

A gentle, slumbering bear.

Jackson is more sensitive than I would have given him credit for; his passion for football runs deeper than his passion for anything else, and that's what makes him fantastic.

But there's more to him than that, and I believe he's just starting to realize it. He is discovering things about himself he didn't know before. Like there is life after football if you open yourself up to it.

There is life off the field. People can love you for more than what you can give them; they can love you for you.

Love.

It's too soon for that, but the stirrings are there—I can feel them every time I'm with him. They grow every single day, every time he says something sweet in that Southern accent of his. Charming. Aloof.

Jackson is shy.

It took me some time to realize it because I was judging him solely by his size and appearance—huge, towering giants of men don't normally give off a timid vibe, but now that I'm learning more about him…

I see it. I see him.

A sweet boy who wants more than the ball he throws around.

Jackson Jennings doesn't give a shit about money or fame; all he wants is his father to be proud of him. Wants his mother to show him affection. He's craving it.

Well I have some news for you, Jackson Jennings: I'm proud of you. And I want to show you affection.

I just wish he would tell me how he felt so I knew…

His arms tighten around me, slowly snaking down to my midriff and hugging me gently. The low snore in my ear is oddly satisfying.

We're both content.

I sigh.

Lie there quietly thinking, trying to settle my brain so I can rest, not even sure what woke me in the first place.

Stifling a yawn, I close my eyes—it's too dark to see, anyway—choosing a spot in my mind so my thoughts can wander back to sleep. Classes. Fall. It's going to rain tomorrow. Sweaters. The holiday. Jackson, Jackson, Jackson.

Ugh. Go back to sleep, Charlie! Turn off your brain!

It takes me a good while. Listening to Jackson's breathing pattern helps; it's constant, the rhythm soothing. I feel safe and secure wrapped in his arms, and he shifts, his large form behind me, nose still buried in my neck.

I lie still as he readjusts, hands unclasping from my midsection, one of them working up my hip, my arm, until his fingers are brushing the long strands of hair away from the column of my neck where his face just was.

He kisses below my ear.

Lies in the dark, coming awake, stroking my hair, fingers raking through it tenderly. Quietly, not making a sound.

My body relaxes, drifting. Weightless.

Then.

Jackson speaks.

It's a low whisper—just my name.

"Charlotte."

I remain still; for some reason, I remain completely unmoving. Unflinching.

Curiously, I wait.

"Are you awake?"

I pretend to be sleeping, control my breathing.

His fingers lightly play with the hair by my ear, coiling it around his index finger, trailing it down the skin of my cheek.

His chest makes a sound, and though we're pressed together, he moves closer still, lips on my shoulder. Hand on my upper arm, he presses another kiss on my skin.

I hear his breath pause. His mouth opens. "What are you doing to me?" he asks out loud, softly.

What am I doing to him? *What does he mean?*

"I thought I had everything figured out. What am I supposed to do now?"

What on earth is he talking about?

"I've never met anyone who made me want to change."

Oh.

Oh!

I try to keep my breaths even to hide the fact that my heart begins beating in overtime. It's racing inside my chest as I wait for him to keep talking, silently begging for more words.

He's opening up because he thinks I'm asleep and can't hear him. Should I say something? Is it wrong that I'm lying here pretending?

"You're so pretty," he coos near my ear. Kisses my hair. "God you're gorgeous. I could stare at you all day, do you know that?" He chuckles deep in his chest. "Of course you don't know that, you're sleeping."

Oh my god, could he be any more adorable? Guh!

"I don't know how to give you what you want, but I want to try," he continues. "Don't hate me when I fuck it up, please. You're the only one who gives a shit about me right now."

My heart.

My heart…

It clenches. Breaks for him. *That's not true!* I want to shout, not knowing if it's actually true or not. It's his truth, and that's really all that matters.

A tear escapes the corner of my eye when he lays a soft kiss to my temple.

"I wanna do right by you, Charlotte Edmonds."

Do right by you.

So Southern I want to swoon—and I would, if he knew I was awake and I could gush over his words.

I continue playing dead.

"What do you want from me? Tell me and I'll give it to you."

Don't talk like that, I want to say. *You don't have to give me anything—just your…just you.*

"I'm not fallin' in love with you." Jackson pauses. "That *can't* be what this is."

I think he's done—because what more is there to say? He practically admitted he's falling in love with me—but he keeps talking to the bedroom, spilling his guts to the dark.

The walls have ears…

"You like me, don't you? Me for me, not because I play ball? You'd stick with me if I decided not to play in the pros; I know you would." He's wishful-thinking out loud, but he's one hundred percent right. I would stand by him, no matter what. If we were in a relationship, it wouldn't matter to me what Jackson decided to do.

Besides…

Being a professional football player is dangerous. Why would I want to send him off week after week with the possibility that he'd get injured? I'd be a nervous wreck watching him on the field every week—waiting for the career-ending hit to take him down. Could my nerves handle that?

Doubtful.

"I don't love you." Pause. "Do I? Shit." Then, "Do you love me?"

My breath—it escapes me completely, and my body goes completely still.

"Do you love me? Of course you don't."

Jackson laughs, this time louder than before. If he thinks I'm sleeping, it's certainly loud enough to wake me up. Does he care? Does he know what he's saying? What he's asking me?

"Love." He tests the word, his voice deep and baritone and smooth. "Love."

Luuv.

I can hear him thinking as the seconds tick by. He sighs into my hair. "I'm an idiot. What the fuck am I even talkin 'bout?"

Tawkin bout.

This boy…

He's breaking my heart, but not in a bad way; rather, it's bursting. I'm feeling everything all at once, another tear sliding across my cheek. Down my face and wetting the column of my neck where he just laid his mouth.

Jackson stiffens as the salty tear meets his lips.

I hear his inhalation—feel it against my back when his body

stiffens. "Charlotte?"

Oh god.

"Jackson?"

His pause is painfully long. "Are you awake?"

I pause, too. "Yes."

I swear I can hear the second hand on a clock somewhere in this house, loudly counting the seconds away. Tick. Tock.

Tick.

Tock.

"Charlotte?"

"Yes?"

I can feel his heart pounding in his chest, the beats pressing into my back.

"Nothing."

He isn't going to say it, and he isn't going to ask if I heard his private confession. But I heard him, and I loved it, and I don't want him to pretend he didn't just say the words no guy has said to me before, because it was beautiful.

"Jackson?"

"*What.*" He sounds miserable. Pouty, almost.

"I heard you."

"Heard me *what*?"

I roll my eyes in the dark; silly boy, playing dumb. "I heard you tell me…" I inhale. "I heard what you said."

"Oh." Nothing more, nothing less.

It's fine; I understand. I understand he has no idea how to express himself. Hasn't had to.

Extricating myself from his hold, I shift to my back. Then roll to my side so I'm facing him in the dark. I can't see his face, but I don't have to. I know what I'd see there if the lights were on: devastation that he confessed what's in his heart because he's not confident I feel the same way.

"Jackson," I whisper in the dark. "Jackson." I say it again, my voice…full of pain and longing. I'm choked up, not having spoken in so many hours, the words stuck in my throat. "I love you."

My fingertips feel for his face, and I smooth them down his cheeks. He grabs them with his hands, kissing the tips before they can continue their course down.

"I *love* you," I whisper again.

I've never said it to anyone but my parents and my friends, but I find that I mean it, and he so needs to hear the words.

"Say it one more time." He's whispering back.

One more tyme.

That I can do. I shiver.

"I love you." I cup his face with my palm, his hand still wrapped around my wrist. He kisses the heel of my hand as it moves past his mouth. "You're beautiful," I tell him. "And smart." My hand sneaks to the back of his head, and I bury my fingers in his hair. "And sexy."

"I am sexy," he admits for the first time, a bit bashfully. "Broken nose and all."

"Especially your broken nose." I lean in, feel for it in the dark, and plant a kiss there. Then another. Then I plant one in the corner of his gorgeous, pouty mouth—my favorite spot. I can't see it, but I can visualize it: full bottom lip, a bit petulant. Cupid's bow on his upper, both the ends tipped up into a natural smirk, kind of like the joker. Or the Grinch.

It's a sassy mouth, ready for sarcasm and banter, not always pleasant, I'm sure. Jackson has never directed any curse words in my direction, but I can't imagine he's always this sweet and pleasant. Or nice.

In fact, I have a feeling he's a real asshole with most people.

A giant douchebag because his guard is always up.

Everything about him turns me on. Everything.

I kiss his mouth, and he accepts it, meeting my tongue.

Suddenly, it's different. *Better.* We care about each other—and that makes all the difference. His touch makes me tingle in a way it didn't just hours ago.

He loves me.

It's intoxicating knowledge to have. Makes me bask, knowing I can touch him freely, knowing nothing is off limits now that we've established how we feel.

Nothing is off limits.

Including S-E-X?

Guess we'll find out…

I kiss his majestic nose again. Again. Loving every second of it, cherishing this moment, hoping to remember it forever, no matter what ends up happening with us. We may not have a happily ever after—only time will tell—but we're happy now, and I want to touch his soul—and his body.

He smells delicious. His incredible body is pressed against my front, breasts smashed against his broad chest. There's hair there; Jackson isn't the kind of guy who grooms or manscapes—he is who he is and doesn't make a fuss about it. He's masculine and wonderfully male, which is the same thing, I get it, but whatever. He's sexy and I love it.

The hair on his chest tickles my boobs, but in the best way, and I wiggle a bit so I'm rubbing over him. Lean in and find the pulse in his neck, sucking the skin below his ear.

He shivers. Grips my hips and tugs.

Runs his hand over my hip, down to my ass, pressing into my skin along the way. Grips my butt in his big palm. Squeezes. Moans.

Mmm.

Our mouths somehow discover their way together in the dark, locking. Opening, two simultaneous moans filling the space between us, creating tension that wasn't there before.

Sweet, sweet sexual tension.

The longer we make out, the harder Jackson's dick becomes; it's long and hot against my thigh, but he makes no move to grind on me or grab my hand and draw it down south.

The longer we make out, the wetter I become *downstairs*. I'm hot and impatient, wanting more than this innocent kissing. Okay, not so innocent since we're mostly unclothed, in bed together, in a dark room and not officially in a relationship.

But we've known each other for weeks, possibly our whole lives, my brain argues. *You're ready for whatever Jackson wants.*

I know he's not going anywhere—I wouldn't be here with him now if he wasn't interested. He's gone twenty-two years without so much as having sex with someone, and he isn't taking this 'thing' with me lightly.

So I push.

Do a little gyrating to see how he responds. Where will he move his hands if I do the seducing?

I'm still wearing my bra—he hasn't officially touched my bare breasts, or seen me completely naked. I've seen his dick in the near dark but haven't had it near my center.

You couldn't fit a dime between us, so inching closer is

impossible, but I take a palm and press it against his pec, pushing a bit so he knows I want him on his back.

Reach for the bedside table and feel around for the small lamp I know is there, fumble for the switch. Its low glow gives off just enough light for me to see his expression, and I want him to see me. I want him to watch when I climb on top of him and remove my bra.

Watch his face change when my arms reach behind my back and release the tiny clasp. Work the straps down my shoulders, letting them sag over my upper arms before shimmying them all the way down.

I'm sitting on top of him as if I'm in a saddle, tossing my bra to the floor; it lands somewhere nearby. Jackson isn't wearing a shirt, so when I move my body forward and let my boobs smash his chest, he inhales. A sharp intake of breath that spurs me on.

I line up our privates; only our underwear separates us, and let's be honest, mine is merely a scrap of material that conceals nothing. I feel everything—the head of his dick, the shaft, his balls.

The tip rubs my clit in the most pleasurable way, and I bite down on my bottom lip, loving it.

My breathing quickens.

"Dry fucking should become a sport." Jackson sighs, out of breath.

"*Only* dry fucking?" The words slip from my tongue and say what I don't have the nerve to vocalize: *Let's have sex.*

Our gazes meet, and I continue bearing down on his dick, round and round, my eyes closing as I tip my head back, face toward the ceiling.

They're still closed when Jackson's giant palms cup my breasts, thumbs stroking my nipples.

"Your tits are…"

Amazing—yes, I know.

"Can I…" Jackson hesitates. "Can I…"

Can you what? Finish your sentence before I die from the pleasure of having your hands caressing my boobs.

He doesn't finish his sentence, but he does say, "Lean forward and grab the headboard."

Um. *Yes, sir.*

I lean forward, grasping for the headboard, and Jackson meets my body, mouth latching onto one of my nipples.

Ahh, I see. 'Can I suck your tits?' is what he wanted to ask but didn't have the guts to say.

"Oh Jackson," comes my soft murmur. It feels…it feels…

My toes curl. I throb; my vagina actually has a heartbeat I can feel, blood rushing straight to my crotch as I rotate his tip along my slit.

Wet. Hot. Dry fucking.

With his mouth still sucking on my nipple, Jackson's other hand reaches between us. Hooks my underwear with whatever finger he's using, draws back the fabric.

"I want you so bad," I moan—or more like croak.

"I want you too."

Yes, please. Yes. *Fuck me.*

Everything with Jackson is thought out; he is the least impulsive guy I've ever met, if you don't count the time he stole my damn chicken sandwich in the cafeteria, although I suspect he planned that out, too. Waited until it was done, watched it cook before snatching it.

But sex? He isn't just going to have sex with me unless he's already given it thought and has come to a conclusion about it.

"What if I fuck it up?" He's referring to sex.

"You won't, baby." I take a hand down off the headboard and rake my fingers through his thick hair. "You won't."

"But what if I do?"

"How could you possibly?"

"What if I come after two minutes?"

Er, I'm not liking the sound of that, but I'm also not about to tell him that. He'd be crushed.

"Then we do it again when you're ready." I bend forward, hair hitting the pillow behind him. "We'll wait."

"I don't want to."

"Okay. Then we won't." A bubble of laughter. "You tell me what you want, Jackson, and we'll do it. I don't want you to feel pressured." I kiss his temple. His cheekbone. The corner of his mouth. "I love you."

This boy—he slides a hand up my chest, over my collarbone and behind my neck. Pulls me to him and kisses me soundly on the lips.

It's like a drug, a potent one that's making me weak everywhere. This kiss is everything—it's giving me life and I suspect it's giving him life, too.

Slow and meaningful. Emotional. Beautiful.

Jackson tries to move his body into a sitting position, dumping me to the mattress on my back. Shucks off his underwear, pushing it down his ridiculous thighs until they disappear somewhere beneath the covers, never to resurface.

He begins to peel mine down, sliding them slowly over my hips, thighs, and calves.

We both hold our breath; this is a big fucking deal, and the significance is not lost on me.

When we're both naked, Jackson Jennings, first-string wide receiver on the Iowa football team and future second-round draft pick in the pros, lays his giant body next to me and props himself on his elbow to study me.

Naked, naked, naked.

Before we go any further, "Do you have a..." The word gets stuck in my throat, but I have to ask. "I'm on the pill, but...I mean, it's up to you. I know you don't have any STDs because you haven't had sex yet—can you get one from gym equipment?" I laugh at my own stupid joke. "Should we, you know—put one on?"

Shut up, Charlie, you're babbling and sound like an idiot.

"Plus, I really like you and love you, but we don't need Jackson Jennings Junior Junior Junior running around. Wait—how many juniors would that be? Three? Is that how that works?" Oh my god, I'm so nervous. "My point is, do you have a condom?"

First, Jackson stares. Then, he grins, his white teeth blinding in the dark. He's so gorgeous when he smiles, and my stomach flips all over again.

Then Jackson frowns. "I didn't grab one—they're in the bathroom. I...I didn't think we'd be screwin'."

Nervously, I bite down on my lower lip. "Um. I did? I'm sorry, I just didn't know? And I knew you wouldn't because you're a gentleman—"

I can't even finish my sentence, because Jackson is rolling me on top of him, slapping me firmly on the ass and laughing. Loudly.

Loud enough to wake whomever is sleeping in the next room over.

"Gentleman? Darlin', no one's accused me of bein' a gentleman in my entire life."

Darlin'.

Ma entyer lie-ff.

He makes my heart race, this guy, with his playful banter and sweet talk—and that slap to my ass was icing on a scrumptious Jackson Jennings cake.

I set the condom on the bedside table when the light was turned off earlier, instincts telling me to be prepared, and I'm glad because the last thing I need is a baby. Sure, I'm on the pill, but those fail, and I don't need any surprise pregnancies. I don't need to be that statistically low number—you know, the one your gynecologist warns you about when they're writing your prescription. One percent chance of still getting pregnant and blah blah blah.

This isn't a romance novel, *this is my life* and his, and a baby at twenty-one wouldn't be cute. God, he would think I was trying to trap him, and that would kill me.

The talk hasn't ruined the mood; talking about sex and screwing hasn't made his dick limp, thank God. In fact, Jackson looks more aroused than he did before, pupils dilated—and not from the dim light.

He palms my breast again. "I love your body, babe."

Babe. He *babed* me and I didn't hate it.

I always thought I would—literally roll my eyes when I hear my friends' boyfriends say it. Babe. Babe. Babe.

Barf.

Except...I don't hate it, not even a little.

He tears the condom open and I watch, nervously tucking a strand of hair behind my ear. Lick my lips in anticipation, though I'm kind of scared shitless.

We're about to have sex and he's never done it…

"Have you ever put one of these on before?"

"No. I'm a fuckin' virgin, remember?"

"Yeah, but don't some guys practice?"

Jackson laughs. "Some guys probably do when they're younger, but I never did."

In the dim light of his bedroom, I watch Jackson Jennings—a big, beautiful beast of a boy—set the condom on the tip of his penis and slowly roll it down. He sucks on his bottom lip in concentration as he does it, nostrils flaring.

I love that. So sexy.

When the rubber is entirely covering his, um, dick—our eyes meet. Somewhat bashful. Shy. Then I do the only thing I know to do; I lie flat on the bed, on my back, and motion him over so he'll crawl on top of me.

Spread my legs when he gingerly covers my body with his. I drag his head down with the palm of my hand and kiss him soundly on the mouth. The kiss is deep, wet, tongues twirling in a sloppy tangle.

Jackson is hard, hanging stiffly between our bodies. His erection brushes my pussy but doesn't push.

I spread my legs wider, ready.

Ever vigilant, his thumb finds the top of my clit and moves in slow circles while our tongues dance, the motion getting me soaked. Has me tossing my head back and presenting him with the column of my throat that loves lips on it.

He obliges at the same time he drags his cock back and forth over my best bits.

Reaching between us, I grip him with my entire hand, pumping leisurely to keep him aroused—as if I need to. Which I don't, because he's so turned on he can barely breathe normally. Labored. Rasping.

Harsh.

Yes, his breathing is harsh, like he can't catch his breath and isn't trying to. Sexy, sexy, sexy.

As a big boy himself, Jackson's dick is obviously *huge*—not so big it's intimidating, but bigger than the only guy I've ever had sex with. Naturally I expect it to hurt when he eases in, despite the fact that I'm lubed up from foreplay.

I slide his erection up and down, up and down while he watches me, tension gripping his entire body. Shoulders taut. Back rigid. Ass flexed. Thighs tight.

He's frozen above me.

"You sure you want to do this?" I ask as gently as I possibly can, not wanting to spook him, not wanting him to change his mind and not…well, fuck me.

I want him to fuck me, so hard.

"Yeah, I'm sure." Perspiration forms on his brow; I can see it glistening.

"You're not going to hurt me."

He looks skeptical. "But you're so tiny."

I stifle a laugh.

"I'm not, though." I carry a few extra pounds, which I've never cared about, and I'm certainly no delicate flower, not as fragile as he seems to think I am. No other guy has made me feel small and delicate before, and I relish how petite I feel lying under Jackson.

He blows out a puff of air, his bangs blowing back. Braces himself above me, finally lowering his hips. Pelvis.

Pushes a bit.

I line him up, making sure he's heading for the right hole.

Guiding to avoid a catastrophe and embarrassment for both of us.

The head is thick and throbbing.

I tip my pelvis up, wordlessly helping him out. Giving him the access he needs to confidently push forward and penetrate me.

Penetrate me.

I giggle nervously; what a stupid word to have in your head when you're about to be *penetrated.*

I laugh again.

Oh my god, shoot me now.

"You little brat." Jackson kisses me full on the mouth, pushing forward, easing in.

Another few centimeters. More.

More.

He pushes in another inch before stopping. "Holy fuck you're tight."

"Am I?"

I swear his brows go up. "*Aren't* you?"

I am. It's been so long since I've had sex, I swear my vagina went and closed back up from being out of commission.

"Does it feel good?"

"Yes."

I preen, happy that I'm able to make him feel good, happy his first time is with me and it's going to be memorable for both of us, because we're in love.

Jackson groans when he buries himself to the hilt, sucking in an audible breath and moaning, "Fuck. Oh my fucking god."

He grunts, letting his head drop, a bead of sweat hitting my bare chest. I run a hand through his hair at the same time I adjust my hips on the bed, making more room for him between my legs.

He takes up every inch of me, inside and out, a monolith of strength and power about to begin pumping in and out of my body.

I know it's coming—I remember how it goes—but Jackson is slow and doesn't thrust like I expect him to. Slowly—so slowly it almost kills me—he pulls out. Slides back in. Slowly slides back out. The speed—or lack thereof—with which he glides in and out is going to kill us *both*.

Instead of groaning like he did before, it's almost like he's holding his breath. Measures every motion, committing it to memory. Every action deliberate.

The sides of his hips flex. Ass, too, and I put my hands on his butt cheeks and squeeze. It's a glorious ass, rock hard and strong. A squatter's ass. *Ass, ass, ass…*

In.

Out.

Painfully. Slow.

I want to die.

Run my nails down his backside in an attempt to encourage more speed; he doesn't comply. He wants to take his time, second by second, studying the movement of his own body tucked intimately within mine.

It's excruciating.

Bliss.

"*Charlotte*," he whispers. "God, Charlotte." Crooning into my ear, kissing my temple as he rhythmically thrusts.

Jackson's first go at sex isn't sex at all—it's making love. At least, I think he's making love to me, and I want to pinch myself.

He goes on like this for a few minutes. The fact that he hasn't come yet has me baffled; I assumed that because he was a virgin, he wouldn't last longer than three minutes. I realize this isn't giving him any credit, but how much stamina can a guy actually have when he hasn't had his dick in anyone's vagina?

I wouldn't last this long if I were him.

I'm also not close to coming, so I give his chest a push, wanting and *needing* to be on top. When I was younger, I once read a magazine article about the statistics of the female orgasm, and seventy-five percent of women can only orgasm on top.

All right, I probably made that up, but the number is high, and I, for one, am among that percentage of girls who can't climax on the bottom. That I'm aware of.

Jackson stops. "Is everything okay?"

"Yes. But..." I hesitate. "Can I be on top?"

His beautiful blue eyes widen and he rolls, taking me along for the ride, our bodies still connected.

Whoa. I've only seen that done in the movies.

Sexy.

"Scoot up closer to the headboard," I tell him bossily.

"Yes ma'am."

I sit up, arching my back, leaning forward a bit, hands grabbing hold of the headboard. It's wooden, an inch or two from the wall, and easy to grip.

Finding my rhythm, I ease back and forth over his body, pelvis automatically grinding into his. Watching as he lies there, looking up at me with a look of wonder on his face, the nonverbals playing over his eyes and mouth in flashes.

Jackson's lips part when I rotate my hips in circles, hands pressed against the headboard. Bearing down. Operating solely on instinct, I try to pretend I know what I'm doing when in reality, I don't. He might be the virgin, but it's not like I have all that much more experience.

Plus, he's athletic and I'm not—as if that makes a difference? Shouldn't he just be naturally good at everything physical while the rest of us mere mortals have to work at it?

With me on top, he's buried to the hilt—thick and deep, and I moan because the sensation is…incredible.

"Charlotte. *Fuck,* Charlotte," he moans, because really, are any other words necessary? Is there anything else to say?

"You feel so good, baby," I murmur above him, lost in him. Lost in us. Lost in the fact that I love him. "Are you gonna come?"

"Yes." His nod is jerky. "I think so."

He thinks so, he thinks so. Oddly, I'm filled with a sense of satisfaction that no other girls have come before me.

I am his first and always will be.

A GAMEDAY

JACKSON

"J, your dad is downstairs in the kitchen."

My *what*? Did I hear that right?

There's another knock, followed by the door opening, and Tyson sticks his head through, peering down at Charlie and me as we lie on the bed. I'm beat; we just had a game against Penn State—which we lost—and the ice bath did nothing for my sore muscles. I ache, I'm tired, I'm hungry.

I have to learn to lock my door.

Raising myself to a sitting position, I run a hand down Charlie's slumbering thigh protectively.

"Your dad, in the kitchen?"

"My dad is here?" That's freaking weird. What's my old man doing here? He never said anything about coming to the game.

"I mean, yeah? Looks like you but way angrier?"

Yeah—that's Pops all right.

Shit.

I scoot to the edge of the bed and stand, pulling on my discarded Iowa t-shirt, grateful the bastard didn't come into my room unannounced. The last thing I fuckin' need is him walkin' in on me with a girl in my room. He would absolutely lose his shit.

Bending, I kiss Charlie on the temple and she rolls, half naked in my direction, cracking an eyelid. It's the third time this week she's spent the night, and I've lost count of the times we've fucked.

I kiss her again.

"Wait here, I'll be back."

Her smile is groggy, her little wave sleepy. Her hand flops up then back down on the mattress, and I give her one last glance before slipping through the door and closing it softly behind me.

Hit the stairs, making my way to the kitchen.

My father is standing by the sink, staring out the window, out at the street, hands on his hips. He looks more like a drill sergeant than someone's father, brisk and at attention. All business and no pleasure.

"Pops. What are you doing here?"

He makes no move to hug me.

"Came to see your game against Penn." He turns, pulls a chair out from the table, and sits, legs spread, thick arms folded across a chest that used to be as broad as mine. Years of not going to the gym and eating crap have worked against him, adding about thirty extra pounds and loads of pent-up resentment.

Pops always wanted to play ball; just never had what it took. If he did, he'd still be in shape instead of a burnout living vicariously through his son.

I lean against the counter.

"What'd you think?"

"I think you should have won." He plucks a grape from a bowl in the center of the table, the fruit Rodrigo's sister brought when she arrived this morning for a tailgating party with her friends.

Yes, we should have won, but we didn't.

I don't know what to say.

"You played for crap."

Actually, I didn't—I had one of my best games of the season, running the most yards. But I keep my mouth shut because it will only serve to piss him off if I defend myself. He's just sore I'm playing for Iowa, and not at Notre Dame or USC.

I wait patiently for him to bring those schools up, his standard lecture on the rare occasions he comes to visit.

"You don't seem upset," he criticizes.

"There's nothin' I can do 'bout it now." What's done is done—the game's been over for hours.

"Have you watched the tapes back yet?"

He knows we won't watch those until practice this week. "Not yet. But I will."

"Send them to me."

Not likely, but, "Sure. I'll see what I can do." The air is filled with silence, and I rack my brain for a way to change the subject. "Where's Ma?"

"Home."

Well no *duh.* Why didn't she come along? "Oh."

"She had to work."

Right. Because her job at the craft store is *so* goddamn important she couldn't make it to one of her son's football games. I try not to begrudge her, but it's fucking impossible; Ma should have been my saving grace against my father, but she didn't have the spine to stand up to him, either, letting him 'have' me instead. Our relationship isn't normal, and I'm just now realizing it.

Depressing.

"I'm gonna need two tickets for my friends Daryl and Patsy for the game against Ohio in October. They'll be in town visiting her cousins that weekend."

No *please*. No *thank you*. "Sure."

"Send 'em to the house so they don't have to get them at will call." He talks at me like I'm his employee.

God forbid his friends retrieve their free tickets themselves. Or actually pay for them.

"You hungry?" he finally asks. "Got any food in this place?"

Yes, but I didn't pay for it and I'm not going to let him root around in the fridge and eat shit on someone's else's dime.

"No. We'd have to go out."

He grunts, unsatisfied with that answer. Pops could easily lean forward and pry open the fridge, but he's too lazy to make the effort.

We regard each other a bit longer, letting the strain mount. It's always present when he visits; no amount of time in the other's company has ever bridged the gap that's been widening over the years. Not since I realized my independence regarding attending a college of my own choosing and living in housing with my friends.

My pops is chewing gum, and he gnaws on it with his mouth open, filling the air with his smacking gums.

My ass cheeks clench, eyes hitting the staircase when Charlie appears, barefooted and sleepy-eyed, her tentative smile growing shy when she lays eyes on Pops.

Fades, unsure, especially when his speculative scrutiny lands on her. There is nothing welcoming about him, nothing friendly, every sign he's throwing out a warning.

Charlie sidles up next to me, bumping our hips in an attempt to be cute.

"Who's this?" He silently judges her, mouth slipping into a frown, lips finally closing in distaste around his spearmint gum.

"This is Charlotte." Tentatively, I slip an arm around her waist. Pop's eyes don't miss any detail—how my fingers loop inside the waistband of her jeans, how close she's pressed into my side.

He's aggravated. "*Fine*. Can you tell your friend this is a private conversation?"

"Pops." I try to slip a warning into my voice, but it comes out weak instead. Like a boy still intimidated by his father.

"Pops, what? I want to talk to my son—I don't need no jock chaser standin' here while I do it." He flicks his gaze at Charlie. "No offense, sweetheart. I'm sure you're a great girl."

Did my father just imply that my girlfriend is a slut who sleeps with anyone who's an athlete? Yeah. I think he did.

"Charlotte isn't a cleat chaser." I feel the need to explain, though it's pointless—he's going to believe what he wants to believe, because he doesn't want me dating. Charlie could be standing here in a nun's habit and he'd still hate her on sight. Nothing I say is going to resonate with him. "We're datin'."

Pops leans back in the chair, balancing on two legs. Releases his hold so they crash back to the ground with a loud thud of his weight and metal.

"Since when are you allowed to date?" The arrogant asshole looks smug.

"I'm twenty-two."

"I'm twenty-two," he mocks in a placating voice. "You think you have it all figured out, do ya? Are you sleepin' with her?"

Why is he doing this in front of Charlie, where everyone else in the house can hear us? Not many guys are back from the game yet, but they will be, and the last thing I want is them walking in on this argument.

It makes me look like a pussy with no control over his life, a boy whose father tells him what to do.

Because I've always allowed my father to tell me what to do.

"I asked you a question, son. Are you sleepin' with her?"

Beside me, Charlie's fingers dig into my hips—a warning squeeze I can't translate. Does she want me to be honest, or does she want me to lie? Or, does she want me to say nothing at all? I can't fucking tell.

"Charlie's my girlfriend."

"You're datin' a girl with a boy's name?" He studies her crudely, as only my father can do. "You ain't one of them alternative girls, are ya?"

Jesus Christ. Could it get any worse?

"My son is not allowed to date. I hope the ride was worth it, because the fun is over." Pops shoots me a look over the top of her head. "Grab your bags—we're movin' you out of here. If you can't focus, we'll find ya somewhere you can."

It's official; Pops is nuts. "I'm not leavin'."

"I'll call in a favor. We'll get you in an apartment."

"I'm not moving into an apartment." Then I do something I've never done before: I roll my eyes at my father.

Pops stands. Rises to his full height and attempts to look me in the eye.

Charlie grips my waist harder.

Shit, she's anxious. I can feel the stiffness in her grasp, even without looking down at her. I squeeze her back, offering up some reassurance; it can't possibly be comforting, but it's the best I can do if she wants to stay standing next to me. I actually have no damn idea how this is going to end, but one thing's for damn sure: it's not going to end well.

"If this is the behavior you're goin' to exhibit while having a goddamn girlfriend, then you won't fuckin' have one."

I pull a face; is he seriously trying to tell me to dump Charlie? With her standing two feet away? My father is officially off his rocker. "You're out of your damn mind if you think I'm breakin' up with my girlfriend because you're tellin' me to."

"You'll not only do it, you'll do it today, before I leave this house."

I tip my head back and laugh. "Whatever."

Jackson Jennings Senior's nostrils flare, pure contempt shining in his blue eyes. He looks like me—or rather, I look like him—and it's freaky as fuck watching him as his blood boils. It used to scare the shit out of me as a kid, but now that I'm taller and bulkier, it's not so scary.

"Pops, you should probably go."

"What did you just say to me?"

I swallow, choking down the fear rising in my throat. I've never so much as spoken down to my father, let alone kicked him out of my house. The thought of it makes me want to vomit all over the fucking kitchen floor, nerves destroying my stomach.

"I said, you should probably go."

He laughs, tipping his head back like I just did. "You keep talkin' to me that way and I'll knock your teeth so far down your throat you'll be spittin' 'em out single file."

Jesus Christ—does he have to talk like this in front of my friends? Rodrigo's sister materializes in the corner of the living room, eyes wide as she pops a potato chip in her mouth, totally watching the action with interest. Horrified.

I mean, Rodrigo's been in some loud fights with his family in the main rooms of our house, but his parents have never threatened to bash his teeth in in front of his friends.

I'm so fucking embarrassed, the flush on my chest rises to my cheeks, burning my skin along the way.

Shit.

Charlie's hands rub my back, but I just need her gone.

Want my dad gone.

Want to disa-fucking-ppear into myself, the drama too much for me to handle.

This is not what I signed up for when I started dating her. Not what I wanted to happen the first time she met my family—not that I expected it to go well, but I thought it would be at least slightly better than this shit show.

"Dad." I've never used that word to address him a day in my life, and it has his full attention now. "Would you calm down?"

"No, Jackson, I won't calm down. I rode halfway across the damn country to watch you fuck up half your plays, and now I'm standin' here starin' at the reason why." His eyes rake up and down critically, starting at her feet. "She don't even look worth it."

That's not true; I had a great game, and he's just being a salty motherfucker. She is worth it, and I can't believe he'd say something like that in front of her.

I've never been so humiliated in my entire life.

"Pops, tone it down. People can hear you."

He laughs. "You mean the idiots who lost you the game? Are you forgetting you're the only one on this team entering the draft this year?"

Not this year, next year—I want to graduate with a degree first. But I haven't told him that, and I'm not going to do it now.

I've never seen Charlie's eyes so wide. She's one part terrified, another part disgusted, and fully ready to flee.

"Jesus, Pops, keep it down," I hiss, desperate to diffuse the growing argument.

"Don't fuckin' tell me what to do."

"Maybe I should go." Charlie sighs beside me, speaking barely loud enough for me to hear as she slips away. I can't catch a breath or turn my head to watch her go because my father is in my face, breathing fire.

I throw my arm out to stop her, but my father stops me instead.

"Let her walk away, Jackson. You'll let her go if you know what's good for your career."

Exactly—it's *my* career. *My* life.

Not yours, old man.

I don't know where Charlie runs off to, if she left out the front door or the back, if she returned to my room and will be there when I finally return—if I return. I have to clear my head. Maybe I should just get the fuck out of here…

This behavior from my father isn't healthy, I know this. But until the bastard leaves, I deal with it the best I can so he doesn't lay me out in my own house.

My career, my life. My career, my life…

More of my friends have arrived since this argument started, but—bless them—they've cleared the room, giving us our privacy. Besides, they're just as embarrassed hearing the shit spewing from Pop's mouth as I am listening to it. No one wants to stand by and watch their friend get railroaded by a parent, but sometimes, it's best to step aside and excuse yourself.

I know for a fact, any other day, Rodrigo or Tyson or Greg—or anyone else on the team—would have stood up for me. They're doing me a favor by leaving, and I'll thank them for it later.

I don't have any more time to wonder where Charlie is, because my father gets confrontational.

"When's the last time you spoke to Brock?" He's asking about my agent, the one I called last week to discuss removing my name from the draft.

"I'm supposed to talk to him this week." It's a lie that won't get me in any more trouble than I already am, and what Pops doesn't know yet won't get us into another fight.

"Good. I'm going to call him—I want to talk numbers. He's getting too much as far as I'm concerned, and I want to renegotiate his salary."

What? No.

Hell no.

No one is renegotiating my agent's salary, least of all my father. Brock is the only adult male looking out for me right now besides my teammates and coaches. Not only that, he's been dealing with my father's bullshit from the time I was a junior in high school—the dude deserves his fair cut. I'm not a kid anymore, and Pops can't touch my contracts now that I'm legally an adult.

Thank God.

"Anything else you want me to tell him?" *Not that I'm going to.*

"No." My father is agitated to the point of an impending blowup. "Didn't I just tell you I was going to call him?"

Jesus, *sorry.*

Why is being in this room with him making me so damn nervous? I have the upper hand here; he's living through me, not the other way around. He needs me—I no longer need him.

I straighten to my full height. "Glad you made it today."

My father nods importantly, pompous and full of importance. "Fucking embarrassment is what it was."

Wow. Okay.

"Anyway." I cross my arms and stare at him, nothing more to add.

Pops tilts his head to study me. "You gonna break up with that girl? I want an answer."

"You already told me I was."

"Don't get smart with me."

"Fine." I huff, petulant. "No, I'm not."

"Jackson, I'm warning you…"

"Warning me about what? What are you gonna do about it, Daddy? Whoop me?" I spread my arms wide. "I'm bigger than you. Ain't much you can do about it, but you can sure try."

My father's face turns ten shades of maroon, heat rising from the collar of his blue, plaid, button-down shirt. It's tucked into a pair of Wranglers, brown leather belt pulled through all the loops, a championship football belt buckle front and center, almost the size of a dinner plate. He earned it as a child—in high school—after winning the state title and has reveled in it since.

In my opinion, those days are gone. He's a miserable sod of a man, living in the past, and if I let him, he'll make me miserable, too.

"Think you're tough shit, do ya?"

"No. I just think it's time for you to lay off."

Jackson Jennings Senior's nostrils flare in my direction. "Everything you see around you, I helped build."

A laugh escapes my throat. "Really? You helped build this house you didn't want me livin' in? Weird."

"Watch your mouth."

"Then stop pissin' down my back and tellin' me it's rainin'," I smart back.

I expect him to hit me—or at least lash out, but he doesn't. "If your mother could see you now, she'd be beside herself."

I laugh again. "Like Mama gives a shit. She hasn't been here not once, and do you know why? She'd have to sit in a car with you for sixteen hours, and we all know she can't stand you." I smirk.

He can't even deny it. "Who raised you to talk to your elders like this?"

I raise a shoulder and shrug. "You did."

My father stands and stares at me a good, hard minute before grabbing his jacket off the back of the chair and heading toward the front door, one last glance over his shoulder before storming out the door.

It slams, damn near shaking off its hinges.

Silently, I wait for the wake to settle from his thunder, alone in the kitchen, red faced and mortified. I hate this part of my family; resent the part that was never normal. Never nurturing. Always mercenary and greedy.

I often wonder if my life had been different had I not been talented at sports; what would Pops have done with me then? Made me miserable anyway? Drilled me and trained me regardless, hoping I'd improve?

Life would have been worse, I muse.

It's cold as balls outside, but I don't grab a sweatshirt when I walk out of the house, my truck parked on the road facing main street. Without thinking twice, I climb behind the wheel and start the engine, determined to clear my head.

AFTER THE FIGHT WITH HIS DAD

CHARLIE

It takes barely any time to find Jackson once I discover he's missing from the football house after I return a bit later—when the coast is clear of his father—his truck no longer in his parking spot. No one saw him leave; he texted not a single soul.

I know, though.

Because I know him.

I turn down Jock Row, easing it along the shoulder, letting the few cars on the road pass so I can stay loitering in the general area, expecting my boyfriend to come along. Hoping he comes along.

Patiently, I wait him out, wondering where the hell he could possibly be. Our college town isn't large, but it's in the middle of nowhere, surrounded by cornfields and silos, with plenty of places for a guy to get lost in if he didn't want to be found. All he'd have to do is hit the city limit and keep going...

Jackson wouldn't do that.

I don't think.

I drive up and down the same road four times before I catch sight of that familiar black truck and pull onto the same shoulder of the road where I first laid eyes on him. Well, the second time I laid eyes on him—the first was in the cafeteria, when he took my food and pissed me off.

At first I don't think Jackson is going to notice my car; after all, it's gotten dark out, and the street lamps aren't that bright. Plus, why would he expect me to be parked on the side of the road?

The black truck passes; in my rear-view mirror, I watch his brake lights go on. Watch his truck stop. Then…he does a three-point turnaround in the road, pulling up behind my car and killing his headlights.

They're just as bright and blinding as I remember them.

I watch him in my side mirror, sitting behind the steering wheel, a frown on his face. Shoulders slouched, defeated.

My hand grapples with the handle of my door, and I shove, pushing it open, stepping out onto the street, one foot hitting the pavement at a time. Slam my door shut, hit the remote to lock it, and mosey toward Jackson's truck.

His window rolls open. Head hits the seatback as he regards me. "What are ya doin' on the side of the road?"

I fumble with my key fob. "Waiting for you."

"How'd you know I'd swing by?"

Swing by? What an odd way to put it—like the side of this road is a destination he frequents.

I reach up and finger the sleeve of his black, threadbare Iowa t-shirt. Run my palm down his bicep. "Because you're upset, and driving is how you clear your head."

This answer earns me a reluctant smile. "You think you know me that well, do ya?"

"I think I do, or I wouldn't have found you here."

Jackson stares down at me. "You should get off the road. It's not safe."

"I know." I rest my hand on the window ledge, glancing over my shoulder when a kid on a scooter motors by. "I just wanted to make sure you were okay."

"I'm fine."

He's not fine; I can see it in his eyes. "You don't have to be fine, Jackson. You're allowed to be pissed off."

I want to tell him he can confide in me. I want to tell him I'm here for him. I want to tell him his dad is an asshole who doesn't deserve a son like him—

But I zip my lips shut because deep down inside, he already knows. It's not necessary to say the words out loud.

Jackson's eyes bore into me, deep and blue. A bit troubled, a bit *something else entirely*. "Get your sweet little ass inside the truck for a second."

Aww. He thinks I have a sweet little ass? "Why?"

"Just 'cause."

I laugh—that's not an answer, but I miss him and love him, and if he wants me to leave my car on the side of the street to climb in his, I'm going to.

I hear the doors unlocking as I make my way around to the passenger side before Jackson leans across the cab and shoves the door open. Grabs at the crap in the passenger seat: cups and his backpack. A navy binder that says *Playbook*.

Everything gets haphazardly tossed into the backseat.

I hop up, slamming the door closed behind me, a pair of hands going around my waist. Pulling me closer.

"Someone is happy to see me!" I giggle, tilting my head so he can lay his mouth on my skin. He breathes me in, exhaling the pent-up tension building inside him.

"I missed you," he murmurs, face buried in my hair. I reach up, raking my fingers through his blond mane, eyes sliding closed. "I really freakin' missed you."

The poor baby. He's taken a real beating today, first on the football field, then from his father—his horrible, horrid father. Ugh.

"It's only been an hour, but I missed you, too." I scratch at the nape of his neck. "I was so worried about you."

He doesn't lift his head. "You were?"

"Yeah. I didn't know if I should stay, or leave, or what to do. Then when I went back to the house and you weren't there, I thought maybe the Children of the Corn got to you before I did."

"Shut up." He stifles a laugh in my neck. "That movie scares the shit out of me."

"Does it?" Jackson Jennings is afraid of horror movies? This is news to me…

"Yes. If I watch scary movies, I have nightmares."

"Aww, come here. I won't let anyone get you." I pat my lap so he'll readjust and snuggle into me, but he doesn't. Instead, he sits up, shoves the center console so it's flush with the row of front seats, and drags me over.

"I'm so sorry I left, Jackson. I'm so sorry." I kiss his temple. Nose. Chin. Everywhere to apologize.

"Darlin', don't worry about it."

"I'm going to worry about it—I panicked, and I should have stayed."

He runs a hand over my hair, smoothing down the waves. "Truthfully, your stayin' would have made him angrier."

"You're sure you're not mad?"

"No babe, I love you too much to be mad."

He loves me.

Jackson Jennings loves me. My heart sores at he pats his lap for me to climb on top.

"Are you out of your mind? There's no room in here for me to climb into your lap!"

"I can lie down if that would help?"

"You're huge—we'll never fit."

"Won't know until we try." *Spoken like a true hormonal maniac.*

"We're not fooling around in the middle of the road."

"What about if we just have sex?"

Just have sex? I've created a monster. "We can't have sex in the middle of the street! Someone will see us—everyone knows what your truck looks like."

"Technically we're not in the middle of the street—we're parked on the side of it."

"You know what I mean. Don't be so literal."

"I have to be literal 'cause I'm tryin' to get inside your pants."

What, like it's hard? "Let's be real here: it won't take much."

"Are you tellin' me not to be a quitter?"

I bite down on my bottom lip, chewing. Thinking.

Having sex in his truck, in the exact spot where we met does seem romantic, in a weird way. What would be the harm…?

His hand snakes inside my pants, down the back, fingers sliding over my ass crack.

"Yes, I'm telling you not to be a quitter."

"So what you're sayin' is you want to have sex in my truck."

Jesus, is he going to make me say the words? I can't. I press my lips together and shake my head, little jerky movements back and forth.

"Come on, Charlotte—say it."

"I can't." I'm not going to tell him I want to have sex in his truck; he already knows it's what I want, so why is he trying to make me say it?

Ugh. Guys and their egos, I swear.

"Do you want to *do it* or not?" I stubbornly press.

"Do." He nods. "I do."

"Then knock it off."

Jackson's eyes wrinkle at the corners. "Yes, darlin'."

Pleased that I was able to assert myself, I lower myself to the seat, feet in Jackson's lap. He removes my shoes first, unlaces the ties of my sneakers, setting them both on the floor in front of me.

Starts on the waistband of my bottoms, tugging. I watch, amused. "You're not wasting any time, are you?"

"Nope." He's only halfway paying attention to me, fixated on the task in front of him.

When my leggings are stripped off, I shiver from the cold—until Jackson rises up on his knees, crawling forward to settle between my legs. Hands working the fly of his jeans.

It's not as easy for Jackson to shuck his pants—the guy is well over six feet tall, jammed into the cab of a truck, twisted up like a pretzel. Still, together, we manage it.

His giant, calloused hand slides under my shirt, warming my skin and getting me hot all over. I love his palms. I love his fingers.

"I love you," I whisper into the cab of the truck as he sets about removing my shirt. Drapes himself over my body, kissing my flesh along the way. Saying it back, quietly. Tenderly.

I slide my hands over his back, pressing my fingertips into his ass; grasp his t-shirt and pull, dragging it over his head so we're both naked.

God, his body is ridiculous—firm and taut. There won't ever come a day where I tire of it.

"You feel so good, babe," Jackson coos above me, reaching his finger between our bodies and pressing his thumb over that hot button on my clit until I moan.

"God, if you're not careful, I'll come before you're inside."

He smiles into my hair. Kisses my neck. Nips at my shoulder with those pearly white teeth.

Mmm.

An excited, impatient moan escapes my throat when Jackson shoves his blue boxer briefs down over his hips.

My pussy throbs at the thought of him pushing his way inside me, and I lift my hips to meet the tip of his slowly descending cock.

He's toying with me, and I don't like it.

Jackson drags the tip along my slit; I'm still wearing my gray panties, but it doesn't matter—I can feel the rock-hard erection pressing against me.

"Stop teasing me!"

He hangs his head to stare down at me. "Well, well, well, look who the feisty one is." His lips kiss me full on the mouth; his dick flirts with the valley between my legs. Pushes.

I help it along, spreading myself, pulling my panties aside without having to remove them. Spread my legs, too, propping my heels up on the arm rest on the driver's side door.

Basically, I look like I'm at the gynecologist, about to have a full exam of my vagina.

Don't. Care.

I want him inside me…

I want him…

I want…

A set of blue lights in the back window catches my eye, and I pause, the throbbing sensations between my legs relegated to the backburner as my brain registers what the hell I'm seeing.

Is that…

Are those…?

My head pops up, eyes damn near popping out of my head as a squad car pulls up behind the truck, lights blazing.

I blink.

Blink again, mind slowly processing the situation. I give his shoulders a gentle push.

"Jackson, stop." Tap, tap. "Stop! Jackson, the police!"

He twists his head slower than molasses, gazing out the window, squinting at the car behind us. Relaxes his countenance, pulling his t-shirt over an incredible set of abs.

"Huh?" The lummox kisses me on my bare shoulder. Ugh, stop! This is no time to keep fondling me!

"What are you doing? We're about to be arrested for public indecency!"

"Relax, babe, it's the campus police."

"Is there a difference?" Why does it sound like I'm panicking? BECAUSE I'M PANICKING!

His nonplussed laugh is ill timed. "Yeah, the badges aren't real and they can't actually arrest us."

"They can't?"

"No, babe. All he can do is write me a warnin' on a slip of paper, which I'll immediately toss in the waste bin."

"Oh. Then what am I getting all worked up for?"

"Don't know, but it sure is cute." He grabs a scrap of material and tosses it at me. "Here, put your shirt back on. He's getting out of his car."

"Gee, thanks."

"Relax babe. I wouldn't let anything happen to you."

"Aww." I coo as the campus security officer approaches the truck. I can see him taking a notebook—or ticket pad out of his back pocket. "And I wouldn't let anything happen to you, either."

"What's going to happen to me? I'm six foot three and a million pounds."

He exaggerates worse than I do. "I won't let anyone hurt your feelings. I'll be the defender of your honor because I was the defender of your virginity."

"No, you were the *thief* of my virginity. Huge difference."

Thief of Jackson's virginity? Kind of has a nice ring to it…

There is a knock on the window and Jackson powers it down, resting an arm on the doorframe, pasting on a patronizing smile I can see, even with just a side view.

"Anything wrong, fake officer?" He chuckles at his own joke.

The kid ignores his barb and adjusts the sunglasses perched atop his head, despite the fact that the sun went down hours ago. "Do you know who that other vehicle belongs to?"

I give a little wave around my boyfriend. "Yeah—me."

"Everything okay?"

"Yup, everything is fine. We're just—"

"—Trying to have sex on the side of the road."

"Jackson!" I smack him on the arm, embarrassed. "Sorry about him, he's new at all this."

The security guard doesn't so much as crack a smile. "So you have a disabled vehicle on the side of the road so you can have sex in your truck?"

Jackson nods. "The side of the road is kind of our thing."

I groan. Unfortunately, it *is* kind of our thing, and I wonder if we have years of anniversaries ahead of us that will be celebrated along this very stretch of street.

The thought warms me, and I scoot closer to Jackson. He looks down at his lap when I slide my hand into his. Give it a squeeze.

I love you, I mouth to him as campus security writes us each a warning for having two vehicles parked on the side of the road.

Love you, too, babe, he mouths back. Takes the tickets when they're handed to him through the window. Balls them up when the campus patrol saunters away, tossing them into the back seat of his truck.

"Hey!" I begin. "We should save those! They're mementos!"

"Really?" He looks skeptical. "You want to keep two slips of paper threatenin' to tow us next time we get caught on the side of the road?"

"Yes. It's romantic—we met on the side of the road."

"No, we met in the cafeteria."

True. "But I didn't realize I liked you until I saw you on the side of the road."

"No, you couldn't stand me."

Also true. But now he's just being literal. "You and your big, dumb truck."

"You love this big, dumb truck."

He's right, I do. "Come over here and give me some sugar." I tap the side of my mouth with the tip of my finger.

Jackson snickers. "Yes, ma'am."

Yes, ma'am.

EPILOGUE

JACKSON

Goddamn I'm hungry.

Nothing new there; I could always go for food. Trouble is, I'm too far from home to dash there real quick, even with my truck on campus—fuck if I'm willing to lose my parking spot next to the athletic building over a snack—and I'm not jogging home for the frozen burrito I'm craving, even if it would burn off the calories.

Like a bear sniffing out food after a long winter, I skip the athletic dining hall—that's too far too because this is an emergency.

The on-campus cafeteria for regular students will have to do.

I turn my nose up at the thought, dreading the flat hamburger patties and stale lettuce I'll surely find when I get there. Chicken sounds appealing; so do a few fatty hot dogs.

I quicken my pace, not sure where this fucking joint is located; I haven't eaten there since…well, since I stole Charlie's food the first day we met.

Still. She's here somewhere; I just have to…

My eyes scan the union, in search of my girlfriend, and when I find her, I weave my way through the crowded dining hall, sneaking up behind her.

Stand gazing down at the crown of her pretty blonde head. Grin as her foot impatiently taps on the tile floor, meet the eyes of the kid grilling behind the counter.

He inwardly groans, recognizing me, doing his best to ignore the furtive, hungry glances I'm making toward the chicken and burger patties sizzling on his cooktop.

Go away, dude, he's telling me.

I don't go away.

I'm too fucking hungry. Plus, my girl is standing here, hungry, too.

When a patty is ready, the kid palms it, slapping the chicken into the center of a bun. Closes it, wraps it securely in foil. Extends his arm, holds it over the counter and into my waiting grasp.

I snatch it, immediately unwrap it, and shove the first warm bite into my mouth.

Holy shit, it's pretty damn good.

"Hey! What the hell—that was mine!" Charlie whips around, eyes already narrowed, daggers aimed at my chest. "You asshole!" She laughs, smacking me on the arm. "Give me a bite."

My girlfriend opens her mouth so I can feed her.

Playfully, I turn to walk away. "You snooze, you lose."

She grabs me by the waistband of my mesh track pants and tugs. "Oh no you don't, pal. You owe me."

"Owe you for what?" I take another bite, holding my hand out for the next sandwich coming off the grill then handing it to Charlie. She takes it, rising to plant a kiss on my jaw.

"You owe me an orgasm."

"I do?"

"Have you already forgotten the last time we tried to have sex, when your roommate walked in on us?" Charlie's brows go up as she reminds me—for the third time this week—that Rodrigo came in "looking for a pencil" while we were having sex.

"Who even uses pencils?" I muse, stuffing the chicken into my gullet.

"Exactly. Who?" Charlie drones on, walking toward the exit and pushing through the glass doors, out into the courtyard. "And the time we were busted by the campus police."

Yeah—and she's still way too dramatic about that whole thing. It wasn't the real police, so I don't know what she was so upset about.

"You *have* to let that go."

"Maybe, but you know what I *don't* have to let go? The fact that the security guard wanted you to sign his clip board—and then you *did* sign it while we were both barely dressed."

"You had a shirt on."

Charlie rolls her eyes. "Just a shirt, Jackson."

"Babe, you're hot."

If she rolls her eyes one more time, they're going to get stuck in the back of her head. "My bare ass was sticking to the seat."

"My *balls* were sticking to the seat," I joke.

"I would say your balls are cute, but that would be a lie." She laughs into her bun.

"My balls are cute—what are you even talking about?"

"Newsflash, babe: no one wants to see your balls, except maybe Tyson and Carlos."

Yeah, that's probably true. I've seen enough cock and balls in the shower to last me a lifetime, but they're always whipping that shit out.

"I love it when you say balls," I tease her.

My girl blushes, the roots of her blonde hair turning pink.

Adorable.

Yum.

"I have to get to class, you pervert." She hikes her backpack onto her shoulder and folds up the leftovers of her food, extending the foil package as an offering. "You want the rest of this?"

"You know it." I take it, bending at the waist to kiss her. "But that's not all I want."

"Oh yeah?"

"Nope." Her eyes close when I brush my lips over her temple. "I want to give you the jockgasms I owe you."

"Jockgasms, eh? Is that what we're calling them now?"

"Yup, unless you can come up with something better."

Charlie goes up on her tippy toes, pulling me down so she can whisper in my ear. "Are you sure you can't haul me off right now instead of making me wait?"

"You know it's better if you have to work for it."

"Fine. My house, nine o'clock—you can jock dirty to me then."

I hate to break it to her, but, "That's not really workin' for it, either."

"I'm not an athlete babe. I don't make the rules." Her little shrug is nonchalant and blasé.

"You're so cute when you make no sense."

She boops me on the nose. "That's what you love about me, isn't it?"

I love when she does this—puts me on the spot and makes me admit my feelings. The way she made me finally open up about my parents and how shitty my dad always makes me feel, and how fucked up it is that my mom lets him. Charlie is the one person who has been here for me—she's my best friend—and I finally realized *none* of it was my fault.

I slide my arm around her waist and give her a squeeze. Kiss the top of her head. "Yeah, that's one thing I love about you, babe."

Sweet. Sexy.

Mine.

THE END

OTHER TITLES BY SARA NEY

The Kiss and Make Up Series

Kissing in Cars

He Kissed Me First

A Kiss Like This

#ThreeLittleLies Series

Things Liars Say

Things Liars Hide

Things Liars Fake

How to Date a Douchebag Series

The Studying Hours

The Failing Hours

The Learning Hours

The Coaching Hours

The Lying Hours

Jock Hard Series

Switch Hitter

Jock Row

Jock Rule

Switch Bidder

Jock Road

For a complete updated list visit: https://authorsaraney.com/books/

ABOUT SARA NEY

Sara Ney is the USA Today Bestselling Author of the How to Date a Douchebag series, and is best known for her sexy, laugh-out-loud New Adult romances. Among her favorite vices, she includes: iced latte's, historical architecture and well-placed sarcasm. She lives colorfully, collects vintage books, art, loves flea markets, and fancies herself British.

For more information about Sara Ney and her books, visit:

Facebook

Twitter

Website

Instagram

Books + Main

Subscribe to Sara's Newsletter

Facebook Reader Group: Ney's Little Liars